Callie held up  Ireland. Your dad has promised me this trip ever since we were first married. Isn't it the best gift ever?"

While the McBride clan offered congratulations and suggestions for the best trip ever, another voice entered the chaos.

"What a wonderful surprise. I'm sure you will enjoy every minute of the trip." The woman Callie had noticed earlier across the room, addressed her, and walked toward her.

All eyes turned to the woman. "I'm sorry, young lady, but this is a private party," Charlie said. "Who are you? I don't think we know you."

"Oh, but you should know me." She hesitated. "My name is Paula McBride and I'm your daughter."

Love and Lies

by

Jeanne Moon Farmer

Shamrock Beach Series, vol. 1

Love and Lies

Cover Art by *Tina Lynn Stout*

The Wild Rose Press, Inc.
PO Box 708
Adams Basin, NY 14410-0708
Visit us at www.thewildrosepress.com

Publishing History
First Edition, 2023
Trade Paperback ISBN 978-1-5092-5030-1
Digital ISBN 978-1-5092-5031-8

Shamrock Beach Series, vol. 1
Published in the United States of America

Dedication

For Kay and my fantastic nieces and nephew, Jolyn, Bo, Leanne, and Kathy

BOOK ONE

*"In family life, love is the oil that eases friction,
the cement that binds closer together,
and the music that brings harmony."*
~ *Friedrich Nietzsche*

Chapter One

The pre-dawn stillness magnified the sound of the Atlantic Ocean waves crashing onto the shore, and as she walked the sleeping street, she was mesmerized by how loud the waves sounded when they had no competition. Captivated by that sound as she always was, she walked on toward the beach before returning home.

She crossed the dunes, and her tiny flashlight shone on fragments of seashells and a tardy crab scurrying to the safety of his home in the sand. Her feet zigzagged on the constantly changing edge of the tide, seemingly daring the unfurling waves to touch her old walking shoes. She was the only person on the beach as the sun created a hazy line between the earth and sky.

It was first light on the east coast; first light of the day she, Callie McBride, wife of Judge Charles McBride, struggled to believe had arrived. It would be the judge's retirement day and that thought clashed with everything that defined her.

She had a strong work ethic, a passionate love for the people she worked to protect, and a fear of turning to granite if she wasn't serving others. There was only one person she could talk to and that was *not* the judge.

She shook her head as she realized that her line of thought was not productive. While her own retirement would not be recognized or acclaimed when it arrived, the very public retirement of her husband, a federal judge, was being celebrated by a hundred people at a dinner later this evening.

Today he planned to pack up his office, turn over the gavel to a younger version of himself, and, God forbid, try to decide what to plant in a garden. She laughed out loud at the thought of it—tomatoes on a vine, corn growing higher and higher, rows of beans waiting to be picked.

"What a waste of energy and brain power" were the words he'd mumbled to her last night. What would today mean for their future as a couple? She loved her husband of forty-four years, but what would they talk about every day for the next few decades after they'd said, "good morning"?

Of course, they'd travel, continue to play Bridge every other Thursday night, and walk three blocks to church every Sunday morning. But none of that would fill up the hours they'd be spending together.

She sighed and pulled her light jacket tighter around her. Charlie expressed plans to go back into private practice with their son, Connor, as soon as possible, but she begged him to take some time before jumping on that idea. After all, she'd argued, it might be time to let the younger attorneys in town have a break from his iron fisted interpretation of the law. He'd laughed at her, and reluctantly agreed to give the idea some more thought. But at seventy, he wouldn't commit to taking too much time.

Glancing across the water, she breathed in the salty

freshness of the new day. It was a beautiful sight; one she'd enjoyed almost every day since she moved to Shamrock Beach when she and Charlie married. It was now home, and she'd grown to love it, though there was a time when she wasn't sure she'd ever fit in.

She'd made some of her best, and worst, decisions here. Marrying Charlie and welcoming their four children into the world were just a few of the memorable events in her Shamrock Beach life. But there were so many lies and secrets that, if revealed, would shatter her life in this town.

Her McBride identity was the public part of who she was, and soon she would submit a letter of resignation that closed the part of her life that no one in Shamrock knew about. Not even her beloved husband. She was retiring from the other half of who she was; her secret life was coming to an end. Like the air she breathed, that secret had been her purpose for all her adult years.

As the sun rose higher above the horizon, her eyes once again scanned the waves slowly rolling toward the shore and she whispered a prayer that she would be up to the tasks of her retirement and his.

She wanted to linger there on the cool sand and forget about all the hoop-de-la that was planned for the day. In a few minutes, she'd walk home to be there when the kids began to arrive, and she'd spend the afternoon bustling around making everyone happy.

Sighing, she knew she was already behind on her checklist of things that must be done. But seeing her sons, Brock and Connor, and her daughters, Adalyn and Dara, would lighten her mood and help her get it all done. Plus, her daughter-in-law and grandchildren kept everything lively whenever they came to visit.

She smiled at that thought and turned away from the water. Today's chaos would be easy compared to the event planned for tonight when hundreds of people would gather at the country club for Charlie's retirement dinner. There would be boring speeches, back slapping, and well-wishes. He would be roasted, toasted, applauded, and made out to be a hero.

It's going to be a nightmare. At the thought, she looked back out to the sea and wished she could hitch a ride on the shrimp boat she'd been watching.

Beyond the dunes, a lone figure watched every step Callie took and silently fell in behind her, at a discreet distance. His job was to watch and wait, and to make sure she didn't see him.

****

This morning, like a whisper on the wind, she heard her mother's voice calling as if she was walking behind her, but her mother was dead for twenty years. When Callie turned there was no one there, and she tried to shake off the eerie feeling. *What is the voice saying? Why does it feel like a warning?*

By the time she reached the back door of her house the wind had died down, it was six thirty, and she had too much to do to give in to the feeling that she was being followed.

She passed Charlie in the yard as he left for his morning walk, a ritual as old as time. He'd walked the sands of Shamrock Beach every morning since they married and moved into this house. It was his quiet time and he never asked her to join him. When she was young and newly married, she thought it was her duty to jump out of bed to go with him, but he gently told her he would rather she stayed at home. She had felt two seconds of

4

rejection before snuggling back under the covers for thirty more minutes of sleep.

"Good morning, sweetheart. I wondered where you were," he said with a smile.

"Too much on my mind, Charlie. I couldn't sleep, so I tried your old trick of walking on the beach. I can see why you go out so early in the mornings. God used His paintbrush to color us another perfect sunrise."

He nodded. "It'll all get done, Callie. Try to relax." Then he blew her a kiss as he continued toward the beach.

Callie sat down in the rocker on the porch. Only a moment, she thought, reluctant to go inside and tackle her "to do" list. She figured by the time Charlie returned from his walk, they'd have an hour to eat breakfast, shower, and dress for the morning before Grace Samuels arrived to help finish the preparations for the arrival of the children.

Officially, Grace had worked for the McBrides two days a week since Callie had gone back to work full time. Truth was, she was Callie's friend, more like a family member than an employee.

Yesterday, they changed the bedsheets in all the bedrooms and hung fresh towels in all the bathrooms; they dusted, vacuumed, hunted down all stray cobwebs, and made a long list of the food to be purchased at Publix and the farmer's market—and all while laughing and trying to figure out how the judge was going to adjust to his new life.

Callie chuckled when she thought of Grace's retelling of some of Connor's misadventures.

"Callie, do you remember when we couldn't figure out why the bedsheets were beginning to fray in the

middle?" Grace laughed as she recalled a time from years past. "I went over and over it in my mind. Frayed at the edges, I could understand, but in the middle didn't make any sense. Then, one night, the sheet got hung up on a loose board and left Connor dangling from a second story window of this house. Every time I think about it, I chuckle. Woke up the neighborhood, he did, with all that yelling for somebody to save him. You'd a thought he was hanging from the top of the courthouse the way he was carrying on. The judge had to get the ladder out of the garage and help that boy get down to the ground." She laughed louder. "I bet that boy was more afraid of what was going to happen when he climbed down the ladder, than when he was hanging out there like a fool. He was wearing out every sheet in the house when he was using them as his fire escape."

In her mind, Callie could still see the moment she was awakened by Connor's shouts for help and Charlie's angry words when his son finally put both feet on the ground.

"But, Callie, you know the worst time of all was when Connor decided to go through my pocketbook to find a piece of chewing gum and found my gun instead. I had the hardest time trying to explain why I carried a gun. That boy asked too many questions. I finally satisfied his curiosity when I told him that black women sometimes had to defend themselves. I told him it was our secret. I reminded him I knew some of his secrets and I'd trust him to never go near my pocketbook again. To this day, I don't think he has ever again touched any of my things."

Callie abandoned her rocking chair, stretched her legs, and moved into the kitchen. Her mind continued to wander to other crazy moments and close calls with her kids as she cracked the eggs for breakfast. But then she cleared her head of memories and began to review the tasks that had to be accomplished before those kids arrived.

As always when she thought of her kids, she started at the top of the alphabet: Adalyn would be there for the week; Brock, Marti and the twins, Mandy and Max, would only be there overnight; Connor would be there for meals and family fun since he lived two blocks away; and Dara and her new friend, Edward Jenkins, would be with them for three days.

As much as she loved them, it was always hectic to get ready for their visits, and she knew she was lucky to have Grace's help as well as her friendship. With each beat of the eggs, she clicked off items on her mental list.

Adalyn and Dara would occupy their old room, Brock and Marti would be in the boys' old room, the grandkids would bunk in the playroom in the attic, and Edward would take the daybed in the den. She and Dara had argued over the matter of sleeping arrangements during last week's phone call.

Dara knew she would lose, but she presented her case anyway. Callie stood her ground. "A rule is a rule, Dara. There is nothing more to discuss. If you and Edward share a bed at your house that's your decision, but this is my house, my rules."

The slamming of the porch door jarred her from her thoughts, and she turned to smile at Charlie as he made his way toward her. "You smell like sea air and salt, honey. I hope you enjoyed your walk this morning."

He grinned. "Callie, do you think they'd miss me if I didn't show up today?" He grabbed her around the waist. "We could run away, just the two of us. I know a great place."

"Charlie McBride, you know in your heart you don't want to miss seeing the family and being the center of attention at the dinner this evening." She laughed out loud. "You are the 'man of the hour' today. Everyone will say nice things about you, several will even cry that you won't be on the bench anymore, and one or two will be smiling secretly because you'll finally have more time to go fishing with them." She wiggled out of his grasp, placed the plates on the table, and turned to grab the coffee pot. "Sit down and eat while it's still hot."

"You know how much I'm dreading this, don't you?" He twirled a fork in his hand as he talked. "I'm not ready to retire."

"I know, but it's Parker's turn, and the time has come for you to bow out gracefully." She placed her hand on the arm that was mindlessly twirling the fork. "Remember, we have plans that have waited too long already." She sighed. "I'm sixty-eight and you're seventy. If we don't start now, we won't have time to do all we've planned."

Again, his regal head inclined in her direction, but he turned his attention to his breakfast and coffee. She was glad for the quiet, a moment to take a breath and enjoy their food. But his restlessness was something she had big concerns about.

When he'd finished his coffee, he pushed back his chair and stood. "Thanks for the lecture and for breakfast. But don't you think you're too young to be married to a retired, old man?"

She too stood, then smiled. "Sweetheart, you may be retired tomorrow, but you are not an old man. Stop carrying on like this is the end of the world." She wrapped her arms around his neck and gave him a passionate kiss. His response was full of heat, and she knew she'd made her point.

He pulled free of her embrace. "Now I've got to take a cold shower and head to the office. But you hold that thought for later." He looked like a pouting two-year old. "You know how Valarie is. If I'm not there to pack things up, she'll send all my stuff to the dump."

He rubbed his chin and chuckled to himself. "You know she's going to stay on to help Parker settle in. Poor fellow, he won't know what hit him when she walks in and tries to get him organized. When I go into private practice I'm going to have to try and persuade her to come with me. I can't imagine trying to practice law without Valarie to keep me straight."

Callie watched him leave the kitchen and heaved a big sigh. She knew he'd play some golf, go fishing with his buddies, and they would do some traveling, but how was it going to be after all these years to have him home all the time?

The main thing he really cared about was the law. He didn't have hobbies and he'd proven over and over that he wasn't handy around the house, no matter how good his intentions. Maybe she shouldn't have tried to talk him into waiting several months before going back to private practice.

Chapter Two

"Anybody home?" Connor shouted as he slammed the porch door and brushed his feet on the welcome mat. "Hey, Mom, I picked up the rolls you wanted from the bakery. Where do you want me to put them?"

Callie walked into the kitchen to give her son a hug and her mouth flew open. "Connor, did you buy out the whole shop? You must have four or five dozen rolls in that bag."

"Five to be exact. I know how food disappears in this house and I wanted to make sure I got my share." He laughed as he gave his mother a kiss on the top of her head. "You get shorter every day," he teased.

"You're messing up my hair, and, short or tall, I can still whittle you down to size, kiddo."

As Connor turned around to take the rolls to the pantry, he bumped into Grace. "Hey, good-looking, what you got cooking?" he sing-songed as he grabbed her with his free hand. "How you doing, Miss Grace?"

"Let go of me, boy. You always think you can get an extra dessert by sweet-talking me." Grace stood back and did a once over of Connor. "You are skinny, my man. You need to come over to my house sometime and let me fatten you up some. You are something else. Hand me my pocketbook out of the pantry, Connor, I've got to head home."

Connor nodded his head. "That's the invitation I've

10

been waiting for. You want me to give you a ride home, Miss Grace?"

"Naw, baby, I've got my car today. You give your mom a hand with all this food. See you all tonight at the big shindig."

As Grace walked out the back door, Connor turned to his mother. "I'd love that lady even if she didn't make the best pecan pie in Florida." He continued to chew on the chips he'd grabbed from the bag in the pantry. "Am I the only one here?"

"Adalyn flew into Jacksonville, and she's hired a car to bring her home. She'll be here in about an hour." Callie was always surprised that her actress daughter occasionally flaunted her wealth and success to the family. "I don't know why she can't just rent a car and drive herself."

"Because she's a lousy driver," he shouted from the pantry. "And who drives themselves in New York, anyway?"

He walked back into the kitchen munching on another handful of chips. "What time are my no-good brother and his bratty kids getting here? I haven't had a good wrestling match with Max in months. You'd think with Gainesville only an hour away, Brock would bring his kids over here more often."

"If I didn't know how much you love your brother and the twins, I'd take offense at your remarks."

"I miss seeing them. The kids are growing up so fast, they'll be gone before we know it." He let out a big groan. "By the way, who's this guy Dara is bringing home? Is he the flavor of the month or is she serious about him?"

The familiar sound of a car horn let them know that

Brock was in the driveway. He had announced his homecoming that way since he bought his first car. Connor headed for the front door with Callie close behind, his questions about Dara unanswered.

"Who wants to know you're here, Brock? Do you have to blow the horn and disturb the whole neighborhood?" Connor laughed as he grabbed his older brother in a choke hold and dragged him out of the car. "Hey, bro, you've added a few more pounds since the last time I saw you."

"Let go of me, you Neanderthal." Brock managed to squeak out a few words as his feet hit the driveway. "Don't try to show me up in front of my kids."

"Kids, does your dad tell you he's a doctor? Don't believe him. He's faking, you know. He's really a beach bum who lost his surfing license."

The hugging, laughing, and teasing continued as Marti and the twins climbed out of the car and headed for the house. Mandy and Max ran to Callie and almost knocked her over with all the energy they'd stored up on the ride over.

"Nonnie, I've missed you," whispered Mandy. "I hope we're having lemon pie for dessert."

The eight-year-old twins looked alike, but were as different as night and day, thought Callie as she opened her arms for their hugs and kisses.

Mandy was quiet, thoughtful, and creative. Max was loud, energetic, and more boy than she remembered either of her own sons being. Mandy observed and planned; Max ran headfirst into life without stopping to think. Together, they were the best gifts she'd ever been given, and after they tired her out, she could send them home.

"Momma Mac, are you ready for this hurricane?" Marti grinned as she greeted her mother-in-law. "A good run on the beach ought to settle them down some."

Marti had coined "Momma Mac" when she and Brock became engaged, and it had stuck. Callie liked it and was grateful Marti felt so comfortable with her.

"It's great to see them happy and healthy," Callie called to Marti as they began unloading the car. For preemie babies that had such a rough beginning, she thought, their energy was refreshing and welcomed. They'd been born two months early and it was almost three months before they'd left the NICU.

Amid all the craziness, Dara and her new boyfriend, Edward, drove up in front of the house. Dara barely had the car door open when, without a signal or look between them, Brock and Connor stopped in their tracks and yelled, "Lock the door, Mom, there's a Seminole in our front yard!"

"Doesn't that ever get old?" Dara yelled and began to dance an Indian war dance around her brothers. The rivalry between the University of Florida Gators and the Florida State Seminoles would play out as long as the three of them lived. "Edward, I told you my brothers were insane," Dara said breathlessly to her companion. "Don't believe a word they say. Brock will try to convince you he's a doctor and Connor will do everything he can to imitate a lawyer. But it's all a joke." She grabbed one brother and then the other and gave them each a slobbery kiss on the cheek.

"Well, you think you can pass yourself off as a professor at FSU," Brock teased and turned with hand extended to Edward. "Welcome to the Shamrock Beach Asylum. The McBrides will ensure that you have the

13

time of your life while you're here."

Edward stood in a daze for a few seconds before he recovered and shook hands with Brock and Connor. "Your sister warned me, but I didn't believe her."

Dara introduced Edward to her mother and Marti and smiled. "Once he gets used to all of us, he'll fit right in," she assured them. "Where are my favorite niece and nephew?"

"Hopefully they're running off some energy. I told them not to go to the beach, so they better be in the back yard." Marti looked toward the screen porch to check. "Mandy, Max, your Aunt Dara is here. And she brought a new boyfriend for you to harass. Come up to the house and start asking him all the questions it isn't proper for the rest of us to ask."

Dara swatted her sister-in-law across the shoulder. "You are so mean! Give the poor guy a chance before you try to run him off."

"Edward, welcome." Marti reached over to shake his hand. "I wish I could tell you that it's an off-day for this bunch. But I'd be lying. It's always like this. If you're fond of Dara, it won't be long before you'll be fond of us, too."

Dara turned to her mother and smiled. "Aren't you glad we're here? I've missed you."

"It's not every day I have the pleasure of being a warden in an asylum," Callie retorted. "Edward, I'm the only sane one here, so if you need something, let me know. To see us at our most humorous, hopefully, lets you know you're not a stranger."

"Where are Dad and The Queen?" Dara called out as she grabbed for Edward's hand and gave him a look that told him everything would be all right. "And is Miss

Grace here today?"

"Your dad is in a meeting with the new judge, Adalyn should be here soon, and the last time I looked, Grace was getting ready to leave. We don't have to wait for anyone, so when you're hungry make yourself a sandwich. I'll put the iced tea pitcher on the table and ice is in the bucket on the buffet."

Callie's heart beat with joy as she stood in the doorway and watched her family delight in being together. Her happiness would be complete when her oldest child, Adalyn, arrived. This is what it's all about, she thought. Family is everything. Including those who will never be with us.

****

The noise died down somewhat while they ate. There was never silence when the kids were in the house, but Callie thought the low hum was manageable. No sooner had she thought that, when the front door opened, and Adalyn announced her arrival.

"The queen is in the house, and she expects her loyal subjects to kowtow to her every wish."

Everyone but Edward stood up from the table and bowed in Adalyn's direction. "Oh, wise and beautiful queen, you need but ask and we will do your will—or not," Brock shouted as the others booed their sister.

Adalyn was regal as she waltzed into the room. No one could deny that she was beautiful or that she was the older sister who had lorded over them for most of their younger years. They gave her a moment of glory and then sat back down to eat.

"How's that corny soap opera going, sis?" Connor ventured forth. "I thought they might have killed you off by now."

"Oh, darling, Connor. The ratings would go down if I wasn't around. My job is not to be killed, but to kill off as many husbands as possible, amass greater wealth, and terrorize my children. Which I learned how to do by terrorizing you," Adalyn broadcasted in a most dramatic manner.

"Oldest child of mine. I'm glad you're home." Callie walked over to her daughter and gave her a big hug. "Join us for lunch and then your loyal subjects will see to your luggage."

Callie looked around the table and smiled. Everyone was talking at once, the grandkids were trying to sneak as many cookies as possible, and Edward looked like a deer in the headlights. It was always like this for the newcomers, but she knew her family well enough to know that in some way or another they would soon make Edward feel like one of the crowd.

Every time she glanced around the table, Edward was staring at her in a way that made her feel uncomfortable. She tried to smile and hoped she was covering her discomfort. *The poor man must be overwhelmed. This bunch takes some getting used to.*

"How's Dad taking all this retirement business?" Adalyn's southern drawl flowed naturally. "I can't imagine he's happy about it. Where is he, by the way?"

As the words left her mouth, Charlie walked into the room. "Callie, you didn't tell me we had started taking in boarders."

The uproar began again as they all commenced talking at once. "All here and accounted for, I see. Max, count noses for me just to make sure." Charlie tousled his grandson's curly hair as he passed by his chair. "Are there any crumbs left?"

"Daddy, would you like me to make you a sandwich? Mom made sure your favorites are on the table. Ham and cheese on rye, heavy on the mustard, light on the lettuce, right?" Dara dutifully offered.

"This is my friend, Edward." She gestured in Edward's direction. "He's been waiting to meet you. I've told him enough stories about this family that he thinks you're the only sane one in the bunch."

"Welcome. Everything my lovely daughter has told you is true." Charlie extended his hand to Edward. "Callie's kids are crazy, never dull, and will make this weekend one of the best you've ever lived." He accepted the plate Dara had prepared and took his place at the head of the table. "Hopefully, we'll have some time to talk later, Edward."

"Of course, Judge. Any time it's convenient." Edward glanced back at the table. "Mrs. McBride, I'm sure you must be pleased that your husband is retiring. Have you considered when you might retire, also? Your work must call you away from home more often than the judge likes."

"Edward, I retired as curator of the local museum just recently. However, I still work as a volunteer anytime they need an extra hand. But I'm not often away from home. In this small town, my job never took me more than a few blocks from this house." She stood and walked toward the kitchen telling herself the man was just trying to make small talk. "Yes, Edward, I'm looking forward to having Charlie around here more often."

After lunch was over and the kitchen cleaned, everyone began going their separate ways. "What time is this shindig tonight?" Brock yelled down the hall. "I'm taking the kids to the beach, and I want to be back before all the hot water's gone."

"We need to be ready to go by six thirty," Callie responded. "You all know the drill and which bathroom you're to use. Showers should start around four, so you have plenty of time to enjoy the beach."

****

"Callie, how do you do it? Everyone is organized and all the loose ends are tied up nicely." Charlie smiled at his wife as he buttoned the last button on his dress shirt. "It's like old times listening to you and kids."

"We do fall back into our old routines, don't we? I'm so glad we still live in this house. It's familiar. I guess that's why it's easy when everyone is home. Marti learned the drill easily enough, and if Edward hangs around long enough, he'll learn it, too."

"From his expression at the lunch table, he may be in shock right now. Hopefully, Dara prepared him for all the guff he'll have to take from her brothers." Charlie pulled up his suspenders and laughed. "I did manage a few minutes of conversation with him after lunch. The man doesn't talk much about himself, but he sure asked a lot of questions about Shamrock and this family. He wanted to know all about your job at the museum and what kind of law Connor practices. He seemed interested in some of the cases that came before me in court."

"Do you think he and Dara are serious? He's older than she is and I'm having a hard time seeing them as a couple."

"You're jumping the gun, my dear. Dara will let us know how things are between them when she's good and ready. You know how tight-lipped she is about her love life."

"You're right. Our kids aren't kids anymore."

"Except when they all get together at our house. Then it's hard to think of any of them as adults. Who do they take after, anyway? Look at us, Callie, so quiet and reserved. We're the model of dignity and decorum." He kissed the back of her neck and pinched her bottom.

Callie swatted his hand. "Right, they sure didn't get their obnoxious ways from us."

Chapter Three

"Who's riding with me?" Connor shouted as he closed the front door behind him. "I've got room for anyone but Brock."

"That's good news, cause I'm taking my own car. I wouldn't ride with a maniac driver like you." Brock smirked at his younger brother and turned to round up his family for the short ride to the country club. "Adalyn, I've got room for you, if you can lower yourself to ride with my group."

"That works. Then I can take Mom, Dad, Dara, and Edward with me." Connor looked at his dad for approval. "Is everyone ready to go?"

It was only a few miles to the country club where the retirement dinner was being held, but Charlie groaned at the idea of everyone being stuffed into just two cars.

Callie caught the look in Charlie's eyes and whispered, "Get over it. You can sit in the front with Connor, and I'll ride in the back. Don't be an old grouch."

She smiled at him, put her arm through his, and took a quick look at her family as they headed for the cars. "Wow, we're a good-looking bunch. How did I get so lucky?"

She was proud of what she saw. Charlie and her boys were handsome in the dark suits that accentuated their tanned skin, fair hair, and big blue eyes. Her grandchildren had cleaned up nicely after their time at the beach and their mother had made sure they stayed quiet and clean while everyone else was getting ready. And, her girls, including her daughter-in-law, looked stunning.

She'd been afraid Adalyn would forget this little dinner at the Shamrock Club wasn't a New York gala, but her daughter had chosen a simple emerald green, flowing dress that was perfect for her auburn hair and green eyes. Her daughter was a beautiful television star, a fact that Callie had to remind herself of often, but Adalyn usually didn't hold her family hostage to her success. At five-feet-nine, forty-year-old Adalyn was a commanding presence wherever she went. Tonight, she had styled her shoulder length hair in soft waves that framed her face but did not hide her beautiful eyes.

Dara and Marti were lovely young women who never tried to compete with Adalyn's beauty, and Callie was pleased each of them had chosen a style that matched their personality. Dara was on the low side of flamboyant in a fitted navy, floor-length dress. Her light brown hair was pulled up in a messy top knot that somehow made her appear taller and more sophisticated than she usually looked. Often, she made a uniform out of slacks and a blazer. She wore the diamond stud earrings that the family had given her when she earned her doctorate degree.

Marti looked chic in an ivory halter-style top and calf-length black pencil skirt. Even with two children she had managed to maintain a stunning figure that was shown to its greatest advantage by the style she'd chosen. Her short blond curls and blue eyes stood out in contrast to Adalyn and Dara's darker looks.

Callie wondered if her ankle length blue-gray silk dress looked frumpy when compared to the dazzle of her family. Her only adornment was a filigree necklace shaped like a shamrock that was framed in diamonds and emeralds. It had once belonged to Charlie's grandmother. He'd given it to her on their first anniversary and she tried to wear it on special occasions because she knew it meant so much to him.

Like her daughters, her hair was a brownish red that had the added distinction of a few gray strands. She thought of each gray hair as earned interest on a life well lived. She was not as tall as either of her daughters, but with years of dieting and exercise she had managed to keep her weight under control. She and her girls were beyond the clothes-sharing phase, but she knew she could probably wear anything in either daughter's closet, a fact that made her smile.

The drive over went quickly and as they walked into the foyer of the club, Charlie leaned over and kissed his wife on the cheek and whispered, "Mrs. McBride, you have a marvelous looking family, and you look prettier than the day I first met you. Thank you for wearing the shamrock. Love you."

Callie looked lovingly at her husband as she tried to forget how much she disliked this place. The Shamrock Club, with its pretentious foyer, chandeliered dining room, and "born-to-money" board members always made her feel like an outsider. Neither she nor Charlie had grown up with money. His dad owned the downtown drug store, where he was the pharmacist, and his wife was the cashier, until their deaths many years ago. And Callie's family didn't count since they didn't live in

Shamrock Beach.

Everyone in town knew they couldn't have afforded to belong here, but when Charlie was made a senior partner in the law firm, one of the perks was a lifetime membership. Although it had been years, there were still a few families who resented that decision. Charlie accepted it all in stride and never felt like an outsider. He made the place belong to him.

The dining room was stunning, as usual. Expensive linen tablecloths, china, crystal, silver, and elegant flower arrangements at the center of each table reflected in the windows, and gilded mirrors made the room glimmer. Callie was impressed so much effort had gone into making this a special occasion for Charlie. He was, after all, a hometown boy that had made good.

They were shown to tables in the center of the room, marked Reserved. The chairs around those two tables were positioned so no one had their back to the stage. By some unspoken agreement, her family found their seats and sat down as other guests began to fill the room.

"I think the whole town is here," Charlie whispered. "Must be a slow night on television. What's on tonight's agenda, anyway?"

"Dinner is first, then the speeches, and after dessert, the guests will go into the big lounge for drinks and dancing."

"Are you serious? We'll be here all night. What about the grandkids? Surely, we can't expect them to live through all of that."

"You're right. Mandy and Max, and any other kids that are here, will be entertained with a movie and popcorn in one of the meeting rooms. It'll all work out. Can't you stop grumbling and just enjoy this?"

While dinner was being served, people meandered around the head tables, slapping Charlie on the back, complimenting Callie on her beautiful outfit, and catching up with the kids. A few brave souls asked Adalyn for her autograph. In between courses, Callie surveyed the room to see who showed up and was surprised there were faces she didn't recognize.

Her eyes lingered over several guests at a table near the back of the room. A lovely young woman and several men were sitting silently watching the action, especially around the head table. She shook her head and decided they were probably family members of one of Charlie's former law partners. She turned back to her table as the next course was being served.

When the meal was over, the mayor walked up on the stage and began the program by asking Charlie to stand and be recognized. To thunderous applause, he stood and took a small bow, smiling to all sides of the room.

Callie noticed the pink in his tanned face, something she didn't ever remember seeing. "He is enjoying this!" she whispered to herself.

One by one, guests took the stage and either roasted or toasted the retiring judge. There was laughter and a few tears as people showed their appreciation for the years of work that Charlie performed from the bench.

The man who was taking his place, Parker Preston, blew up Charlie's ego trying to let everyone know that filling Charlie's place on the bench would take all the energy, talent, and intellect he had, and then some. It was a touching tribute and a perfect speech to end with.

The mayor took the podium to conclude the dinner portion of the evening. "Ladies and gentlemen, don't you think we've said enough nice things about the judge? We don't want him to go into retirement with his head any bigger than it already is." He paused to let the laughter fade away. "Please follow me to the ballroom where the real party will begin."

Callie stood up and turned to Max and Mandy. "Come on, kids. Let's go to the room where they set up the movie." She took their hands and started for the door.

"When you've delivered the kids, please come back here. I've got a little surprise for the family, and then we can all go to the ballroom together." Charlie smiled at his wife and motioned to the family to sit back down.

"What's going on, Dad?" Connor whispered as he leaned toward his father.

"I've got a surprise for your mother."

They talked among themselves until Callie walked back in the room, then they stopped talking and waited.

"Sit down, sweetheart. This will just take a minute." Charlie stood and held the chair for his wife. "Callie, I have a little gift for you for putting up with me all these years. It's my retirement gift to you." He kissed her cheek and handed her a small envelope.

She sat with a stunned look on her face. "Oh, Charlie, what is it? You didn't have to do this."

Adalyn called over to her mother, "Mom, open the envelope. We want to know what's in it."

Slowly, Callie opened the envelope and drew in her breath. "Charlie, really?" She stood and threw her arms around him. "This is the best gift ever."

Everyone shouted at once. "What is it, Mom?"

Callie held up two airline tickets. "Tickets to Ireland. Your dad has promised me this trip ever since we were first married. Isn't it the best gift ever?"

While the McBride clan offered congratulations and suggestions for the best trip ever, another voice entered the chaos.

"What a wonderful surprise. I'm sure you will enjoy every minute of the trip." The woman Callie had noticed earlier across the room, addressed her, and walked toward her.

All eyes turned to the woman. "I'm sorry, young lady, but this is a private party," Charlie said. "Who are you? I don't think we know you."

"Oh, but you *should* know me." She hesitated. "My name is Paula McBride and I'm your daughter."

BOOK TWO

"I will look after you and I will look after anybody you say needs to be looked after, any way you say.
I am here.
I brought my whole self to you."
~ Maya Angelou

Chapter Four

Callie felt her face lose all color. She couldn't catch her breath and a vice slowly closed around her body squeezing tighter as the seconds passed.

The silence in the dining room was deafening. It hurt the ears with its piercing intensity. The sound waves of disbelief and shock shimmered across the two tables and hung precariously in the crystals of the chandelier.

She didn't look to the right or the left, her point of abject astonishment directed to the young woman standing behind Charlie until she was shaken awake by his hand on her arm. The sound of his voice brought the world back to life.

"Holy heavens, Callie, who is this woman?"

Callie searched for Grace who was still seated at the next table. When their eyes met, Grace, who'd overheard the woman, shook her head in a side-to-side motion as though to let Callie know she should relax.

Turning to Charlie, she realized he'd been trying to get her attention. "I'm sorry, Charlie. What did you say?"

"This is a crazy prank. Who came up with this stunt?" Charlie looked at her, then at each of his children.

"Did one of you pay this woman to embarrass me?"

The shock was evident, but others in the room who had also heard, were gradually regaining their senses. They gasped and turned in Charlie's direction. Voices sparingly disrupted the silence, cautiously at first and then, erupting into a cacophony of chatter.

But Callie knew it was no joke. She didn't know what was going on, but somehow, her intuition told her it was not a prank on her husband. On herself, perhaps? She wondered as Brock rose from his chair, cleared his throat several times, and then spoke.

"What is the meaning of this, lady? Have you been sent here as a joke?"

He walked forward and faced the woman who was standing like an avenging Joan of Arc, her expression one of smug arrogance.

"Sit down and be quiet," Charlie shouted and finally got the attention of his family. When they were settled, he cleared his throat again. "That's better. Thank you." He turned to the young woman. His voice shook in anger. "I'll ask you again. Who sent you here to perform this tasteless joke?"

She stood her ground, lifting her chin in defiance. "I assure you, sir. This is no joke. I came here tonight to claim my place in the esteemed judge's family. What better way to claim my stake than in front of all the people who are important to you?"

Her demeanor remained calm as she looked directly at the man she claimed to be her father. "Tell them, Father. Stand up finally and tell the rest of your family who I am."

Her words were darts being thrown across the room at a target. Each one was pointed and directional.

Charlie shook Callie's hand off his arm. He stretched himself to his full height and assumed the stance of a judge in the courtroom. He regained his equilibrium, and his manner became cool and reserved. "My dear, you are a lovely young woman. But, so sadly mistaken. My two daughters are sitting here beside me. However, if you will join us, I'm sure we can find a way to unravel the riddle of your parentage." He leaned on the table as he lowered himself to the chair, slightly shaken, but still in command of his emotions. "Callie, this is a mistake," he declared to his wife and then quietly addressed his children. "You do not have a sibling that I've been hiding away for the past however many years. This person is not my daughter."

He looked around the table at the bewilderment on the faces of his family. They looked back at him with a variety of emotions on their faces—surprise, shock, disbelief—and no words to accompany their expressions.

Before anyone could speak, Paula pulled her chair closer to Charlie. She set her glass of wine on the table and turned to Callie. "You are so beautiful. I almost wish that you could have been my mother."

Connor jumped to his feet, almost knocking his chair to the floor. "Wait just a minute" His voice contorted with rage. "I don't know who you are or why you're here, but one more word to my mother and I'll find a reason to have you hauled off to jail."

"Calm down, Connor." Callie reached her arm toward him. "Surely, this fiasco can be settled without an attorney and the sheriff." Her words were soft, but steely. "This young lady seems to have been given some misleading information and we can help her make it right if we all stay calm."

Callie kept her gaze on Connor until he sat down, then she turned to Charlie. "Honey, this isn't the time or place to deal with this. I suggest we invite Paula to meet us at Connor's office in the morning to continue any conversation." She took a breath. "Don't you agree?"

"Dad, don't say a word. Mom has a good idea and I'm fine with it." Connor didn't look at his father but turned his attention to their uninvited guest.

"Miss, whatever your name is, I'm escorting my family home and I strongly advise you to leave this area, or I will have you arrested for disorderly conduct and harassment. After all, you are an uninvited guest at a private party in a private club. If you have cause to disrupt us further, I suggest you be at my office at nine in the morning. I will rearrange my day to give you one hour. If you have other ideas about intruding on my father's life and following us, be warned, I will have you arrested."

Motioning to his family, he started to move with them toward the door. "If you'll excuse us, this party is over."

He handed the young woman his card and herded his family out of the room. Before he exited, he walked toward the ballroom. "Sorry, folks. I'm taking the family home. You all feel free to dance the night away. We've had more than our share of excitement for tonight."

As the family left the dining room, the roar of voices from the ballroom became deafening.

Charlie stepped toward his son and his relief showed. "You handled that like a master, Connor. I hate to leave my own party, but God help me, if I'd had to stay in that room another minute, I would have become a person I don't want to be. I know you were thinking of your mother, and I'm grateful."

They rode home in silence. Both carloads of McBrides were at a loss for anything to say to each other. As they piled out of the cars and walked slowly toward the house, Callie broke the silence. "I suggest we change out of our party clothes and meet in the kitchen for a family meeting in about fifteen minutes. Max and Mandy, there's a new video in the playroom. Go change your clothes and I'll bring you some snacks and drinks." They all nodded and moved away from her, probably relieved that someone had taken charge.

After Callie and Charlie closed the door to their bedroom, she looked at the lines and scowl on her husband's face and felt the burden of age fall on her own shoulders. She sagged in tiredness and sat on the edge of the bed. She realized the fatigue had nothing to do with whatever Charlie's secrets might be. Her own suddenly felt like they weighed more than Atlas could bear.

"I'm counting on you to clear this up, Charlie. I saw the look on your face the moment that woman made her announcement, and I hope you don't know more about this than you were letting on at the party. If you have something to tell me, please do it now, not in front of our kids."

Chapter Five

Charlie shed his coat and tie before he turned toward his wife. "My mind has been searching every possible scenario for answers and I don't have any. I'm as shocked as you are." He crossed the room and sat down next to her. "Callie, this must be a joke and, I promise, we'll get to the bottom of it. I wouldn't hurt you for the world."

"Charlie, right now, I'm almost sick to my stomach. I can't think of another moment in my life when I've been more undone, shocked, and fearful. I look at our children and I can't begin to imagine what they are thinking or feeling, but I will do whatever I have to do to protect them. So, if you're harboring some deep, dark secret, you and I need to find a way around it that doesn't hurt them."

Quiet tears rolled down her cheeks and she clenched her hands so tightly they began to ache. Her mind raced to another secret—her own—and she prayed the young woman at the party wasn't unraveling something Callie wasn't able to deal with. Her chest tightened. Grief? Guilt?

Charlie rested his hand on her shoulder. "This whole thing is crazy, and I'd bet two cents that someone set this up to embarrass me. You'll see, Callie. It's part of some sick joke. Please don't be upset."

She stared at him for reassurance but instead, his air

of denial hit her like a slap across the face. She thought perhaps he was protesting too much.

When he reached for her, she pushed his hand away. "I've got good instincts. There's something going on here that could change our lives, and you're acting like it's all a joke of some kind. How can you do this to me, Charlie? How can you do that to us?" She jumped up and raced to the bedroom door. "I've got children to face. Somehow, I've got to reassure them that their lives aren't going to change, too."

"For crying out loud, Callie. Our children are adults, not children. They don't need you to reassure them of anything." His voice was harsh and ragged. "If anything, I'm the one who needs to see what their questions are and how Connor thinks he's going to handle this in the morning." He followed her toward the door. "Don't make more of a drama out of this than has already happened." He opened the door, muscled his way past her, and stormed out of the room.

How interesting. He'd always left her to keep their children on the solid path. And they would always be her children. Sitting back down on the edge of the bed, she felt abandoned and empty. Where was that feeling of unity that had gotten her through so many down times in her marriage and so many worrisome moments with the children? Charlie had anchored her life, even in the times his work took priority over the family, even when he was far away from home for weeks on end. *Even in those times when my secrets seemed overwhelming.*

Standing up, she walked toward her dressing table hoping a change in position would transform her attitude. For years she'd not allowed her emotions to control her reactions. This wasn't the time to fall apart, and she knew it, but something had shifted in her.

Halfway across the room, she changed directions and walked toward her nightstand where she always kept her Bible. Placing her hand on the worn cover, she closed her eyes and whispered, "God, help me. You know I'm being unfair to Charlie and our family. God, if all this chaos is really aimed at me, please don't let it harm my family."

Withdrawing her hand, she straightened her shoulders. She didn't dare look in the mirror right then. She marched toward the door. If Charlie had betrayed her, was it really any worse than what she'd done? She swallowed past the lump in her throat and stepped into the hallway and back to the family.

****

She listened to Charlie's heavy footsteps ahead of her as he crossed the house and entered the kitchen.

"Hey, kids, your mom will be here in a minute. What are you passing around to drink?"

"We've got options, Dad. Look on the counter and choose your poison. We've got soda and iced tea," Dara offered. "Or I can pour you a glass of wine and bring it to you."

"Wine will do, sweetheart," he responded and took his chair at the crowded table. His children were in their life-long places. Dara had changed into her pajamas but had forgotten to remove her jewelry. Brock sat with his back straight and his anger easily readable. Adalyn, elegant as always in a stylish robe and slippers, delivered a performance of laisse faire as she sipped her wine. Connor was the one pacing the room and holding family court. Marti and Edward were absent, and Charlie wondered if that was by choice or at the request of the others.

"Dad, we've been talking, and we think you need to be the one to meet with this woman in the morning. Mom doesn't need to be there and neither do the sibs," Connor began. "We can handle this better without the interruptions and we can fill them in after it's over."

Callie entered the kitchen as Connor was making his suggestion. "Why don't you want me to be there tomorrow? I'm part of this craziness, Connor."

"No offense, Mom. Connor is convinced this can be settled in a few minutes. That's all. There's no conspiracy to keep you away." Adalyn placed her arms around her mother and gave her a hug. "We're convinced this is a set-up and between Dad and Connor, they can get her to tell the truth."

Brock cleared his throat and looked at his sister. "This is just like your soap opera, Adalyn. We ought to let you meet with this kook." His look softened when he saw the expression on his mother's face. "Mom, I'm not trying to make light of this. Really. We know there's not even a smattering of truth in this and it will be over by ten o'clock tomorrow."

Dara stood behind Charlie but directed her questions pointedly. "Wait, I want to hear from Dad. Was there ever some hanky-panky going on that we need to know about?" Her hands were on her hips, and she was leaning into her father. "I've heard my siblings' opinions on the matter, but you're the only one who can possibly shed some light on this. I want answers, Dad. Are you the person we think you are?"

Charlie jumped up, knocking into the table as he turned to where his daughter stood. "Hold on, Dara, I'm as anxious to get to the truth as you are. I'm disappointed in your lack of faith in me. You're an adult and entitled to answers as they pertain to you, but, as my child, you are not entitled to make the demands you've just made." After venting, his demeanor softened somewhat. "We'll have to wait until tomorrow to know where this Paula person is headed and what she wants from me." He sat back down and took a huge swig of the wine Dara had poured. "I'm sorry she ruined the party for all of us. We should be dancing and having a good time instead of sitting in our kitchen looking like dogs without a bone." He slapped his hand on the table and drank the rest of his wine. He waved his hand toward his wife. "Callie, tell your kids that everything is going to be all right. They always believe you."

Dara moved away, silenced but not defeated. "Fine, Dad, I'll shut up. But I know I'm not the only one who has these questions."

"Mom, are *you* okay?" Adalyn glanced at her mother as she shook off her father's sarcasm and her sister's posturing. "This is probably rougher on you than any of us, and we're ignoring that fact. Let me fix you a glass of wine." She moved over to the counter where the wine and glasses had been set out. "There's a red and a white. At this point do you have a preference?"

"Adalyn, I'll have a little of the white. Thanks." Callie had tried to hide her feelings from the children, but Charlie's sarcasm was a low blow and it still hurt. She felt she needed to defuse the rising tension in the room and send them all to bed for her own sanity if for no other reason. "I'm shocked and upset, like all of you. But I believe your father, and before I let my emotions run wild, I'm going to have a sip of wine and then go to bed. You all need to do the same. I'll deal with whatever is coming, but not tonight." She took a fleeting glance at her children and gave them a weak smile. "Stop worrying about me and stop giving your father the third degree. We need to save our energy for what's coming tomorrow. It could be nothing but a misunderstanding or something more, but no matter what, the McBrides will get through this together."

"I've kept out of this, but, Charlie, I want you to know I'm in your corner," Marti said as she walked into the kitchen and hugged her father-in-law. "Momma Mac, you know I'd follow you to the moon and back. This family will give you all the support you need, no matter what happens." She turned around and smiled at Brock. "I'm taking your mother's advice and I hope you all do the same. This has been one long day and stirring the pot before we have any more information is only going to make it longer. If I can have faith in this family, surely all of you can muster a show of unity. How can you let one moment erase who you are?"

Brock blew her a kiss. "Thank you, sweetheart. For a few minutes we all reacted and forgot to trust in each other." He walked over and poured himself another glass of wine. "Like several others in this room, I need some assurance that I'm not going to have to deal with another sister." He joked, but his expression was serious. "Dad, one word from you and we'll all go to bed without continuing the inquisition."

"Give it up, Brock. Take your wife's advice," Adalyn demanded. "If we can't trust Charlie McBride, then who on this earth can we trust?"

****

He stood silently in the shadows and watched as the lights in the house were turned off. He wished he could have heard the conversations that must have taken place between the McBrides tonight. He would have to congratulate his boss. Embarrassing the judge and his wife was way too easy.

Chapter Six

"Good morning, Dad," Connor said before he looked up from his computer. "Take a seat and I'll finish up what I'm doing so we can talk."

Charlie looked around his son's office and smiled at the similarities to the one he himself had occupied when he was a practicing attorney. Connor had a corner office on the second floor of a building in the downtown business corridor of Shamrock Beach.

The view was worth the price of the space, thought Charlie as he looked at the windows that made up the corner of the room. If he looked in one direction, he could see across the rooftops of several one-story buildings all the way to the dunes, the sea oats, and the ocean.

In the other direction he could see a few of the buildings that overlooked the town square. Connor's massive desk took up space in front of the large window that faced the street, and comfortable leather chairs were placed where the occupants had a choice of views. Mahogany bookcases, filled with law books, lined two walls behind him and Connor's degrees hung in simple black frames over the lower bookcase. It was a space that spoke success without boasting.

The glare of the morning sun was softened by the blinds that covered the windows and, as much as Charlie tried, the angle made it impossible to read the screen of

Connor's computer. He wasn't trying to be nosy, he just wanted to know if his son was doing research for their meeting.

As a lawyer, he knew better than to interrupt or ask any questions. He would wait until Connor was ready to offer suggestions or explore options. The steady rhythm of Connor's fingers on the computer keys was somehow calming and for a few minutes he forgot why he was sitting in his son's office. He could see Connor's profile, the furrowed brow caused by intense concentration, and he wondered if this meeting would unearth something that had the potential to damage his relationship with the family. But then, how could it? He was deep in that thought when the clicking of the keys stopped and Connor shifted his position.

"Sorry, Dad. I needed to finish some notes before we meet with this Paula McBride person." Connor shook his head and swiveled his chair so he could face his father. "She doesn't exist as far as I can tell. No social security number, driver's license, or home address. I haven't had a chance to look for birth records, but I'll do that if necessary. I think we're being scammed."

"Connor, I didn't sleep a wink all night and still couldn't come up with any ideas on what this is all about. It will be interesting to hear what the lady has to say when she has only a small audience. You know how vulnerable we are as lawyers, and this could be a stunt pulled by somebody who feels they were treated unfairly in my court."

A buzzer on Connor's desk interrupted their discussion. "Mr. McBride, your nine o'clock appointment is here."

"Thanks, Annie. I'll be out in a few minutes. Please

ask her to take a seat," he responded, then turned to face his father as though trying to figure out what was going on in his father's head, but Charlie's face didn't hold any clues. "Dad, are you ready to let me do most of the talking or is this going to be your show?"

"Connor, I want this meeting to be as professional as possible. I want this lady to understand the legal and moral ramifications she may face if she continues her accusations. And I want to know who is behind this. I know you can handle all my concerns, and I'll try to be the observer." He watched a smile creep slowly across his son's face.

"Don't laugh, Connor. I can do that. Now go and invite this Paula to the meeting."

Connor walked around the desk and placed one hand on his dad's shoulder. "You know we're with you, right? This might turn out to be fun."

He opened his office door and took several steps into the reception area. "Good morning. Thank you for being on time." He extended his hand. "You've read my card, so you know I'm Connor McBride. Please follow me."

****

His face was expressionless as his eyes scanned the young woman standing before him. She was about the same height and body structure as his sisters, and something about her eyes caught his attention.

As he walked behind her, he was surprised by her poise and air of self-confidence. Her clothes looked fashionable and expensive, her hair was neatly knotted in a small bun at the nape of her neck, and her fingernails were manicured. She had dressed the part. He had to admit, she was pretty, and her eyes could draw a person in.

Motioning for her to take the chair beside his father, he sat down behind the desk and took a deep breath. "Apparently, no introductions are necessary, so why don't we begin with your story. Believe me, we are interested in every detail."

"Good morning." She nodded in Charlie's direction. "I'll start with the facts. I am Paula McBride, the daughter of Sandra Duncan and Charles McBride. I was born in Tallahassee on October 25, 1972." She spoke clearly and carefully, making sure each word was enunciated precisely.

Connor watched his father's face as the young woman spoke. His expression didn't change, but he began to blink his eyes rapidly as he watched what seemed to be a well-prepared performance. Connor knew his dad was struggling to remain an observer. "Do you know the circumstances of my father's association with your mother? Did your mother ever tell you that Charles McBride is your father?"

"My mother, who died last year of cancer, told me the story of my father over and over. She loved to tell me about him; she believed one day he would claim me as his daughter. She knew he was married, but never doubted that he had loved us. I have copies of letters he wrote to her when he was not in Tallahassee. Each one is dated, and in several of them, he even mentions his desire to become acquainted with me in some father–daughter way."

Charlie couldn't hold his tongue any longer. He leaned forward and faced the young woman. "I have never met anyone named Sandra Duncan, and I have never written to anyone in Tallahassee that wasn't part of a case that I was working on. May I see those letters?"

"Naturally, I didn't bring the letters to this meeting. I couldn't take a chance on their destruction." Her voice hardened. "After the rudeness and the reception I received last night, I didn't know what awaited me at this meeting." She stood and placed her hands on Connor's desk. "I assure you, I have the letters, my birth certificate, and copies of support checks that were mailed to my mother during the first two years of my life."

"I will need to see all of those. And of course, I wonder why your father—whoever he may be—only sent checks for two years. But my questions to you are who are you and what do you want with my father? We all know your claim is ludicrous, so please state your true objective and we'll go forward from there."

She shook her head slowly. "My reason for being here is very simple. With my mother's death, I have no one. I want to be recognized as Charles McBride's daughter and I want to take my place as a member of his family."

She leaned closer to Connor, her look seductive, her voice sultry. "However, now that I have met you, I almost regret that you are my brother."

Chapter Seven

After Paula left the office, Charlie and Connor sat in bewildered silence for a few moments before Charlie stood up and started pacing the room. "This is unbelievable. Support checks, letters, birth certificates. There is no way these things are genuine. I would certainly know if I had done these things. They're fakes, I tell you, and she's going to pay for this one way or another."

"Calm down, Dad. She'll trip herself up if we give her the space to do it. We just have to figure out why she's doing this and what she really wants." Connor stood up and walked to where his father was standing. "As your attorney, I need to know if there is *any* way her story is true. I need you to tell me again that you don't know Sandra Duncan, you never had an affair with her, and you never sent her any type of financial support. Things can happen that we don't plan on—I've seen it often enough. I just need to know the truth." He backed off to give his father space, but he didn't change his stance. "Your answer will be attorney-client privilege, not father to son. I don't care what the answer is, but I've got to be sure we have a legitimate challenge to her allegations."

Charlie ran his fingers through his hair and turned back to look at the ocean. His silence lingered before he finally spoke. The sigh that preceded his words was long and deep.

"I don't remember meeting anyone in Tallahassee by that name and I've *never* had an affair. At least, not in a sexual context. There was a woman who worked in one of the judges' offices in Tallahassee that I became friends with the year I worked there. We met for coffee occasionally, and I took her to dinner several times. I was lonely but it was innocent as far as I was concerned." He paused. "She knew I was married. I talked to her about your mother and our life together. It was a crazy time in our marriage. We were renovating the house, your mother was pregnant with Adalyn, and I was away for weeks at a time."

He swung around and faced Connor. "I promise you, son. I never laid a hand on that woman. I can't even remember her full name. It was Julie something. I know it wasn't Sandra Duncan."

"Does Paula look anything like Julie, Dad? Do you see a resemblance? She could be her daughter even if you aren't her father."

"When I first saw her last night, I thought she reminded me of someone. But, when I saw her today, there wasn't even a hint of Julie or anyone else that I know for that matter. Connor, I'm being set up. This woman is not my child."

Connor nodded. "Okay, I believe you. Does Mom know about this Julie person?"

"Well, no. I never thought there was a reason to tell her." He backed away from the look on his son's face. "I know. I know," Charlie said, putting his hands in the air. "Taking a woman to dinner who's not my wife wasn't the best decision I've ever made. I can see that in hindsight, but I promise you, I didn't think I was doing anything wrong at the time. Don't judge me too harshly. It wasn't romantic and it was a very long time ago."

"Back down, Dad, I'm not judging you. And I believe you. I just hope your innocent dinner dates don't take a bite out of you now." Connor sat down and turned to his computer. "Dad, don't take this wrong, but I'll understand if you think it would be better for another attorney to handle this. I realize there may be sensitive things your son doesn't need to know."

"For goodness sakes. Are you telling me you have some doubts about my side of this story?"

Connor looked him in the eye. "Not at all. I don't want this to get awkward between us, and it's better for me to step away now instead of later. That's all I meant."

"Son, I have nothing to hide. For my money, you're the best attorney in town. There's no need for me to seek different counsel."

"Great. I was hoping that would be your answer. I can't think of anything I'd rather do than take on this case." Connor jumped to his feet, gave his father a hug, and began moving him toward the door. "Why don't you go on home. I've got a full day and I need to do some more research on Paula McBride. We'll see what happens when we meet with her tomorrow, and she brings us her papers. No matter, we can always try for DNA testing. In this case, we'll be disproving paternity. Don't get yourself worked up about this and try to enjoy your first day of retirement."

"Oh, yeah, retirement. Who else starts their retirement in the midst of a fiasco like this? Do you really think I can go plant a garden when all this is swirling around me? I'm going home, but I'll do some research on my own. I've got to find out who she is."

"Better than that, Dad, if I were in your shoes, I'd take Mom to lunch and tell her about Julie. It may never come up, but I think she needs to be prepared for any and everything." For the first time that morning, Connor smiled. "Good luck with Mom. I know what a tiger she can be when she's upset about something."

****

Charlie had a hard time keeping his eyes off Callie as the sun's rays streamed in the restaurant windows that were behind her head. They created a spotlight effect that highlighted her hair and face.

She was dressed in her casual style and, from what he could tell, she was wearing very little make-up. He wished he could capture the moment and frame it. He also wished he wasn't about to ruin it. Hurting Callie was the last thing he'd ever wanted to do.

"You look pretty. Sitting in the sunshine, you look the same way you did the first time I saw you. Sunshine becomes you."

"Thank you. If I remember correctly, you stumbled over me, scattered my books, and blocked the sunshine. It wasn't one of your grand entrances."

"Your memory is correct, but you couldn't see yourself the way I saw you." He took her hand and held it. "Now that I'm retired, we can do this more often. It's been a long time since I've taken you out for lunch. It's been a long time since I've been out to lunch. Valerie always had something sent to the office so I could go over the docket between court sessions."

"Charlie, we've got a house-full of people waiting to find out what went on at Connor's office. I was really surprised when you called for me to meet you at the café. What's the real reason you've decided to take me to lunch?" She gently pulled her hand away and glanced at the menu. "This isn't a typical lunch date, is it?"

"I thought it would be best if I talked to you first, then we can go home and face the inquisition." He began to fidget. "And I really did think it would be nice to have lunch with you."

"I've known you a long time, Charlie McBride. Your flattery is not convincing. Just tell me what's going on. What happened with Paula?"

"Paula was on time, she was smartly dressed, and she is sticking with her story. She told us she has the paperwork to prove she is my daughter."

Callie gasped. "How is that possible?"

"We don't know—I don't know—but we're going to find out. Paula says her mother's name is Sandra Duncan and she passed away last year. She claims she is now alone in the world and wants to be part of our family. She told us she was born in Tallahassee in 1972."

"That's crazy! But something is bothering you. What haven't you told me?"

"Before you begin making all kinds of assumptions, just hear me out. That's the right time frame for when I was working in Tallahassee, but I don't know anyone named Sandra Duncan."

"Only one question matters, Charlie." She threw her napkin on the table and stared angrily at her husband. "Did you have an affair with someone while you were in Tallahassee? No matter what her name is or was? Were you sleeping with someone while I was pregnant and trying to keep the house renovations on track?" Her voice began to rise, and he could see her bottom lip begin to quiver.

"You know better than that. What have all our years

together meant if you can ask me that question?"

"Stop stalling and give me a straight answer! You haven't denied anything."

"Callie, I did not have an affair with anyone at any time. When you've calmed down, you'll remember the vows we took and what you've always meant to me." He tried to reach for her hand, but she withdrew. "I do have a story to tell you, but it isn't as dramatic as what you're imagining."

"I haven't shed any tears over you in a long time and this story better not be the reason I begin today. Yes, I remember our vows and I have trusted you all these years without any question. I've never doubted you." She hesitated and her shoulders sagged. "I didn't sleep much last night and I'm trying not to overreact."

"Thank you for those words. For a minute, I thought you'd already convicted me." He looked at her with sadness and saw in her face the impact last night's event was having on her. "I'm sorry that last night was spoiled for us. More for you and the kids, than for me. Somehow, I'll make it up to you."

"Tell me your story, and let's go home. I'm not hungry."

He nodded, then cleared his throat. "It happened so long ago, and at the time I didn't think it was a big deal. But today when Connor was interrogating me—" He stopped and tried to make light of the situation. "—he was shocked I hadn't told you about a woman named Julie that I'd met when I was working in Tallahassee. I don't even remember her last name. We became friends, Callie, nothing more. My life was in chaos, and she was easy to talk to. I was away from you and our home so much, you were pregnant, the house renovations needed my attention, and I wasn't happy with the caseload I was carrying at the time. She and I sometimes went for coffee during our lunch break, and I took her to dinner a couple of times. She knew I was married. I talked to her about you and how excited we were that a baby was on the way. She shared some of the hardships she was going through as a single mother. She had a son, a cute little boy that I met one afternoon when I picked her up for dinner." He took a deep breath. "That's it. That's all there is to my story. No sex, no torrid affair, just coffee and a couple of dinners."

The moment between them stretched into an over-powering silence. Callie dropped her head and stared at the floor. Charlie's relief at finishing his story turned into wishing he was anywhere but at lunch with his wife who was obviously more than a little upset with him.

Her voice was soft and low when she finally spoke. "Only one little thing, Charlie. You didn't bother to tell me about Julie at the time, and you're assuming I'll believe you now." She stood up and looked down at him, her heartbreak evident on her face. "I'm going home."

****

Sweat ran down the back of her neck and beaded up on her forehead, an annoying reminder of Florida's humidity and year-round sunshine. As she neared the house she turned slightly to see if Charlie had followed her, but the sidewalk behind her was long, white, and empty.

Oh, well, so much for making it up to me. It felt good to walk briskly, her muscles eager to be stretched after the tension of the past thirty minutes. The knots had loosened some, but her stomach felt like it was working against the rest of her body.

The exertion of pushing herself forward did nothing to clear her mind of the words she'd heard at lunch. Such little words, spoken in normal conversation, had sucked the air out of the room. They twisted her out of shape, and she didn't know why she was being so emotional. After all, having lunch with a woman who wasn't your wife paled in comparison to what she'd neglected to share over the years.

But she was tired in a way she'd never been before. A sign of aging, perhaps? Of too many years of secrets? Too many years of disappointment? She shrugged.

Charlie had hidden something from her that might have the power to blow her world apart. But it was nothing compared to all that she'd hidden from him. She had secrets of her own. So, why was she over-reacting? How much of her life had she been forced to keep from Charlie? Now that the shoe was on the other foot was it fair for her to be so hypocritical? Could she accept his words at face value like she had in the past or was there something more to this Julie thing than he'd been willing to share today? And did it really matter if there was?

One thing was clear as she approached her front door, she wasn't ready to let the kids see her distress. They had questions that needed answers, they wanted their world to remain intact, and they had always depended on her to be the family stabilizer.

As she climbed the steps to the front porch, Adalyn's voice startled her. She lost her balance and stumbled on the steps.

"Mom, are you all right?"

She prevented a fall by catching the railing and it gave her a moment to pull herself together. "Sure, sweetheart. I wasn't paying attention and caught my heel." Callie stepped up on the porch and walked toward the swing where her daughter sat.

"Aren't you warm sitting out here in the hot sun? I'd have thought you would be inside soaking up the air conditioning."

Adalyn was beautiful, even with no make-up and hair pulled back in a girlish ponytail. She was wearing cut-off jeans and a halter top that had been in her closet since she was a teenager. She called the outfit her "*I'm home now clothes*" and Callie knew they would never go in the thrift store basket that always sat in the hall closet. Year after year, it amazed her that her daughter could still fit into them and look so good.

"Too many people in the house and too much talk I was tired of hearing. I forget what living here always sounds like. Noise, noise, and more noise." Her voice softened and the attempt at humor melted away. "How in the world did you live through the years when we were all at home? I'd never thought about it until today, but we're a vocal bunch. Didn't you ever yearn for silence?"

"Today's noise is filled with tension and suspicion, sweetheart. It's not the noise that usually fills this house. And, besides, when you were living at home, you were one of the loudest voices. You could make yourself heard above the roar of your brothers and your father." Callie tried to spin her remarks in a way that didn't add to the worry she saw reflected in her daughter's face.

"Are we going to have a family meeting? Are the judge and my lawyer brother going to let us in on the big meeting they had this morning? And are you going to share what happened during your lunch with Dad?" She turned to look down the street. "By the way, where's Dad?"

"My goodness, Adalyn, you do have a ton of questions." Callie sighed. "First, there isn't a meeting planned that I know of. Second, it'll happen when it's supposed to." She was anxious to change the subject, and Adalyn didn't need to know that she had no idea where Charlie was. "Did you all have lunch? There was so much food left over from yesterday…."

"Yes, Mom. Everyone found their way to the fridge. Stop worrying about us." Adalyn patted the empty space next to her. "Sit here with me for a while and try to wind down from whatever is eating away at you. We'll get through this together. Just like you taught us to do." She draped her arm around Callie's shoulder and pulled her close. "You're always reminding us that family sticks together through thick and thin. It's the McBride motto, remember?"

The warmth of Adalyn's voice and touch were calming, and she allowed her daughter to be the comforter for a few minutes. She smiled from the inside for the first time since the horrible moments of the previous evening. "Hey, sweet thing, I'm the mother here. I'm supposed to be taking care of your worries. Not vice versa."

Adalyn tenderly squeezed her mother's shoulder and let out a big sigh. "Just think, Mom. You've raised adults who think, care for others, and want what's best for you. Bet you never thought *that* would happen."

Callie pulled away, chuckled, and pushed a stray hair from her daughter's face. "Adult or not, you will always be my baby girl and don't you ever forget it." A heart-warming smile connected mother to daughter like it had done since Adalyn was a small child.

There was a moment of quiet before Adalyn began

moving her legs to make the swing rock slowly back and forth. "I've always assumed you and Dad had a perfect marriage, or at least, a good marriage. I never thought it could be otherwise, but I'm having a hard time wrapping my head around the fact that if Paula McBride is the real thing, my dad was involved with another woman. That's the stuff my soap opera life is made of, not my real life. If her story is true, then it pulls the rug out from under all of us, doesn't it?"

"Adalyn, our family is on solid ground, and I think I know your father very well. I'm sure there are many women who feel that way and then discover an infidelity, but I don't think this is one of those cases. This young woman's story doesn't add up and I'm not giving up on any of us. Let's wait and see what happens before we make a leap in the wrong direction. Okay?" The doubts of the previous hours seemed to vanish as she made that declaration to her daughter.

"I'm trying. I guess I've read too many scripts where it doesn't work out and there's no fairytale ending."

"You're the oldest, Adalyn, and I'm counting on you to help me hold us together." Callie turned and looked toward the house. "What's the scuttlebutt inside? Are your siblings ready to explode or is it safe for me to go in?"

"You take the risk of being bombarded with questions if you venture inside. Dara is loaded for bear and Brock can only hold her in check for so long. I had to get out of their way, that's why I'm out here." She cleared her throat. "On another subject, what's the deal with this Edward character? He hardly seems like Dara's type and he sure is playing it low key. I don't feel comfortable around him, Mom. He's lecherous."

"All men look at you that way," Callie chided her daughter.

"You're right. I'm used to that look, but not in my own house. And certainly not from a man who is dating my sister."

"All I know is I don't know. They've been dating for several months, and Dara said he practically insisted that he come with her this weekend. If he wanted to meet the family, I'd think he'd be a bit more proactive. But he's staying pretty much to himself." Callie stood up and started for the front door. "I wouldn't be surprised if we overwhelmed him, and I'm sure he didn't expect all the drama that's going on now. Come on, sweetheart. We'll have to cut him some slack."

"I'll try as long as he's not a keeper."

"Be kind, Adalyn," Callie scolded. "He's Dara's choice, remember."

****

"Edward, did you get lunch? I'm sorry I wasn't here to make sure all the leftovers made it to the table." Callie practically bumped into Edward as she went through the door.

"Yes, Mrs. McBride. Lunch went well. In fact, you may not think it, but everything is going extremely well." He looked her in the eyes. "I will say, Mrs. Mc Bride, you are different from what I'd pictured." He laughed as he went out of the house.

Callie stared at his back. She wondered what in the world he had to laugh about and what he had expected of her. *What had Dara told him about her and had she done something to change that impression?*

****

Across town, Grace sat in her living room and

waited for the call she knew was inevitable. As she waited, she tried to imagine what was going on at the McBride's house and wondered who was playing games with whom.

She was quick to answer when her cell phone rang. "Is there something you forgot to tell me?" Her mind raced as she listened to the voice of the caller. "And how does this change our carefully made plans? How much do I tell Callie?" The answer was what she expected, but as she continued to listen, she scowled. "She's coming to my house for how long?" Again, she listened. "I hear you. Just make sure Callie and I are kept safe. I don't care how long it takes. It's another month before the trial begins and a lot can happen between now and then."

****

She proofed the letter for possible mistakes, reading it several times. When satisfied with the words and phrasing, she placed it in the envelope she had addressed to the field office in Miami. The loose ends would soon be tied up and she could let go of a mountain of lies.

Hurrying down the sidewalk, she held the letter tightly against her chest. *Grace must read this before it's mailed. She'll know if I've made my intentions to retire clear and definitive. I've got to talk to her. Like always, I've got to talk to her.*

To Callie's surprise, the door opened before she could ring the doorbell and Grace was pulling her inside.

"Callie, why are you here?" Grace whispered. "You should have called first."

Callie drew back in alarm. "Since when do I have to call if I want to visit? What's going on? Is something wrong?"

"I don't know what's going on, but something is,

56

and it's got me on edge." Grace took a deep breath and tried to smile. "I'm sorry. It's been crazy around here since the night of Charlie's retirement party. I didn't mean to alarm you." She let go of Callie's arm and walked into the living room. "Have a seat and tell me why you're here."

"All I wanted to do was have you read my retirement letter before I mailed it. You're the only one I can talk to about any of this." Callie took a deep breath. "Something's shifted inside me and fallen like a broken gyroscope."

Grace took the letter out of Callie's hand and adjusted her glasses.

Shamrock Beach, Florida
March 31, 2012
Dear Martha,

The time has arrived for me to inform you of my decision to retire after forty years of service. July 31, 2012 will be my last day of service. My duties as a witness in the trial of Mario Villa will have been concluded prior to that date.

My partner and I have celebrated our successes knowing that lives have been saved and many have been restored to a normal existence. We mourn our failures knowing the heinous crime of human trafficking has not ended, but our efforts have resulted in reduced pain and suffering for many victims.

I have finally accepted that my daughter is one of the unlucky victims who will never be found. If she is still alive, she is lost in the maelstrom of evil that we have not been able to eradicate.

Thank you for supporting me and those with whom I have served. Thank you for always believing.

Sincerely,
CEM

"I know it's that time in our lives," Callie said softly, "but I'm having difficulty coming to terms with the fact we will be leaving years of work behind us in a few short weeks."

Grace put the letter on the coffee table. "You were such an innocent when we first met. I thought I had found a solution for you and for me when I made all those suggestions so long ago. What if, all these years later, I created the mess your family is in today? What if I'm to blame?"

Callie reached out and took the hand of her friend. "I have regrets about some of my decisions, but not the one that made us friends. Not the ones that let me lead a life that has helped these victims."

Grace nodded slowly and withdrew her hand. "Thank you, my friend. I know we can't go back and change anything, anyway, I'm just sorry for your sadness and how this has shaken your foundation. And remember, Callie, Charlie and your family are your foundation. Nothing's changed there. Please trust in that and relax." She got to her feet. "But, Callie, things are happening that I can't explain, and you must not come here again. It's not safe." Grace looked at her for understanding. "I'll see you tomorrow at your house. And your letter is fine. I'll drop it in the mail for you. Now go home and be very watchful as you go."

Callie stood, too, not sure why her only confidant in the world was giving her the brush. "Grace, I had lunch with Charlie, and it was like we were on different planets. He confessed he had a friendship with some woman when he was working in Tallahassee all those years ago. He promised me it was nothing more than a friendship, but it's making me crazy. When you add all my lies to his, it seems like we have some real trust issues." She looked at her old friend and sighed. "I have the strangest feeling that it's all connected somehow."

"Callie, this is so unlike you. You're talking nonsense. You know Charlie McBride has never been unfaithful to you. You're trying to put pieces in this puzzle that don't belong." Grace started walking to the door. "Go home and stop over thinking every little thing that comes your way. Don't you unravel on me now."

Chapter Eight

"Hey, Matt, it's Connor. You're on speakerphone, so be careful what you say. I need a favor."

"Well, good morning and to what do I owe the pleasure of doing business with you? I'm not ready to start my day, and I wouldn't have answered the phone for anyone else. If you're calling this early, it must be life or death."

"Are you still in bed, or what?"

"Yes, I'm still in bed. What's it to you? And perhaps I'm not alone. Did you even think about that?"

"You crazy galoot. Who in their right mind would be in bed with you?" Connor laughed out loud. "Seriously, Matt, I need your help. Or, if you'd rather, I'll take my business to someone who's awake."

"You have my attention. What's going on?"

Connor McBride and Matt Granger had been buddies most of their lives. The Grangers lived on the next street and, as boys, the two had been inseparable. They'd played football together, were roommates in college, and had never lost touch, even when Matt moved to Jacksonville to join his older brother, Tom, in a successful private detective agency.

"For one thing, I'm working on forgiving you for not being at my dad's retirement party last night. You better have a good excuse for that. And for another thing, if you'd been there, you would already know why I need you."

"Oh no. Was that last night? I'm sorry. Really. I had planned on being there."

Connor thought he heard his friend slap his forehead.

Matt continued, "I've been working on a big case, and I was doing surveillance until late last night. Please let your dad know that I'm sorry."

"Will do. But that's not the reason for the call." Connor recounted the details of the previous evening and heard Matt gasp on the other end of the phone.

"You're making this up, right? Your old man has a love child? No way."

"Stop right there and just listen. This Paula person says she can prove that my dad is her father and the only thing she wants is to be part of our family. Dad denies the whole thing and I believe him. She's setting us up for something, and I need you to find out what and why." Connor pounded his fist on the desk. "Matt, get out of bed and get down here now. I need your help."

"Let me check in with Tom and I'll be on my way. I'll meet you at your office in about two hours."

****

Callie looked across the room at her kids and tried to lighten the mood. "What would we do with another girl in this family? It would mess up the balance and then we'd have to have another boy. What do you think?"

Brock stood up and put his hand on his mother's shoulder. "That's not funny." He looked around at the faces of his family. "Mom, you don't have to cover up how you're feeling just to make us feel better."

"I'm trying to make *me* feel better, Brock. But you're right. It's probably not a good time to make jokes." She patted his hand and gave him a smile. "You all know how much I trust your father. I believe him." She waited for one of them to make a comment before continuing. "Somehow this is going to work out for the best."

"I'm mad as a hatter," Dara shouted. "It makes me furious that Dad was cheated out of his retirement party by some low life who is looking to make a dime."

"Tell us how you really feel, Dara." Brock motioned to his sister to continue. "What do you plan to do about it? Seriously, do you have some great strategy that you'd like to share with us?"

"Shut up, Brock, and let me vent. I fumed and fussed to Edward for hours and he's tired of listening to me. So, you all get to hear me now. Who is that woman and why aren't Dad and Connor here to tell us what's going on?"

"Dara, they'll be here soon, and I'm sure they'll have some clarifying information for us," Callie added.

"Really, Mom? Just like you won't tell us what happened between you and Dad at lunch? What are all the secrets about anyway?" Dara demanded.

"Calm down, sis, and let the story unfold in its own time. Jumping on Mom isn't going to help." Adalyn stood up and headed for the kitchen. "Anybody want anything while I'm up?"

"Now that you asked, I'll take a double scotch on the rocks. No, make it a triple," Dara responded.

"Right, Dara. And, since when do Mom and Dad keep anything but wine in this house?"

****

Charlie had walked at least five miles since Callie left him standing in the middle of the restaurant with his mouth wide open. The exertion of the walk hadn't helped him resolve a thing. He had never been unfaithful to his wife, but he'd made a mistake by not telling her of his friendship with Julie. Now he wondered if she'd believe anything he told her. His mind traced every year of his life searching for a possible answer, but nothing surfaced.

He recalled girls he'd chased in high school and college, and the one person he had dated in law school before he met Callie. The timing was wrong though and none of them could have been Paula's mother. He thought of cases in court that ended badly and the people who might want revenge. There were plenty of possibilities in that group, but the research would take months. There were no easy answers, and he was tired of thinking about it.

Sitting down on a bench near the pier, he watched the waves hit the pilings. His brain waves were doing the same thing to the inside of his skull, and he could feel the beginning of a headache.

Callie was embarrassed and hurt, the kids were in a state of shock, and he didn't know how to make it right. He would apologize to his wife and explain all the facts, as he knew them, to his children. But what good would it do? He needed hard evidence, and he didn't have it.

Looking down the sidewalk, he watched as his friend, Pete Dawson, approached. On any other day he would have welcomed the company, but today he needed time to think.

"Mind if I sit down?" Pete asked.

"Would it matter if I did?"

"Not in the least. I think you need some company today." His long-time friend sat down heavily next to him. "Why did you all leave the party so early last night?

I was waiting to dance with your lovely wife."

"Are you kidding, Pete? You really don't know why we left?"

"Well, Charlie, I heard a few rumors, but no one gave me any facts."

"Pete, there was a woman at the party last night, apparently uninvited, who quite publicly claimed to be my daughter. She said she has proof of an affair I had with her mother." He stammered. "I can hardly get the words out of my mouth. The whole thing is ridiculous when I think about it." His voice got louder the more he talked. "I've never cheated on Callie. Never."

"Calm down, Judge. Looks like you've got one hell of a mess. What are you gonna' do to get out of this one?" Pete looked squarely at Charlie and slapped him on the back. "All I can say, my friend, is you sure do know how to ruin a party."

"Yeah, Pete, I'd been planning that one for the past few months." Charlie tried to smile but failed. "In fact, I accused my kids of playing a sick joke on me."

"Seriously. Unless you tell me different, there is no way I believe that little gal. She's setting you up and I'll do whatever I can to help you figure this out." Pete leaned back against the bench. "How's Callie taking this whole thing? Sure am glad I don't have to explain something like this to Alice. She'd have me in divorce court, and I'd be penniless before she got finished raking me over the coals." He chuckled.

"Pete, what would I do without you to cheer me up? Callie and the kids are holding their own. They're all real troopers, but I know this is shocking. No matter what happens, Callie didn't deserve any of this humiliation."

"Do you have any idea who this woman is? Or why

she singled you out? Unless you're keeping a lot of secrets, you don't have Fort Knox in your bank account, so there's no reason for her to try to con you out of money."

"She told Connor and me that all she wants is to be part of the family." He hung his head. "I don't have a clue what's coming next. Connor is doing some research to see if he can find out who she really is, and I've been sitting here reliving my life trying to find a crack somewhere that would include someone who calls herself Paula McBride. It still doesn't add up."

"We've known each other for a long time, and you know I'll fight with you. I've seen you in court for too many years and played too many golf games with you to walk away from our friendship now. I'm in for the long haul. You can count on me." Pete stood up and shaded his eyes from the sun. "Go home, old man. Before you get the sunburn of your life. I'll talk to you soon."

As Pete Dawson walked away, Charlie was grateful for such a good friend. They'd met when they were both starting out in law. Pete, who'd spent most of his growing up years in the northeast, had started working in his father's regional law office, had just gotten married, and loved to play golf as much as Charlie did. They'd been adversaries and friends for more years than they liked to count.

Pete had retired two years ago, and his daughter, Madeline, was carrying on the family tradition. She had taken over Pete's practice and was doing well for herself. He and Pete had joked on several occasions that Connor and Madeline would make a great couple, but he didn't think they'd ever been on a date. Maybe he'd give Connor a nudge in her direction.

The few minutes with Pete had lifted his mood, although he'd been reminded that others in town had overheard Paula's declaration. He was grateful that Pete was on his side because he figured there were others in town who'd already taken sides against him.

Watching his friend walk down the sidewalk toward town, Charlie realized the sun was getting lower in the west and he'd procrastinated long enough. He needed to go home and face whatever waited for him.

But what about Callie? A look had crossed her face he'd never seen before. She had always trusted him, believed in him, and loved him. Did he have any idea what new feelings would play out between them? Had he taken her for granted and not realized how much he had depended on her trust and belief? He couldn't erase that look from his mind, and he knew she was hurt.

And what about his kids? They were putting on brave faces, but, at the very least, they had to be embarrassed, too. Would they continue to defend him? His heart was heavier than it had ever been. What if his world was crumbling because of a few words spoken by this Paula woman?

The house was within sight and his pace slowed. Everything good in his life could be summed up in that house; but for the first time, he dreaded walking up the steps and opening the door.

****

"It's about time you got here, Matt."

"It's been exactly one hour and twenty minutes since you called, my friend. You better be glad I didn't get a ticket." Matt walked over and took the seat closest to Connor's desk. "Let's review what you know."

It didn't take Connor long to give Matt the facts.

"Is that all you know?" his friend asked.

He nodded. "I started running her name through every database I could find, and I finally found a source that lets me know one thing. But I can't find her birth records. In Tallahassee, she worked for a few months as a waitress at some diner. No record of her going to college or ever being married. The picture I found on the diner website is a match. The big puzzle is, I can't find anything on a Sandra Duncan. No birth or death records, even though Paula says her mother died last year of cancer."

"Did you do a local or national search? Maybe the mother didn't live or die in Tallahassee."

"If she hooked up with my old man, she had to be in Tallahassee at some point."

"What paperwork did she tell you she has?"

"Birth certificate, letters from my father to her mother, and copies of support checks. Of course, she didn't bring any of them with her this morning, so I set up a meeting for her to bring them tomorrow. That'll give me more time to try and get a read on her."

"What did you make of the interaction between your father and this woman?"

"There really wasn't any. At one point, I saw my dad look as though he might have recognized something in her, but it was a fleeting glance. And you want to hear something funny? She tried to hit on me as she was leaving my office. She told me she was really sorry that I was her brother."

"You're an ego maniac. She wasn't hitting on you. She was telling you she didn't like your looks."

"Not the way she was leaning over my desk. She definitely had those 'come hither eyes' directed at me."

"Forget your high hopes. What do you want to happen and how can I help?"

"Matt, I don't need another sister. I want this woman to be discredited and my father's honor to be restored. This is a scam, and we need to find out what she really wants from my family. She's after something that only my father can deliver, or she would have chosen another person to go after."

"I can put her under surveillance, run down her information, and meet her at the hotel bar for a drink to see if she's forthcoming with any clues. But our chances of uncovering anything are slim to none. She doesn't sound like an amateur. We need for her to make a mistake."

"You're right, and I'm counting on you to orchestrate the trap."

"You've called the best man for the job. Now call your mom and have her invite me to dinner. I need to understand where the family stands on this."

****

"Mrs. McBride, I can always count on you for the best leftovers in Florida. Thanks for adding my name to the pot for tonight."

"Matt, there's always room for you at our table. How are your folks? I saw them at the retirement dinner but didn't have a chance to say a word."

"I'm sure they understand. I don't think they've recovered from the appearance of the mystery guest who spoiled your lovely party."

"Is she the reason you're in town? I wondered how long it would take before Connor called you." Callie walked over and gave Matt a hug. "Thank you for being here. Everyone's feeling a little bit crazy right now, and you might be the voice of reason that we need." She stepped back and looked at him. "If your folks know about Paula, then it must be all over town."

"No, no. I don't think it's all over town. My folks were seated close enough they overheard what happened. And you know my mom isn't the gossip type. When I asked her about what happened, all she said was someone who wasn't invited to the party had upset you and the judge, and you left early." He stopped talking and tried to gauge her reaction. "I'm sure only a few people know what happened. Everybody at the party is probably wondering why you all left so early and didn't stay to enjoy the dancing."

A smile slowly crossed Callie's face. "You're probably right."

"We'll get to the bottom of this, I can assure you of that much. I already have my brother doing a little homework on this Paula person. You keep your chin up, okay? This lady is going to wish she'd picked another family to scam."

"I'll try. Will you do me a favor and call everyone to dinner? You look like you're starving."

****

Callie took her place at the table and watched her children interact with Matt. If she didn't know better, it would be as though nothing of importance was happening in her household except a reunion of old friends. There was laughter, teasing, and everyone talking at once. Just like it should be. Her eyes wandered to the other end of the table where Charlie was in the thick of the conversation. *How can he be laughing when our world seems to be falling apart?* But that was her Charlie. Always the optimist.

She couldn't assess the real mood of her kids in this atmosphere, but she was grateful for the break in the clouds that had been hanging over the house all day. Even her grandchildren seemed to have livened up, so why couldn't she? Maybe because she was worried that she was somehow complicit in this drama….

One person and a few words had changed everything for her. Frustrated, that's how she felt. Frustrated and hurt. And to be honest, she was frightened. Was there a way forward for her? It was hard to imagine a life without moments like this one around her dining room table. She loved her life and all that it had stood for until last night. No matter what happened or what the outcome, she wished Paula McBride didn't exist.

She wished she could turn the clock back to the time before she had ever heard that woman's name. Charlie had waltzed into the house several hours ago and acted as though nothing had happened between them. He'd given her a hug and retreated to the den where the grandchildren were quietly playing games. As unlikely as it seemed, Mandy and Max had been uncharacteristically quiet all day. They'd stayed out of everyone's way, which wasn't like them at all. She guessed their parents had given them a story to let them know there was trouble in the house.

"Mom? Mother? Oh, mommy dearest, where are you?" Brock called to her across the table. "I hate to interrupt your daydreaming, but we need you to be part of this discussion."

"I'm sorry. What discussion? I was having fun just watching you all carry on. I didn't realize you'd gone and gotten serious." She winked at Brock. "You have my attention."

Connor spoke directly to his mother. "Dad and I are being called on to answer a million questions and we thought you might want to hear what we have to say."

She nodded at Connor and wished she could be excused from the table. "Sure, honey, tell us everything."

Brock looked over at his children. "Max, Mandy, now we get to the boring part, so you all can be excused. Close the door to the den and turn on the TV. You know which shows you can watch. Right?"

The twins were out of their seats and racing to the den before he had the words out of his mouth.

"Okay, Connor, tell us what you know," said Charlie.

"It's simple. This woman has no claim on us even though she says she has proof. I asked her to bring her documents to my office tomorrow morning. As far as verifiable records go, she doesn't exist. There is no evidence of a Paula McBride in any database that we've checked except one. And all I can tell from that source is that someone with that name worked part-time for a few weeks at some diner in Tallahassee. Apparently, she didn't work long enough to get a paycheck. There's no evidence of withholdings. I think she must have been paid under the table. I'll let you know more when I've seen these supposed documents Paula is bringing to me. I'll make sure the right people examine them, and then we'll take the next steps."

Edward interrupted. "What next steps are you talking about? She either has evidence or she doesn't, correct?" He smirked and looked Connor in the eyes. "I don't think I've been properly introduced to your friend. You all forgot that part."

71

"I'm sorry, Edward. I forgot my manners. Matt Granger has been my best friend since childhood and his family is one of our neighbors. Matt, this is Edward Jenkins, a friend of Dara's." Connor ignored the sarcasm and steely eyed glance. "Next steps may include forensics and DNA testing. We won't know what we're dealing with until we see the documentation."

"Won't you need court orders to proceed? I doubt if this woman will consent to a DNA test unless she is ordered by the court," Edward continued. "Every trick in your bag, counselor, will take time. Or am I wrong?"

"If court orders are needed, I will try to expedite them in a timely manner, Edward."

As the silence in the room grew louder, Connor turned to look at his dad. "Do you want me to tell the rest?"

"No, son. It's my story, so I'll tell it."

Charlie went on to tell everyone about his friend, Julie. He kept an eye on Callie as he spoke and stuck to the simple facts. "We were friends and that's all. She knew all about your mother and how excited we were to be expecting our first child. She even introduced me to her son who was just a toddler at the time. We were never intimate, and I don't see any connection between Julie and this Paula person. I can't even remember Julie's last name."

Before he could continue, Edward got up and left the room.

Connor shrugged his shoulders and gave Dara a questioning look. When she didn't respond, he spoke to his siblings. "No questions from you guys. Dad's not on trial here. Until we know more, you all aren't going to bombard him with questions and your opinions. Let this thing unfold and let Matt and me do our jobs. After our meeting tomorrow with Paula, we'll have more to go on and, hopefully, some answers for you. I know you have a zillion things you want to say but hold on for now. Until further notice, Mom and Dad are off limits to your curiosity."

He stood up and started out of the room. "Come on, Matt, let's go to my house. We've got work to do." He waved good-bye, then turned. "Thanks for dinner, Mom."

"Connor, you're not playing fair," Adalyn called after him as she heard the back door slam. "He's enjoying the control he thinks he has over us a little too much."

"Connor's right. It won't help anybody or anything if we continue to badger Mom and Dad," Brock offered. "When he knows more, he'll let us know, right, Dad?"

"Thanks for taking his side, Brock. We don't know what we don't know, and speculation isn't going to help. Think of your mother's feelings and let's call it a night." Charlie stood up and held out his hand to Callie. "Why don't we turn in and let our children solve the world's problems?"

****

After Callie and Charlie had closed their bedroom door, Dara spoke up. "I don't know about you, but none of this is adding up. Dad says he's innocent; Paula says he's not. Connor seems to think this is a con, and so far, Paula isn't asking for money. Even though the woman didn't make too much of a spectacle of herself last night, what good is ruining Dad's reputation when he's retiring? I've gone over and over every angle and I can't find the storyline. Am I the only one that seems to be

73

obsessing about this?"

"Dara, calm down. We're as concerned and curious as you are. Let's wait until they've had the meeting tomorrow, and then we can add our two cents." Brock looked around the room. "Hey, sis, what's with your boyfriend, anyway?"

"I think you've scared him away." Dara stood up and headed for the front porch. "He probably needed some fresh air. I'll go check."

"Adalyn, this is beginning to read like your soap opera." Marti laughed as she, too, headed out of the room. "I'm taking the kids up to bed. You all hash this out and let me know if you come up with anything new."

"I'll be upstairs soon, Marti. I have a few questions for Adalyn about changing my career. I think it might be fun to be a leading man on TV."

"Brock, you know I married you for your sense of humor. Adalyn, don't burst your brother's bubble. Let him down easy."

With only Adalyn and Brock left in the room, it felt empty and too quiet. "Okay, sis, what's going on in your life? You haven't been yourself since you got here."

"I don't know what you're talking about."

"Yes, you do. You're putting on a good act, and I know this garbage that we're going through is getting to you, but there's something else. I know you too well. Spill it and get it over with."

"I'm getting old." She stumbled over the words. "I don't feel old, but I'm beginning to look old. I'll be forty in August."

"So what? We're all getting older, and forty is not even middle aged in my book. What's the big deal?"

Adalyn got up and moved closer to where her

brother was sitting at the table. "Your patients don't count your wrinkles or gray hairs. Everything on television is exaggerated. My producers have noticed, and they're making comments that make me nervous."

"That's ridiculous. The role you play calls for an older woman. You've grown the part and it wouldn't make sense for them to bring in somebody younger. I think you're making a mountain out of nothing." Brock looked long and hard at his sister. "You're beautiful, Adalyn. You've got a mature beauty that few women will ever achieve. The producers are crazy if they don't recognize what they've got." He lifted his sister's chin and looked in her eyes. "I don't watch your show, but half my patients do and, most of the time, they come to see me to find out what's going on in *your* private life. Or they schedule their appointments so they don't have to miss the show. They love you."

"Yes, I have fans, but what have I accomplished with my life? You're a doctor, Connor's a lawyer, Dara teaches. All of you are making a difference; you're helping others. What am I doing besides memorizing lines of script?"

He smiled. "For a few minutes of the day, you manage to take people out of their dreary lives. You give them a respite from their problems. You entertain them and you look like what all of them wish they looked like. Believe me, sis, as a doctor I say you are good medicine."

"Thanks for the vote of confidence, dear brother, and for seeing me. Sometimes you really can be sweet."

Brock laughed off the compliment and quickly changed the subject. Talking to Adalyn about her age was a no-win conversation. "Did Dara come back or is she still out on the porch?"

75

"I think she's still outside. Want to join her?"

"For a few minutes, then I better see if my wife is feeling lonely."

"That's too mushy for me. Let's see if the other set of love birds want our company. Make some noise. You know Mom wouldn't let Dara and Edward share a bedroom." She grinned. "Dara had the nerve to ask. You know, she thinks she can get away with stuff that we could never get away with. When will she learn?"

Brock and Adalyn walked across the room hand in hand and made sure the screen door slammed behind them.

"Want some company?" Brock whispered.

"I'd love it. It was getting lonely out here."

"Where's Edward? Brock and I thought you'd be all lovey-dovey out here."

"I haven't seen him. But, on Shamrock Beach, he couldn't have gone too far."

"Are you guys getting serious, Dara? You don't usually bring boyfriends home."

"Kinda' nosy, aren't you, Adalyn?"

"Kinda' touchy, aren't you, Dara?"

"Sorry, sis. It's been a rough twenty-four hours. And, to answer your question, I'm not sure. Sometimes I think we have a relationship and at others I find myself wondering what is going on between us. He's different from other men I've dated and I'm trying to decide if the differences are too much for me."

"Sounds like he's a passing fancy, if you ask me," Adalyn offered. "What do you think, Brock?"

"Like I would know about these things? When I met Marti, she was it for me. There were no doubts then or now." He turned back toward the door. "Lovely sisters of mine, I'm saying good night. This conversation is out of my league. See you in the morning."

"Thought you were headed home tomorrow," said Dara.

He called over his shoulder as he went inside, "With everything that's going on, we're going to hang around for at least another day."

After saying goodnight to their brother, Adalyn sat down on the swing next to her sister. "We haven't had a good chat in a long time. How are you?"

"The university is great. I still love my job, but sometimes I get homesick. Maybe my reaction to Edward is about missing the family. He's not pushing me for a commitment. Which seems strange since he pushed so hard to be here for Dad's party. You know, he gave me the whole bit about wanting to know my family." She laughed. "I tried to warn him, but even my warning couldn't have included this fiasco. What do you think is going on with this Paula person?"

"I wish I had a clue. Dad seems to be taking it in stride, Mom is a bit more emotional than usual, and Connor has taken charge. I'm glad he asked Matt to do some investigating." The more she talked, the more animated she became. "I want to know what Paula's game is. She doesn't appear to be the type that wants to be part of a large family. Can you imagine her sharing a bathroom with this crew?"

Dara ignored her sister's attempt to lighten the mood. "I want them to insist on DNA testing. Any good graphic art student at the university could have forged her so-called papers."

"Connor won't be fooled, and Matt will follow every angle until he knows the truth." She sat quietly with her thoughts. "Doesn't all this make you look at Dad a little differently? What if there *was* another woman? That will certainly shatter our image as the perfect family, won't it?"

"Don't go there. Don't put that thought out in the universe. It's not true and you know it."

"Good evening, ladies." Edward's voice startled Dara into silence. "I'd have thought you would have turned in long ago."

"We waited on you since you don't have a key," Dara responded. "You startled me. Have you been standing there long?"

"I'm surprised you didn't hear me coming up the walk. I wasn't trying to be quiet."

"You must have walked several miles."

"Walked a little, sat on a bench a lot. Things were feeling rather claustrophobic around here. I was hoping everyone would have gone to bed by now."

"I'll leave you all to have your discussion. I'm turning in." Adalyn brushed past Edward on her way to the door and was unsettled by the heavy odor of bourbon that surrounded him. "Dara, I'll leave the lamp on for you. Lock up when you come inside."

****

"What's going on with you, Edward? You've been acting strange all evening."

His voice reflected his anger, and he made no effort to temper the volume. "Are you serious? Your family is in a meltdown, and you think I'm the one acting strange. If I'd known I was walking into a family crisis, I'd have stayed in Tallahassee. I thought your family had prestige and respectability. Instead, I've discovered your father is a sham. This family is counterfeit and so are you."

"How dare you. Families don't fold in a crisis, Edward. They stick up for each other. They stick together, and I'm sorry you don't understand that. If you're uncomfortable, you can go back to Tallahassee anytime. You have the keys and it's your car. I can take the bus or rent a car." Dara's response to Edward's anger was defensive. "Nobody is making you stay."

"Exactly, and I might do that after I've had a few hours' sleep. Don't be surprised if the car is gone in the morning." Edward slammed the door behind him as he went into the house.

The vibrations of the wooden door hitting against its frame rolled across the porch, disturbing the quietness of the night. Dara, her heart racing, felt the impact and hoped the sound had not awakened everyone in the house. What a night, she thought and used her feet to push off in the swing.

Allowing the swaying motion to calm her down, she made no effort to go inside. How many problems had she solved in her youth sitting right here on this porch? The thought relaxed her and renewed her waning energy. There was no point in going to bed because she knew she wouldn't sleep. It was a time of too many questions and too few answers.

She trusted her father, but what if? And the last few hours had helped her realize the relationship she wanted might not be with Edward. Somehow, they weren't the right fit, and it surprised her that she wasn't sad. So what if she was meant to be a spinster professor. She'd learn to live with it, just like she'd learned to live with other disappointments in life.

She was thirty-four years old, had her doctorate in British and Irish Literature, and loved teaching at the university. It made her sad to think that she had no children and most likely would never be a mother; the other parts of her life would have to make up for that loss. She had Max and Mandy to fill the gap.

There had been love in her life. She knew she could give and receive love. But she'd made her choices. Obtaining a doctorate, studying, and living abroad in Ireland had been more important than staying home and marrying Tony Gallagher. Foolishly, she thought he would wait for her, and he did for a couple of years.

Then, he met someone named Janet and had married her. It wasn't until her heart was broken that she realized how much she loved him. Gazing out at the moon rising beyond the dunes, she knew if Tony walked toward her tonight, she'd want him with every cell of her body. No matter what she was feeling, she knew the decision she made years ago was the right one for her. The bad part was holding every other man she met to the standard Tony had set.

Her thoughts raced back to Edward, and she tried to put herself in his position. He had come along with her for a family celebration that had accelerated into an ugly family drama. She tried to imagine how she would react if this was Edward's family, and she was the outsider.

"This is crazy," she whispered. *I need some sleep. There's no telling what tomorrow will bring.* She stopped the swing and headed inside. Tiptoeing to the door of the den, she knocked softly. "Edward, may I come in?"

When she heard a mumbled reply, she opened the door and walked over to the figure sprawled out on the sofa bed. "I'm sorry this has turned into a nightmare visit. You have every right to feel excluded. All the evidence points to more craziness before this is over." She tried to sound as light as possible. "But who knows. By tomorrow this may all be settled, and we'll be laughing at how we over-reacted."

"I'm out of my league here. It's like I'm intruding on a very private family matter and I'm hearing things I shouldn't. It's not you. It's the situation and I'm not handling it well." Edward seemed to struggle to find the right words. "Nothing will be settled by tomorrow and you know it. I think it would be best if I went back to Tallahassee. You know, to give you the time you need with your family without having to worry about me."

"I understand," she whispered.

"It's best for me to leave. I have things to do that are more important than getting involved in your craziness." He turned back to the wall. "I'm tired, Dara."

Chapter Nine

Shortly before first light, Callie stirred. She lay still and listened to Charlie's gentle snoring, wondering how he could sleep so soundly with all that was happening.

She wasn't worried about the outcome, she just felt sad. Sad that her family was facing this battle, sad that her children were being subjected to doubt about their father, and sad that their celebration in Ireland might have to be postponed. This morning she was determined to break the sadness and get on with life, but she knew that would take energy she wasn't sure she had.

The song of a bird in a nearby tree broke into her thoughts. A small bird was welcoming a new day and Callie allowed the song to waken her to the possibility that today would be a better one. Cautiously, so she wouldn't awaken Charlie, she climbed out of bed and grabbed her robe. As she slipped out of their bedroom, she turned to smile at her sleeping husband. Her heart filled with love for the man who had captured her imagination so many years ago.

She couldn't let go of the fact he was a good husband, loving father, wonderful lover, and compassionate friend. He had been there for her when she needed him, had provided well for their family, and had made her proud of the choices he made. Compared to that, this Paula and Julie thing was a small bump in the road. She took a deep breath, quietly closed the door behind her, and ran headlong into Brock.

"Oh, my," she muttered as she regained her balance. "I thought I was the only one awake. Did I hurt you?"

"No, ma'am, but thanks for asking. Where are you off to in such a hurry?" Brock whispered.

"No hurry, honey. I was trying to be quiet." She looked up at her handsome son. "Are you headed for the kitchen?"

When he nodded, she linked her arm through his and together they tiptoed across the house. As quietly as she could, she busied herself with the coffee pot.

"The coffee will be ready in a few minutes. Are you up for a good mother-son conversation?"

"Always. What's on your mind?" He laughed. "Now that has to be the stupidest question I've ever asked."

"You're right. I know everyone has one person on their minds and her name is Paula." She pulled down mugs from the cabinet and got out the cream reluctant to go on. Finally, she took a deep breath and looked at him. "I need your opinion, and I'm open to any suggestions you might have on how I should go forward."

"You don't need me. You're one of the most grounded people I know. But I will say, don't be shy. Be assertive. I'll be here to help remind Dad this isn't just about him. He needs to keep your feelings in the forefront. This woman is some kind of con, I'm sure of that. None of us believe otherwise." He paused. "First off, if I were you, I would make sure I was included in all future meetings. If this woman is the fraud we believe her to be, another woman in the room could have an intimidating effect. She knows you'll see right through her. I hate to say this, but we men can be conned by a beautiful, sexy woman. And she is both of those. I'm surprised she doesn't have Connor drooling all over himself."

"Brock, you ought to be ashamed of yourself. Your brother's not like that."

"Don't kid yourself. Connor loves women and he'll follow them anywhere."

"Drink your coffee and stop with this nonsense." Callie poured two cups of coffee and took her seat at the table. "I like your idea about me going to the meetings. Back me up on this when your father and brother try to convince me otherwise."

Callie turned the conversation to questions about her grandchildren and enjoyed the few minutes of quiet time with her oldest son. She watched his face as he recounted the twins' latest antics, and she knew he was full of love for his children. That made her proud of the father he had become. "How are things with you and Marti?"

"You never told me that love keeps getting better and better. I love her more than I ever imagined I could. In many ways she's like you. You know, the glue that holds it all together. I'm happy. My life is good."

She grinned at him, her heart and spirit lighter. "That's all a mother wants for her kids. I guess one out of four isn't bad. I'm not so sure your brother and sisters would make the same statement."

"Adalyn is worried about growing old, Connor seems content, and who knows about Dara? What do you think about this Edward character? He doesn't seem to want to get to know us. I've tried to engage him in conversation, and he has a way of turning me off before I can get started." He shook his head. "There's something about him that makes me uncomfortable for him to be in this house."

"If he's her choice, then he's her choice. That's all I'll say. I'm just not sure she's happy, and they certainly aren't acting like they're a couple. Let's just say, the jury is still out on this one."

"If he wasn't with our Dara, do you think you'd like him?"

"Not fair. Let's see how it plays out."

The front door closed, and Brock jumped up to see what was happening. When he returned to the kitchen, he was smiling broadly. "I think it just played out. That was Edward leaving, suitcase in hand."

"What are you talking about?"

"Edward just got in his car and drove off. He had his suitcase with him, and Dara is nowhere in sight. Guess this family is too much for him." He sat back down as Dara and Adalyn came in the kitchen.

"Is he gone?" Dara asked. "We waited until we thought we heard the car drive away."

"Yes, he's gone, and you don't seem too broken up about it," Brock said.

"Not at all. I'm glad he's gone. Let's leave it at that. Okay?"

"If you're okay, we're okay." Callie winked at Brock. "Girls, help yourselves to the coffee. I'll get us all a slice of Grace's cinnamon bread to sweeten this day."

"Cut me some, too," yelled Charlie as he came in the kitchen. "I'm on the run. I overslept and I need to get my walk in before my meeting with Connor." He poured coffee into his Yeti cup and grabbed a napkin for his bread.

"Hold on, Charlie. I've decided to go to the meeting with you."

"There's no need for you to be there."

"It's my need, so don't try to talk me out of it. I'll be ready to go by the time you get back from your walk." Callie placed a plate of cinnamon bread on the table and walked out of the room.

"What's gotten into your mother this morning?" He waved the piece of bread at his children. "I don't think it's a good idea for her to be around Paula until we know more."

"Don't make a big deal out of it. She's part of this story, too. Mom handles things better when she knows what she's dealing with," Brock replied.

"Dad, the idea of a possible other woman impacts Mom more than it does us, so I can only imagine what she's feeling. And anyone working to hurt you can hurt her, too. We all believe you, but you're the only one who can make sure Mom doesn't get lost in all this."

Charlie turned to his son. "I hear you. I just hope this doesn't backfire on us."

****

When they arrived at Connor's office, Callie motioned for Charlie to take the chair in front of Connor's desk, and she took a seat on the couch that was across the room.

"I didn't expect you to be here, Mom. If you don't mind, you've chosen the right seat. I think it's best that Paula sits in the other chair in front of my desk."

"I agree, Connor. Where's Matt? I thought he might be here this morning," Callie said. She felt more confident of a good outcome knowing Matt was working to find the truth.

"No, I don't want Paula to see him. Remember, he does his work behind the scenes." He turned to his dad.

86

"Again, let me take the lead on this. We'll make copies of whatever she brings and keep the originals in my safe. I've opened it so she can see where the documents will be held until they're examined for authenticity. If she's skittish about that, I'll call the sheriff and he can take them over to the vault at City Hall. Are you in agreement?"

Charlie nodded.

"Once we have the documents, they'll be turned over for validation. I've been in touch with one of the professors in the forensic lab at the university and she knows to expect someone from the sheriff's office to bring the documents to her. I'll explain all of this to her." Connor turned to speak to his mother. "The downside is it may take a few days for us to receive a report from the lab."

"I thought you were going to insist on DNA testing," Callie said. "The paperwork she has probably won't prove anything." She knew how "authentic" official documents could look.

"That will be our next step. But it's a bit more complicated, and most likely she won't offer to do that voluntarily. I'll need a court order. And court orders require cause."

The buzzer on Connor's phone sounded and he indicated to his secretary that they were ready for her to send Paula in. "Are you ready for this, Mom?"

Callie nodded. *Let the games begin.*

When Paula walked in, she seemed momentarily stopped by the sight of Callie. "Oh, Mrs. McBride, I didn't expect to see you this morning." She walked over and stood in front of the sofa. "I'm glad you're here. I've waited so long for our chance to get to know one another.

After this meeting, do you think we can meet for coffee?"

Callie was astonished, but she also knew how to conceal her reactions. She'd had years of training no one in the room knew anything about. She hadn't anticipated a personal conversation with the young woman, however.

She glanced at Charlie who had risen from his chair to intervene. She gave him a nod of reassurance before speaking. "Paula, let's take it slowly, please. When the time is right, I would be glad to have coffee with you."

Charlie sat back down as Connor began to speak to Paula. "Please take this chair so we might begin the meeting. I'm assuming you brought the documents with you."

Paula placed her hand over her heart. "My goodness, Connor, not even a good morning. I had hoped we could be on friendly terms."

He did not look sorry, but he inclined his head. "My apologies, but I do have a tight schedule today. Good morning."

"That's much better." Paula leaned over the arm of the chair and opened the small briefcase that she'd been carrying. "This folder contains the paperwork I spoke about yesterday. You'll find copies of my birth certificate, letters to my mother, and copies of support checks signed by Judge McBride. I brought you copies. You know it's in my best interest to keep the originals."

Connor shook his head. "Then it looks like we'll be going to court. Copies of documents cannot be used to certify authenticity. And, if we are going to court, I'll also ask the judge to order DNA testing." He leaned across the desk. "Sorry, Paula. I thought you were going to cooperate with us."

"You only asked to see the documents that I have. You didn't tell me that copies wouldn't be enough. I hadn't planned on you taking me to court." She stood up and looked at Charlie. "Are you going to let him harass me like this?"

Charlie's words were formal. "Young lady, this is not harassment. It's the law and we will follow the letter of the law until there is some resolution. Did you really think you could walk in here with copies and we'd accept them at face value? You have made a serious accusation against me, and the burden of proof is on you, Paula. You will have to prove that your claim is real."

She turned to face Callie. "Mrs. McBride, you are the only family I have left in this world. All I wanted is to be a part of something. I'm not asking for money. I only want my father to recognize me as his daughter. Won't you help me, please?" Tears flowed as Paula appealed to Callie. "Don't let them take me to court. One word from you and they'll stop this. Can't you see that?" When she finished, she hung her head.

Callie could feel her heartrate pick up and she could only pretend that she was unaffected. She didn't feel as confident now as she had earlier this morning, but she was determined to keep her end of the bargain she'd made with Connor and Charlie.

"Young lady, you know I can't help you. This is a legal matter that will be settled as the law allows. Once that happens, I might be able to open my arms and give you the family that you seem to want so badly. We both must take steps to ensure that our worlds mesh but don't collide. I'm sure you understand." She was trying not to let everyone see her hands shaking and hoped her voice wasn't quivering. She wanted to run out of the office but didn't know if her legs would hold her if she tried to stand. "Connor, please give Paula a tissue," she said.

He pushed the box of tissues across the desk without looking directly at his parents or the young woman seated across from him. "I'll take the folder you've prepared, although it proves nothing. Where are you staying so you can be informed when the court order is ready?"

"I'm at the Shamrock Inn," Paula whispered as she handed the folder to Connor. She gathered her things and walked out of the office without another word. She didn't look at anyone and didn't turn around when Connor said "good-bye."

As soon as the door was closed, Charlie and Connor ran across the room to Callie. Charlie sat down next to her, and Connor knelt in front of her. Both were talking at once.

"Callie, are you all right? You shouldn't have been subjected to this—"

"Oh, Mom, I'm sorry. You handled that outburst like a champ. If I'd seen it coming, I'd have tried to stop it."

Callie raised her hand to quiet them both. "My mighty protectors, I've had worse moments. I just wasn't prepared for her to get so emotional."

"She was so composed yesterday. I never thought she would go to high drama so easily." As soon as he knew his mother was okay, Connor's frown turned to a grin as wide as his face. He grabbed his mother's hand, gave it a squeeze, and turned to look at Charlie. "I think we've got her, Dad."

****

"Matt, here's the folder with all her paperwork. Hopefully there's enough here for you to work on. We're going to have to get a court order for the originals."

"I can have my friend, Jill, at the lab look these over. She'll be able to spot anomalies and inconsistencies, but we'll need to give her the originals for anything conclusive." Matt began thumbing through the file. "Have you read any of these letters? If I had to guess, the handwriting is more feminine than masculine. I haven't seen your dad's writing enough to recognize any similarities. Does it look familiar to you?"

"Remember, these letters were supposedly written some forty years ago. Doesn't handwriting change over the years?" Connor furrowed his brow.

"There are always markers that identify a person's handwriting. Jill will know what to look for." Matt picked up a page and started to read it. "This mush doesn't sound like your dad. I can't imagine him being this flowery."

My darling, here I sit in my stuffy office trying to concentrate on case notes, but you are in my thoughts constantly. I long to feel your arms around me, your legs wrapped snuggly around me, your beautiful body beneath me. Next week I will have time to spend loving you and touching you. Our love making is always beyond what I had imagined it could ever be. Can you find a sitter for Paula so our passion can run wild?

"Wow. Whatever happens, we've got to make sure your mom never sees this trash."

"I wish *I'd* never seen this trash. This is one of those things you hope to never know about your parent. Don't read me any more and, Matt, I will bodily harm you if this stuff is ever leaked to my mother. How am I going to keep this private, even from my siblings? We've got to rush that DNA test and prove this chick is a fraud before any more damage is done."

"It's time for you to kick into lawyer mode, my friend. You need to start filing those petitions with the clerk of the court just in case we need to have court orders. One of my associates began surveillance on Paula around midnight last night. Sorry it didn't start sooner, but it took a few hours for me to get someone here from Jacksonville. The downside of being a successful firm, I guess. So far, nothing to report. No visitors, nothing unexpected."

Connor picked up the phone on his desk. "Annie, I need for you to start on a *Petition to Prove Paternity*. We'll need to file it as soon as possible with the clerk of the court, and see if you can get me an appointment with our new judge this afternoon. I need to keep Parker updated on what's happening. One more thing, Matt's working with me on my dad's case, so he can have access to whatever he needs. Hold on a minute, Annie." He turned to Matt. "Do you need desk space or anything?"

"No, I'm using the office at my folk's house. Mom cleared it for me this morning. And it's better that Paula doesn't see us connected in any way."

"Okay, Annie, that's it for now."

"I think I need a beer, and the Shamrock Inn serves the kind I like." Matt smiled mischievously as he turned to leave. "We've got this. Stop looking so worried."

****

"Is this seat taken?" He recognized Paula from her picture and sat down next to her at the bar of the Shamrock Inn. "Are you new in town? I don't think I've seen you in here before."

"Just passing through," Paula responded without looking in his direction.

"Gus, I'll have a cold beer when you have a minute." He nodded to the bartender and turned his attention back to Paula. "This is an out of the way town to just be passing through. Not too many folks stop off here."

"I'm the exception, then. By the way, I'm Paula McBride. Who are you?"

Matt was surprised that she used the McBride name but decided to go along with her. "Aha, so you're *the* Paula McBride." He hesitated for effect. "I hate to say it, but you're the talk of the town. I missed the dinner the other night, but I hadn't been in town for two minutes before someone mentioned your name." He extended his hand. "I'm Matt Granger. I used to live here, but like you, I'm just passing through."

"I imagine the gossip is raunchy, isn't it? I heard that folks in town are calling me the judge's love child. Not exactly the way I wanted to be introduced to my new hometown."

"You're planning on moving here? That takes guts. Small towns can be cruel."

"I'm finding that out. So, what do you want from me? It must be something, or you wouldn't be sitting here trying to find out what I'm up to."

"Lady, there was an empty seat at the bar, and I sat down. I didn't know who you were until you introduced yourself. I'll move if that will make you more comfortable."

"No, no. I'm sorry. I'm just a bit touchy after the reception I've gotten. The McBrides weren't too happy to learn of my existence."

"Did you expect them to accept you with open arms?

Apparently, you've taken everyone by surprise. Where are you from?"

"I'm living in Tallahassee. Why?"

"No reason." Matt shrugged his shoulders and picked up the drink Gus had placed in front of him. "Cheers, and here's to better days."

"Why are you in town, Matt?"

"I came to see my folks. I try to see them every few months. And it's a good excuse to enjoy the beach for a couple of days." He finished his beer and stood up to leave. "Maybe I'll see you around. It was nice talking to you."

"Wait. Do you have plans for dinner? I could use some company."

"I'd love to join you, but my folks are expecting me. If you're staying at the inn, maybe we'll run into each other later." He waved and walked out of the bar.

When he reached the sidewalk, he phoned Connor. "Your new 'sister' is a real looker. If this wasn't about work, I'd ask her out. I'm headed to my folks' for dinner, then I think I'll hang around the inn. You never know. I might get lucky."

"You're funnier than you look, my friend," replied Connor. "What's your real opinion of her?"

"She's smarter than I gave her credit for. I'm going to try to run into her again after dinner. I'm sure she'll be in the bar."

****

"Connor, I have something for you. I would have given it to you sooner, but in all the craziness I forgot about it." Dara reached in her bag and handed her brother a wine glass carefully wrapped in a linen napkin with the country club's insignia in the bottom corner.

94

"Thanks. I've always wanted a used wine glass."

"Oh, ye of little faith. This is not just any used wine glass. It is *the* used wine glass of one who wants us to believe her name is Paula."

"What are you talking about?"

"At the dinner the other night, I picked this up off the table and brought it home with me. It's the glass that Paula used, and I know you can get a good DNA sample from it. See that wonderful lipstick mark? I was floored when she came over to our table and stayed long enough to have some wine." She gave her brother a wicked smile. "In a moment of madness, I snatched it off the table and walked out with it. No one questioned me, and I knew we'd need it if things got worse. Well, things are worse."

"Dear sister, you've been watching too much NCIS. You know we can't legitimately use it, but Matt has a friend at the state lab, and I'll see if he can send it for a test. It won't be admissible in court, but it may be what we need to give Paula a scare. Even if she isn't in a database somewhere, it will settle the paternity question." He gave his sister a big kiss on the cheek. "Sometimes you are a keeper. The trick will be to get a DNA sample from Dad without letting him know that we have this glass."

"Leave it to me. He'll have a cup of coffee in the morning and, shall we say, I'll borrow his cup."

"I thought you were an English professor. Are you sure there isn't a touch of criminal forensics in your background?"

"You've got to be kidding. I grew up in a house that breaths investigation and intrigue. Edward thinks this whole thing is a black mark on Dad's reputation and he hinted more than once that Dad might not be so innocent. That's when I told him I was going to push you guys to go after DNA testing and he argued with me. I'm glad he's gone."

"Is that why he left? I'm assuming he wasn't the love of your life."

"We had a minor disagreement that led me to realize we have major problems. Enough said." She turned and walked toward the kitchen. "I will never admit to stealing that glass, by the way."

As Dara left the room, Connor pulled a cell phone from his pocket and dialed Matt. "I've got another favor to ask."

Chapter Ten

"I need to talk to you. When can you meet me?" Paula was desperate and she held the phone tighter. "I know you told me not to call you, but they're coming at me from all sides."

She started pacing the small room. "What do you mean? Why can't you meet me?" She was yelling now. "I don't care what you think. If you can't meet me, I'll have to go home without finishing what you asked me to do." She threw her phone on the bed and walked over to the makeshift bar. Just as she was pouring herself a vodka tonic, her phone rang.

"I knew you'd call me back." She listened to the voice on the other end of the line. "I told you, they want a DNA test, they want to send all my documents to some lab. No," she shouted, "I didn't give them the originals. Those are still here in my room." She couldn't calm down. "I did this for you. You encouraged me to do this." The voice on the other end of the phone was getting louder and more demanding. "I'm sorry I didn't do it the way you wanted. I saw an opportunity and I took it. You know where I'm staying. I'll be out front of the hotel at eleven o'clock tonight. Send someone to bring me some money. My expenses in this two-bit town are starting to add up."

****

Connor woke to the sound of his cell phone and

reached over in the dark to shut it off. When he saw Matt's number, he sat up and answered.

He pulled on his jeans and walked to the kitchen. "What do you mean, your guy was following her on foot until she got in a car with somebody and drove away. Why didn't he follow her and why is this urgent?" He listened for a few more minutes. "Come to my house. I'm putting on some coffee."

Connor was tired and the tension of the past several days was catching up with him. He hadn't slept well since the retirement dinner, and he couldn't slow his mind down enough to rest.

The pieces of the puzzle were not coming together, and he was beginning to doubt himself. Perhaps it was time to call in an experienced criminal attorney. There were so many things about this case that baffled him. *What was Paula's game? Why had she chosen his dad? Did his dad know more than he was telling? And who is Paula's accomplice? Was he too close to it to see what was really going on?*

The back door slammed, and Matt was standing in his kitchen trying to catch his breath. "Is the coffee ready?" he asked between gasps. "Don't you lock your doors? There are some bad guys in this town."

"If you ran over here from your parents' house, you sure are out of shape. That's all of two blocks," Connor said. He pulled two mugs out of the cabinet and filled them with steaming hot coffee. Matt was still bent over, breathing hard, as he handed him the mug. "Don't you ever work out?" He waited until Matt seemed to be breathing easier. "Nobody in this town locks their doors. You've been living in the city too long."

"I ran over here from the Shamrock Inn in record

time," Matt gasped as he straightened up. "I work out four days a week." He opened the refrigerator and grabbed a bottle of water. "I'll do the coffee in a minute. I need something cold."

"What's going on, and how did your man lose Paula? I thought you hired only the best?"

"My guy was standing outside the inn when Paula rushed out and jumped in a car that roared up and then screamed away. He didn't have time to get his own car. But he did get part of a license number. 'DRT 7.' He didn't get the last two numbers. The car was a black SUV. He thinks it might be a Mazda, probably a rental." Matt pulled out his phone and dialed a number. "I know it's late, but I need you to run part of a tag number. Yes, I owe you." He laughed at something. "It's a Florida number and I don't have all of it. What I've got is DRT 7." Again, he listened. "Because I know you can work miracles." When the call ended, he turned to Connor. "Done."

"Really, Matt? Is flattery how you get people to do your work for you? Some poor gal has you all wrong."

"I'll have you know that was not a gal. In fact, it was Phil Gerber. Remember him? He went into law enforcement after he left the university. He owes me big time for a case I helped him with several years ago." He put his phone back in his pocket. "Hey, this coffee actually tastes good."

"After your talk with Paula, did you come away with any vibes? Apparently, you don't think she's legit or you wouldn't be here in the middle of the night."

"She's smooth, but I think someone else is pulling the strings. She's not in this alone and she doesn't think fast enough on her feet to be the mastermind."

"You think it's the person driving the SUV."

"Can't say. The lady was definitely on the prowl when I talked to her in the bar. This might be somebody she picked up after I left. My guy was going back to talk to the bartender."

"Is that why you woke me up in the middle of the night?"

"Connor, what if this is someone on the inside who has access to the judge? Does your dad think he's in any danger?"

"You're kidding, right? The judge has had a few scares in the past and there could be a hundred folks who blame him for their bad choices, but I don't think he's given any thought to danger. Not for himself or for the family. Why are you going down this road?"

"Bad vibes about whoever was in the car. Paula would have already asked for money if that was the end game. Something made the hair on the back of my neck stand up, and I've learned to pay attention when it happens."

"My dad was on the bench a long time. He's sentenced murderers, con men and women, and others who would swear he was biased against them. He's even dealt with a few men accused of human trafficking. There was one case, I remember, where the guy threatened to get even. I think his exact words were, 'Judge, I'm going to take you down.' "

"Those are the kinds of things that make the hair on the back of my neck stand up."

"Okay. Say I buy into the hair on the back of your neck thing, what are you suggesting?"

"I want you to call the sheriff and ask for round the clock surveillance on the judge and the house. Your entire family is in that house right now, except for you, and whoever is behind this has done their homework. I think this Paula is a decoy or diversion for something else."

"He will have a fit if I do that."

"Let him. You've got to protect everyone else. Make the call and I'll go with you to the house to break the news to your dad."

Connor called the sheriff's office and set the plan in motion and then he dialed his dad's cell number and let it ring until his dad picked up.

"Sorry to wake you. Matt and I are coming over to talk to you."

****

"Boys, I think you're overreaching here. You're turning this into something bigger than it really is, don't you think?" The judge sat at the kitchen table and tried to defuse the conversation. "I know there are folks who wish me dead, but I don't think this Paula is one of them."

"We think this is bigger than Paula. Matt has suspicions and so do I. We've already done our own speculating and decided to go over your head. I had a long talk with the sheriff, and he totally agrees. A patrol car is probably parked out front already. You've got to think of everyone who's in this house right now. I know they'll be going home soon, but Mom will still be here when they leave. If you aren't concerned for yourself, at least consider her."

"Sir, when I hear from my friend about the car tag and when we get the DNA test results, we'll know whether we've overstepped with the surveillance."

"Whoa, Matt. What are you talking about? What

DNA tests?"

Connor gave Matt a scowl and then looked at his dad. "I was going to tell you, but later. You're not going to like what we've done."

"You're right about that, even though I don't know exactly what you've done."

"Dara stole the wine glass that Paula drank from the other night and we're sending it to a friend in the forensic lab at the university. I know we can't use it in court, but we need something to work with. We can't find anything on Paula."

"You could be disbarred for this, Connor. What were you thinking? What was Dara thinking?"

"We were thinking we need more information, and this test will prove you're not her father. This will not come back to us as a written report. There isn't anything official. Matt will get a call from his friend and the glass will be destroyed. Dara knows she needs to deny everything. Because Paula isn't in any database, we're still in the dark. We needed to take this chance." He stretched nonchalantly. "You know I'll need a DNA sample from you,"

Callie walked into the kitchen rubbing the sleep from her eyes. "What's all the racket?"

She looked at the serious expressions and wanted to crawl back in bed and pull the covers over her head. "Matt, Connor, it's late for a social call. What's going on?"

"I made a decision to have the house placed under surveillance and I wanted Dad to hear about it from me."

"My lord, why would you do that?" She pulled her robe tighter around her and grabbed the back of a kitchen chair to regain her sense of security. "All of this nonsense is getting on my last nerve."

Connor smiled at his mother's favorite saying. "Things have been getting on your last nerve for as long as I can remember. What's one more?" His expression turned serious. "Just a precaution, Mom. It's no big deal. Just keep the doors locked and try to ignore the patrol car out front until further notice."

"Does that mean no one leaves the house? Your brother and sisters might not like that idea. And what about Max and Mandy? You're going to scare them."

"I'll be here for breakfast and explain this as a precautionary measure. I won't be dramatic."

"Hold on." Charlie scowled. "Will there be a detail following me, too?"

"Yes, sir. Sorry. They'll be discreet. But its best until we know more," Matt said.

"That little gal has certainly gotten to you guys. This is way over the top," Charlie growled.

"It's better to be safe, don't you agree?"

Charlie shrugged his shoulders and glanced at his wife. "I think this whole thing has gotten out of control. I'm sorry we're in this mess. Connor, have them run that DNA test and let's get this over with. We all need a decent night's sleep."

"Dad, drink some of this water and we'll send the glass to the lab." As he handed over the glass, Connor turned to his mom and grinned. "I'm not using your good crystal."

Callie sighed. "What happens when you get the results?" She was almost too weary to care, but she wanted answers. "Can life get back to normal?"

"When we get the results, we tell Paula to pack her bags and move on."

"You mean there aren't repercussions? She can just go on and do this to someone else?" Callie sat down and looked at her son. "That's not fair."

"I know it doesn't sound that way. The sheriff and Dad will make that call, when and if we have some more information."

Connor lifted his mother's chin with his fingertips. "Don't worry. She'll get what's coming to her, and our family will pick up the pieces and go on."

"I'm not so sure about that." Callie, usually so optimistic, felt drained. She knew there were bags under her eyes and tears that she still hadn't shed and not for Charlie or their marriage. The outcome of Paula's parentage didn't seem as important as the damage that had already been done.

She'd worked hard every day of their marriage to be strong, to move past her decision, to even make amends for it, but it was beginning to feel like a mountain on her back. Would she and Charlie ever be able to go back to the carefree trust that they'd built as the hallmark of their relationship?

If only she could retire without having to reveal her own lies. Dare she hope for that? Even if she didn't deserve that grace, her family did, so she'd hope for the strength to hold on.

She shook her head, then shrugged. "If you all are finished, I think I'm going back to bed. I may have a few more hours before Max and Mandy start hounding me for French Toast."

Connor gave her a gentle pat on the shoulder. "Speaking of the twins, were Brock and Marti planning on leaving today?"

She managed a tired smile. Yet another of her

precious children had their world turned upside down by this stranger's announcement. *No, Paula should not be allowed to carry on.* "Brock told me last night they'll make that decision based on what's happening. He has someone covering his practice for the rest of the week. And what happened with Dara and Edward? Does anyone know?"

"Dara told me they had a disagreement. How did she phrase it? Oh yeah, she said a *minor disagreement that looked like a major problem,* and she was glad he was gone. I guess he went back to Tallahassee."

"He is an odd one. Doesn't sound like Dara is too broken up over his departure," Charlie grumbled. "Where does she find these guys? He looks a bit old for her, don't you think?" His question was addressed to Callie.

"She told me he's several years older than Adalyn and that she felt age didn't matter. I don't think she was that serious about him, to be honest." Callie took a few steps and turned around. "For two people who weren't in a serious relationship, I'm surprised she brought him home to meet us."

"Callie, wait. I'll go with you." Charlie moved away from the table before he looked over his shoulder at Connor. "You don't have any more surprises for me tonight, do you?"

"Good night, Dad. Sorry I had to bother you."

Without another word, Connor and Matt found themselves alone in the kitchen. "Well, that went over like a lead balloon. Grab your father's glass and let's get out of here."

****

Adalyn had tossed and turned for the past hour. She

looked at the clock on the dresser and groaned when she read three o'clock. Too early to get up and too late to try and go back to sleep. She'd been going over the pros and cons of returning to New York later in the day or staying in Shamrock Beach until something had been resolved.

Her show was on hiatus, so she wasn't missing any filming, her dog was safely with the dog sitter, and there wasn't a man with open arms waiting to greet her when she returned. In fact, she groaned again, ever since her last divorce she'd sworn off getting involved. Two husbands and several crazy relationships had convinced her she was better off alone. At least that's what she'd been telling herself.

Dara stirred. "What's going on? Go back to sleep, will you? I can hear you thinking."

The years melted away and it was like old times, Adalyn thought. "Nothing has changed. You are still one of the lightest sleepers I know." She threw off the thin summer sheet and sat on the side of the bed. "I was trying to decide when I was going back to New York. How 'bout you? When are you headed back to Tallahassee?"

"Good morning to you, too," Dara grumbled. "Why am I even talking to you? If you're awake, you think I should be."

"I haven't made a sound. But now that you're awake, give me an answer."

"Have you forgotten? I don't have a car. I'm going to have to rent one if I want to go home." She fluffed her pillow and rolled in the direction of her sister. "As soon as I can get my eyes open, we can have a discussion."

"Has summer session started?" Adalyn asked. "Are you in a hurry to get back to Tallahassee?"

"I taught the spring session and I'm taking the

summer off. I've got some research and writing to do, but no classes. Why?"

"If you're not in a hurry to leave, neither am I." The light from the alley behind the house cast a glow across the bedroom and she could almost make out the frown on Dara's face. "What are you thinking so hard about?"

"Do you think Mom needs for us to hang around? It isn't like her to let something rattle her, but I think this is getting the best of her. I'm not worried about Dad; he'll fuss and take it in stride. Mom's a different story and I'm concerned."

"Think about it, sis. How would you feel if you were in her shoes? There's a chance Dad may have broken her trust. I think she's feeling vulnerable and embarrassed." Adalyn's voice broke as she struggled with her words. "Saying it out loud just now helped me make my decision. I'm staying until I'm sure she's all right. I'll make a couple of phone calls after breakfast to clear my calendar and see if the sitter can keep Jazz for the rest of the week."

"If you're staying, so will I. There isn't anything pressing that I can't manage from here on my laptop." Dara groaned and turned her back to her sister. "Now will you please go back to sleep?"

Adalyn listened as her sister's breathing slowed and wondered how Dara could go from light sleeper to deep sleeper so quickly. Her mind still raced as she pulled up the covers, and she couldn't get thoughts of her own moments of betrayal out of her head.

She'd been so young when she married Peter. Young and naïve and trusting. It was still difficult for her to believe that his cheating had started almost as soon as they returned from their honeymoon and had continued the entire four years of their marriage.

And she'd been so vulnerable after their divorce. Her feelings of self-doubt, her wounds of rejection, and her lack of self-esteem clouded her vision and within a year she jumped right back into the same story with David, an actor she'd known for years.

He had lulled her with his promises, his caring, and his words of flattery that fed her battered ego. And it was all a lie. He'd used her to further his career and, when he'd gotten what he wanted, had let the world know that his mistress, not his wife, was going to Europe with him when shooting began on his new TV series. Yes, she had an inkling of how her mother was feeling.

At some point, she fell back to sleep. The next thing she knew, sweet Mandy was snuggling up next to her, whispering in her ear. "Wake up, Aunt Addy. There's going to be French Toast for breakfast."

"Huh? I'm awake." She hugged her niece and felt the warm embrace of a child's love. "This is the best wake-up call I've had in a long time. Give me another hug and then go make your Aunt Dara get out of bed."

****

"The McBride family is gathered around the breakfast table gobbling up their mother's delicious French Toast, enjoying each other's company and making sure everyone is happy." Brock stood at the end of the table using his coffee cup as a fake microphone. He'd endured the silence and solemn faces since he entered the kitchen. "Come on, folks. Wake up and smell the coffee."

"Sit down and act like a rock. You're the only creature on this earth who expends energy at this hour of the morning." Adalyn sipped her coffee and continued to frown at her brother. Then she gave a quick look around the table and started to chuckle. "Brock is right this time. We look like a bunch of zombies." She pushed back her chair and grabbed the cup from her brother. Holding it in front of her, imitating the hostess of a morning show, she began to shout, "Wake up, world! Wake up, McBrides! We have riddles to solve and worlds to conquer this morning. I challenge each of you to smile. Come on, just one little grin."

Everyone started booing, hissing, and laughing. "Of all the families in the world, I had to choose this one. We aren't even allowed to wake up in peace." Dara pretended to grumble, but she was laughing so hard she spilled her coffee. "Okay. Now that you've gotten our attention, what's on the agenda today?" She looked down the table at her father who sat quietly eating his breakfast.

"Don't look at me. I'm not running this show anymore. Call Connor and see what's going on. He said he'd be here for breakfast, but he's probably in his office enjoying a *quiet* cup of coffee." Charlie took another bite. "One other thing. Brock, Adalyn, and Dara, see you in my office when you've finished eating. It'll just take a minute."

"Speaking of Connor, I thought I heard his voice last night. Was he here or was I dreaming?" Brock questioned.

"No dream. He and Matt stopped by to interrupt my sleep sometime after midnight. They thought they had stumbled on something, but it was nothing."

Callie brought the last platter to the table and sat down. "Matt and Connor are working hard to find out who Paula is. They want your father to be updated on everything that's happening. Today, Paula is supposed to bring Connor the originals of the documents she claims she has. Let's wait and see how that turns out."

She took two pieces of French Toast off the platter and sprinkled them with powdered sugar. "Why don't you guys take the twins on a hike down the Matanzas Trail? I'll pack you a picnic lunch. That'll help pass the time till we hear from him."

"You have the best ideas, Nonnie." Max gave a whoop and jumped up from his place. "Can we do it, Dad? Please, please, please."

****

Brock stood by the office door and frowned. "Dad, you've got to be kidding. Connor and Matt are taking this too far. How am I going to explain police escorts to my kids?"

"Make a game out of it, Brock. Kids love play acting," Adalyn offered. "It'll be fun, if you don't overreact yourself." She turned to her sister. "I have dibs on the cutest cop, Dara."

"Adalyn, you're nuts," Dara responded with disgust. "Dad, how long is this going to go on? Do we have to check in with somebody if we want to leave the house?"

"I'll be able to answer your questions as soon as I go out and talk to the officer sitting in the patrol car in front of the house. For now, take it in stride. That's how I plan to handle it."

****

Callie finished chewing her last bit of breakfast and sat back in the chair. How she missed the noisy days when her children lived at home. Today she was grateful for any distraction.

"Charlie, don't you love it when the kids are home,

and the house is bustling with noise?"

He looked across the table at her but ignored her question. "We need to talk about what's going on. You're shutting down, trying to pretend this isn't hard on you. I've known you too long to believe that. You've detached yourself and that's not like you."

"How do you want me to act?" she said quietly as she leaned forward and gave him a hard look. "I'm a doer, Charlie. I'm the one who fixes things for this family and right now all I can do is sit quietly on the sidelines or call for a policeman to follow me to town."

She picked up her plate and walked to the sink. "My world may be falling apart and all I can do is wait for it to happen. I can't go out my front door without people staring and asking all kinds of inappropriate questions. And you look at me with questioning eyes. What is it you want to know? Do you want to know if I can welcome this woman into our home if she is your daughter? Is that what you want us to talk about?"

"Dear God, how could you think that?" For a moment, he sounded defeated. "How do you think I feel? Don't you think this is tearing me up inside? Don't you think it bothers me that my children are looking at me with a hesitation I've never experienced before? Don't you think I know you're hurting? We've always talked our way through things. That's been our strength, Callie. We've always been able to talk, and now you're pushing me away and making assumptions that have no basis."

She willed herself to be calm. To be patient. But she was frightened and not about Paula. The fear was wearing her out. She just needed to hold on like Grace urged.

"You wanted to know my thoughts. Well, I've

emptied my mind. Even said some things that were better left unsaid. I'm not pushing you. I'm just trying to keep my head above the waves that are rolling over me. I don't know what else can be said between us until we have some answers." She had other things on her mind besides Paula. Things that Charlie must *never* know.

"Do you think I'm lying to you?" His head snapped up and he looked at her, anxiety in his voice. "Is that it? You think that girl might be my daughter?"

She shook her head. "I don't know what I'm thinking, Charlie. One minute I know it can't be true and the next minute I'm asking myself all kinds of questions." She paused to rethink where the conversation could head. "I've loved you for so long, trusted you for so long. Never could I have imagined this conversation. These past few days have been some of the hardest I've ever lived." Her gaze traced his face and she saw her sadness reflected there. The tension in her body eased, and she softened her voice. "No matter what, we'll get through this. I love you, Charlie McBride, like I always have. I just need you to give me a little space. You need to help me pretend that things are normal around here. Okay?" His arms were around her the moment she finished her sentence.

"My darling, I can do that. If you think everything will somehow work out, I can give you all the space you need. Heck. I can even pretend with you." He dropped his arms and took a step away from her. His mood shifted, his smile returned, and as if to prove to her that he understood, he whistled as he left the kitchen.

****

Callie slipped out the back door and walked quickly down the alley to the next street. She turned toward town and hoped she'd managed to leave without someone in the house or the surveillance team noticing.

The walk to the church usually took ten minutes, but she knew at her fast pace she would be there in less time than that. She needed the quiet and the peace she always experienced when she entered the sanctuary.

As she walked up the steps, she prayed the church would be empty and she would be alone. The doors were unlocked, as she knew they would be, and she took a deep breath. Gently she pushed the doors closed behind her and turned to face the altar. As she scanned to the right and left, she could see she was alone. Only the altar lights were on, but the defused rays of the sun shining through the stained-glass windows offered an illusion of peace and comfort. They invited her to stay.

She walked halfway down the aisle and took a seat where the rays would fall around her, where she could feel their warmth. As she allowed the stillness to help her quiet her thoughts, she pulled the kneeler down from the pew in front of her and moved to her knees.

Lord, I don't know who I am anymore, and it scares me. I don't understand why I can't roll with these punches like I've done so many times before when a crisis occurred. You know all the hidden places in our lives, all the secrets, all the necessary lies. Please help me see how to navigate through my own circumstances. May I also be forgiven. I need You and I don't seem to be able to find You, even though I know You're with me.

Please help me and Charlie and our kids. I can't do this without Your guidance and help. And, Lord, I ask You to be with this woman who is doing so much damage to my family. Help her to see what she's doing and help me to forgive her for doing it. I have other

113

responsibilities that require my attention right now. You know all that's resting on my shoulders. I must make sure that my priorities are in order, in both my worlds. Give me strength, Lord. Give me strength. Amen.

Easing her way back onto the pew a tingling sensation crept across the back of her neck, and she was caught in a web of fear. Her nerves felt jagged, and heat rose in her face. A shadow or slight movement to her left caught her attention. Yet, when she turned to look, there was no one in the church. Her body stiffened in response, and she braced in anticipation of an attack. *What is going on? There is no one here but me.*

She adjusted her position so she was leaning against the back of the pew and tried to focus her eyes on the lighted cross above the altar. Moments passed before her shoulders began to relax. She listened to her breathing until it gradually slowed, and her heart rate felt normal. Shallow breathes became deeper, and slowly the fear began to dissolve.

Lord, please let me know I'm not crazy. There was someone in this place besides me. My instincts are well trained—my fear was real.

She sat still for a long time, making sure she was in control of her emotions. The sensation had not occurred again, and she finally decided her jangled nerves had played a trick on her. Just as her body began to relax, she was startled by a different sound at the back of the church. It was not a subtle sound, more like a crash, but her instincts took over and she crouched down in the pew. Curling in a tight ball, she prayed she wasn't visible above the seat.

"Callie, is that you?" A familiar voice called out. "I didn't mean to disturb you." The pastor was standing at

the end of the pew looking at her in surprise. "Are you okay?"

"Pastor Mark," she exclaimed. "I'm sorry. I thought I was alone, and you startled me. I'm fine, really. A bit embarrassed that you found me huddled in the pew." She could feel her face turning redder. "I finished my few minutes of quiet and I was about to head home when I heard a crashing sound."

He extended his hand to help her sit up. "I'm glad you had a few minutes of quiet before I barged in here and dropped that box of candles." His expression changed to one of suppressed humor. "You can imagine my surprise to see you hiding in the corner of the pew. You looked like you were expecting someone to attack you." He hesitated. "You know I'm here if you need to talk. I'll support you and Charlie any way I can. The judge is one of the most honorable men I know."

She stood up and moved around him until she reached the aisle. "I did overreact a bit. You know I'll call you if I need anything." As she hurried up the aisle, she knew her tone of voice had been abrupt, and it wasn't fair to someone who was trying to be kind.

When she reached the door, she turned around to see the pastor standing in the aisle with his hands on his hips. She wondered if he thought she was crazy. "I'm sorry, Mark. There is just so much right now… I'll see you on Sunday."

As the church doors closed behind her, she slowed her steps. Her eyes darted up and down the street to make sure there was no one waiting for her. A few people were walking about, going in the shops and offices on the next block, but none of them even glanced in her direction. She laughed and grabbed for the railing to steady herself.

The kids are right. I've been watching too many detective shows for my own good. No one is waiting to ambush me. Me, a wife, mother, and a small-town museum curator. Why would anyone want to hurt me?

Callie never saw the person standing in the shadow of the church, watching every move she made.

Chapter Eleven

"Twenty-four hours has gone by and there's no word from the lab and your guys haven't seen Paula. What's going on? Do you have any ideas, Matt?" Connor's voice was edgy and sharp as he paced his office. "I wasn't worried before, but that's changing."

"I called the lab, and my friend assured me I'd get some info today. She said it'd be preliminary but would give us enough to start our work." Matt's face wasn't readable, but his voice was steady. "On the other front, my guys are frustrated. There's no sign of the woman and nothing has panned out on the partial license plate. We're in one of those lulls that happen just before all the pieces come together. I go through this with almost every case, Connor. It's the nature of the work I do. One little piece of info will surface soon that will pull it all together. Can you be patient until we find that piece?"

"You know how to do your job, Matt. I'm not trying to second guess you. But time is passing, and my dad is still hanging out there. Everyone in town has an opinion, gossip is rampant, and my family is getting restless. They look at me like I'm holding out on them. They're expecting answers and I don't have any."

"What does your schedule look like for the rest of the day? Can you ride with me to Gainesville to check in with the lab?"

"Not today. I'm due in court at ten thirty and I've

still got to tie up some loose ends." He walked back to his desk and pointed to a stack of files. "These will fill my time until court."

"I understand, my friend. I'll call you when I know something."

****

Connor was leaving the courtroom when his cell phone rang, and Matt's name popped up on the screen.

"Great timing. I'm walking out of the courthouse now and I know you have some good news for me."

"This is preliminary, remember? Looks like your dad is not Paula's father. Their DNA is not a match."

"Fantastic. I'm on my way to the house to shout this news from the rafters." Connor paused. "I can share this with my family, right?"

"For now, keep it in the family. Don't let anyone talk about it outside the house. We don't want to tip our hand just yet." He could feel Matt's smile through the phone. "It's like when we played cops and robbers, good buddy."

"Right. I got carried away. It's a relief to know without a doubt that my dad wasn't lying."

"This isn't over, Connor. We still have to find Paula and figure out what this is all about. Depending on what else we find, this could become a criminal investigation. But thank goodness, your dad is off the hook."

****

Connor was glad everyone was still at lunch when he arrived at his parents' house. But realizing the twins were still at the table, he forced himself to keep quiet until they'd been dismissed.

"Are there any leftovers? I'm starving." He pulled out his chair and began filling a plate. He wondered if his mother always set a plate for him, even when it was rare that he joined her for a meal. "One BLT on whole wheat coming up. Mandy, pass your favorite uncle that platter."

"Uncle Connor, I can pour you a glass of tea, too," Mandy said. She had the tendency to be shy, but she liked the attention she received from her uncle. "Is that okay, Nonnie?"

"Certainly, sweetheart. You're a good helper." Callie smiled as she watched her granddaughter carefully fill the glass and carry it to the table. "To what do we owe the pleasure of your company for lunch, Connor?"

"In the neighborhood, Mom, and I wanted to see your lovely face. I could smell the bacon cooking all the way to the courthouse."

"Oh, brother. It's getting deeper and deeper in here." Adalyn rolled her eyes at her brother. "Please tell me you have some news. Anything at all would be greatly appreciated."

"Mandy, thank you for my tea. If you and Max are finished eating, I have a surprise. Max, bring me my briefcase, please." Connor motioned to this nephew who dashed to pick up the leather bag from the hallway bench. "Thank you, my good man. Hopefully this is a movie you haven't seen before. Why don't you and your sister leave us grownups to our boring conversation and go watch it?" He handed the video to Max and watched the twins take off for the den. "It's parent approved," he assured his sister-in-law.

When the kids were out of the room, he turned to his father. "You're off the hook, Dad. The preliminary DNA report says you and Paula are not a match."

There was a collective sigh around the table and Charlie knocked over his chair in his rush to get to Callie.

"Don't cry, Callie. Please, sweetheart, it's over and there are no more reasons for you to doubt." He leaned over her chair and gave her a hug. He held her a long moment, then straightened, but left his hands resting on her shoulders.

"It's not totally over," Connor said. "There could be a criminal investigation, and we still need to get the truth from that woman. We need to know who orchestrated this fiasco and why. It may take more than a few days."

"I know, son. But the important question has been answered for this family." Charlie couldn't stop grinning. "Give us a minute to celebrate this good news before we must think about what's next. And would you go out front and tell that poor policeman he can go home?"

Connor held up his hand and looked around the table. "Celebrate all you want, but this news stays in the house. It's not for public knowledge until further notice. You've got to remember that it will take a court order to run that test for real and for the results to be conclusive." He looked at the puzzled faces around him. "Let's just say, there's a lot of legalese that needs to take place before this goes out to the world. Understood? If we end up in court, I want all our bases covered."

"You mean you're not really a lawyer? Is that it, bro?" The words tumbled out of Brock's mouth, and everyone laughed.

"I paid a lot of money for that fake diploma," Connor said with a grin. "So, don't ruin my reputation."

"Has there been any word from Paula? Do you know where she is?" Dara asked.

"Matt is looking under every rock, but right now we don't have any info on her whereabouts. She hasn't

120

checked out of the inn, and nobody has seen her or heard from her for two days. He'll let us know when he has anything."

"Dad, I know it's not official, but I'm really glad the pressure is off." Brock crossed the room and stood next to his mother. "Mom, the color is back in your cheeks. You can start to breathe again."

"Only my doctor son would notice that I haven't taken a breath in over a week." Callie stood up and gave Brock a pat on the back. "I'm all right. Those were tears of relief." She smiled and took her husband's hand. "Charlie, we need a few minutes alone, don't you think?"

When Callie and Charlie moved away from the table, everyone started talking at once. The somber mood was dissipating with every word.

"Guess this means we can all go home," Dara shouted. "Not that I don't like your company, but Adalyn snores and I miss my bed."

"You're making that up. I do not snore." Adalyn tossed her napkin at her sister. "I only breathe musically sometimes."

Connor cleared his throat and his siblings quieted. "In the next few days, it should be okay for all of us to resume our lives but be cautious. Notice what you notice. We still don't know if our involvement in this drama is over. There's more to this than we've been able to figure out. The only question that's settled is the paternity issue. Somebody's behind this and wants something from Dad. We just don't know what." He knew his siblings needed to leave, but he was reluctant to see them go. He lowered his voice. "Just don't abandon Mom all at once. I think this has been harder on her than she wants any of us to know."

Marti stood up. "I hate to break up a good party, but Brock needs to be home as soon as we can load up the kids. He wouldn't tell you that he's been calling in favors to get his patients covered these last few days. Fortunately, we're just a little over an hour away if we need to come back for any reason." She grabbed Brock's arm. "Come help me pack."

"Hang on a minute." Connor grabbed his brother's other arm. "I didn't want to say anything before, but you need to keep a close eye on the twins. Don't scowl. I'm just looking at this from all angles."

"I get it. We'll be careful." He gave his brother a slap on the back. "By the way, I told Dad I'd go on a walk with him. Can you go in my place?" He waited for Connor to nod before he left to help his wife.

"Do you really think the kids might be in danger?" Adalyn asked. "Or are you being paranoid all of a sudden?"

"Sis, until we have more information, we've all got to be a little paranoid."

"We hear you, Connor," Dara chimed in. "I've got to rent a car, so I'll be here at least another day. And Tallahassee is less than four hours away. You'll call me if you think I need to come back?"

"Sure, Dara. I don't see any reason for you to stay."

"Well, I'm staying," Adalyn said firmly. "I don't need to head back to New York just yet. Connor, you and I can be the support team for a while longer." She sipped her iced tea and winked at him. "How much mischief do you think the two of us can get into without the others around?"

"Let me count the ways, dear Adalyn."

****

122

"Charlie, is it really over?" Callie sat on the edge of the bed and wrapped her arms around herself, trying to hold all her emotions inside. "I feel like I've aged a hundred years in the past few days. My mind didn't have time to get used to one thing before something else happened. Do you think this test is reliable? Do you think people in this town will ever look at us the same?"

"It's not over until we have more answers than we have now. Why in the world that woman thought she could wreck our lives with her crazy story is beyond me." He grabbed his wife's hand and lifted her chin to look at him. "I'm so sorry for all of this. I was born here, raised here. I don't care what other people say, and I know who my friends are. But you came from outside and I didn't realize that even after all these years, you still don't know this is your town, too. I hope I never give you another reason to look at me with doubt. I think that look you gave me in the restaurant is one of the lowest moments in my life."

She swiped at her tears. "I'm sorry. I got caught up in the drama and knocked my common sense out the window. One thing I've learned in all of this, Charlie, is that I won't ever take my life and your love for granted again. I've grown comfortable and complacent over the years, and I've forgotten to appreciate what I have. These past few days have shown me how much I would hate to lose you and all that loving you means. God opened my eyes."

Charlie took her hands in his. "Thanks for reminding me. I've always known you were the best wife in the world, but this week showed me I've also got the best kids in the world. Their support and humor kept me going. With you all in my corner, I think I can handle just about anything that comes along."

"That's good, because we never know what's coming tomorrow. Now reassure me nothing bad will happen to our family and tell me to stop worrying."

****

"My goodness, it's quiet around here. Even the boards aren't creaking anymore." Charlie stretched as he put the morning paper down on the table and picked up his coffee cup. "It was great to get a good night's sleep. I don't think I really closed my eyes all week and it wasn't because of all the noise."

"Our grandchildren did keep up a constant chatter, didn't they?" Callie shook her head and smiled.

Charlie glanced across the table at his daughter. "Adalyn, you're very quiet this morning. It must be hard to go from the lively conversations with your brothers and sister to the silence of boring old folks."

"Right. You and Mom are boring." The look she gave her father was gentle and loving. "When did Dara leave? I must have slept through her leaving."

"I heard her drive out of the driveway around five o'clock. I didn't think she'd leave until after breakfast, but the note she left on the table said she couldn't sleep and decided to get on the road before the rush hour traffic. It gets hectic around Jacksonville."

Charlie lifted his coffee cup and saluted his wife and daughter. "It has been great sharing a meal with you lovely ladies, but I think I'll walk over to Connor's office and see if there is any news." He rose from the table and planted a kiss on his daughter's head. "Thanks for hanging around, Adalyn. It isn't often we have any time with only you. I'm looking forward to the next few days."

After he left the room, Adalyn gave her mom another once over. "You're leaving for Ireland very soon and you haven't started to get ready for your trip. Why don't we head up to Jacksonville today and buy you a couple of new outfits? You deserve a special treat," she prattled on. "We can go to lunch, get a manicure, see a movie. Whatever suits you."

"What about tomorrow? I thought I'd go over to the museum this morning and see if there's anything I can do to help them get ready for the new exhibit that's supposed to open in a few weeks. In fact, why don't you go with me? You know, just a little stroll with you, me, and that nice police officer who's sitting out front."

"I'd love to." She could laugh about the surveillance now that their ordeal was over. "Mom, aren't you retired?"

"Well, yes. But I still offer a helping hand when something big is coming up. Go on, take your shower and we'll leave in about an hour." She smiled tenderly at her daughter. "You used to be the only one I could persuade to go to the museum with me. It'll be wonderful to have you there."

****

The next day as Callie and Adalyn were unloading the packages from their shopping spree, the phone rang. "I'll get it, Mom, and then I'll go out to the car and bring in the rest of your new treasures."

Callie watched her daughter walk toward the phone that was hanging on the wall in the kitchen and wondered why the ringing of a phone could dampen the happy mood she was in.

Her shopping adventure with Adalyn had been the medicine she needed to help her forget the chaos of the past week, but her inner voice told her the phone call was going to reinstate her anxiety.

"Hi, Connor, if you're calling for Dad, he's –" Her brother cut her off mid-sentence. "Oh, he's sitting in your office. Do you want to talk to Mom?" Adalyn listened. "I don't know what to say. Yes, I'll talk to her." She hung up the phone and returned to her seat at the table.

"What is it, Adalyn?" whispered Callie over the nausea rising in her throat.

"There's been a new development. One we didn't see coming." Swallowing hard, she continued, "They've just found the body of a woman floating in the Intra-Coastal Waterway. Her description matches Paula."

"Dear God, what if it's that poor girl? What kind of accident was it? Who found her?" Callie's words accelerated as she tried to grasp what she'd heard. "Where's your father?"

"Slow down. Dad is at Connor's office, and I don't know any more than I've told you. But, Mom, this doesn't sound good."

****

"Dad, Matt got the call because his friend in the Duval County sheriff's office knew he had been asking questions about a woman who matches the description of the one they pulled out of the Intra-Coastal this morning. They're estimating the age of the woman at somewhere between thirty-five and forty-five, brown hair, blue eyes, approximately five feet six inches, maybe one hundred and twenty-five pounds. She was fully clothed. Forensics and the medical examiner haven't released any information. What I just told you is preliminary info that's in the police report. So far, they haven't found a car, a boat, or any reason for her to be in the river. Matt says the police think it's an accidental drowning that needs more investigating."

Connor watched his father's face as he delivered the information. He was looking for any clue that his father might have an emotional tie to what had happened. But the expression on Charlie's face was unreadable.

"Dad, are you listening to me? Did you hear what I said?"

Charlie shook his head and shoulders. "Sorry, I'm listening to you and trying to figure it out at the same time. There's no rhyme or reason for any of this." He shook his head again. "Seems the more evidence we have, the less we know. We've got to get to Paula's documents before someone else gets to the hotel. We've got to find out who she is."

Connor grabbed his phone and punched in Matt's number. "You're right about those documents, Dad." After several rings, Matt answered.

"We've got a major problem," Connor said. "How can we get Paula's supposed documents?" He listened. "No, no. Don't tell me what you're going to do. Just do what you need to do and call me later."

He ended the call then glanced at his father. "It's a good thing we're a team. I totally forgot about the documents." He smiled at his dad and motioned for him to follow. "We need to get to the house. Mom and Adalyn probably have a million questions that we don't have answers for, but maybe our being there will be reassuring. By now, they should have called Brock and Dara, and there will be even more questions."

In the twilight, they walked shoulder to shoulder toward the house both lost in their own thoughts. The ocean breeze blew gently, the birds were returning to their roost, and lights were coming on in the houses up and down the street.

Too early for people to be out on their porches, windows were closed to keep the air conditioners efficient, and the lack of human voices made it eerily quiet. The symphony of the air conditioners almost cancelled out the sound of the waves breaking on the beach.

Connor wished for noise, laughter, children yelling, human conversation—signs of normal life that might help to break up his thoughts. Since hearing the news of the woman in the river, he had felt the jaws of a giant animal closing around his family. His father was right, none of it made sense and their legal minds were being derailed by their emotions.

They walked up the porch steps and Connor grabbed the screen door handle. Before he could pull the door open, his father stopped him. "We need to make sure we don't upset your mother any more than we have to."

"I understand. But she will want to know everything we know, and she won't like it if she feels she's been lied to. We need to be honest with her, don't you agree?"

"Just be gentle with her. That's all I'm asking."

He heard the tightness in his father's voice and realized the toll the Paula drama was having on even the head of his family. "Good advice, Dad. Good advice."

****

"Will it ever stop?" Callie's voice reflected the strain that this new development was having on all of them, but she didn't look surprised. "I've prayed for that young woman since the day she opened this can of worms. At least she isn't being exploited anymore."

"They haven't let us know whether it's Paula." Connor stood next to his mother's chair and reached over to touch her shoulder. "Matt is skeptical. He called because he didn't want us to hear about it on the nightly news. If it is Paula, it leaves a very big hole in our investigation. She held the answers to so many of our questions."

"Connor, let her rest in peace," Callie whispered. "Let the poor woman rest in peace."

"It's not that easy. She made some choices that weren't in her best interest, and we're sure she was the cover for someone who may be a greater threat to our family. We've got to keep digging until we have some understanding."

"Honey, this isn't easy on any of us, and Connor will do his best to keep you and the others protected from whatever danger may be lurking." Charlie paced the floor as he spoke, choosing his words carefully, and keeping his tone of voice as gentle as possible.

"And the plot thickens." Adalyn's sigh resonated across the room. "I came home to get away from the soap opera I act in, and I've landed in a bigger one that we're actually living. The joke's on me."

Connor's voice hardened as he turned on his sister. "It's not always about you, Adalyn."

"Grow up. I was just making an observation."

"This is hardly the time or place for the two of you to start jabbing each other," Charlie scolded.

"You're right." Connor glanced across the room and winked at his sister. "We're all in this one together, Adalyn. One call and your screen writers will give us a happy ending, right?"

"I need some fresh air." Callie stood up and headed

for the front door. "Anybody want to sit on the porch with me?" She looked around the room and hoped no one would say yes. The silence told her everything she needed to know. Her family was lost in their own thoughts, afraid that any more discussion would start the finger pointing that she was trying to escape.

"I'll be in the swing if anyone needs me," she whispered as she closed the door behind her.

She walked to the end of the porch and sat down in the swing. Closing her eyes, she concentrated on letting go of the confusion and chaos that was robbing her of peace. Moments from the past flashed in front of her and she shivered.

Connor is right. None of this is about Adalyn, and as time passes, it doesn't seem to be about Charlie. I just hope it's not about me. Did my choices put my husband and family in danger? Is my carefully guarded life spilling over them in ways I can't control?

Pulling her cell phone from her pocket, she dialed Grace's number. "Did this madness start because of me?"

Chapter Twelve

Dara finished up things at her office and walked the two miles to her apartment. It was late in the day for her usual walk, but a week of her mom's good food and no exercise was going to start showing if she didn't get back into her routine.

She was tired, worried about her family, and, although she didn't want to admit it, lonely for Edward. His actions in Shamrock Beach had been disturbing and, in her heart, she knew their relationship wasn't the right one for her. But they'd had fun together and he had been great company while it lasted. Tonight, she would walk into an empty apartment, wait for the phone to ring, and wonder how she was going to meet someone new.

"Maybe a small glass of wine will take the edge off," she said to the walls as she tossed her keys on the hall table and headed for the kitchen. "I've got to figure out how to get my apartment key back from Edward without talking to him or seeing him." She laughed at that illogical thought.

She poured her drink and was headed to the living room when she saw the note on the kitchen table. "*Call me when you're back in town. Let me try to undo some of the damage I caused. I miss you. Edward.*"

Slamming the note down, she found her cell phone and called her sister. When Adalyn answered, she didn't even say hello, but put the phone on speaker so she could take a sip of the wine.

"Can you believe Edward wasted no time using his key to come in my apartment and leave me a note?" Her tone of voice was anything but pleased.

"Hello to you, too," Adalyn said. "What are you so mad about? Aren't you the one who gave him a key?"

"I never thought he'd use it after abandoning me at Mom and Dad's. It's just not right. He said he wants to repair the damage he caused. Can you believe that?"

"Dara, text the man and tell him to mail you the key. That should take care of it. Or, if you aren't brave enough to do that, call a locksmith and have the lock changed." Adalyn sounded impatient. "Unless you want to continue the relationship."

Dara rolled her eyes. "Calm down. I told you he wasn't right for me. For a few minutes today, I missed him, but there's no reason for me to call him or see him."

"I'll ask you again. What are you mad about? Surely, the sex wasn't so good you'll sacrifice the rest of your life for it."

"Adalyn, that last remark wasn't funny. Why did I think I could vent to you?" Dara considered ending the call but took a deep breath instead.

"Because you know I'd only speak truth to you, little sis. Forget this guy and decide what you want to do about the key." After a minute of silence, she continued. "Are you through venting? There's something we need to talk about."

Dara thought about it for a few seconds and then sighed. "Yes, thanks for being there. I hope it's not more bad news."

"You might call it that. Matt let us know that a body matching Paula's description was found floating in the

Intra-Coastal Waterway. No positive identification, but he wanted us to be prepared."

Dara almost dropped the glass in her hand. "I know you're not kidding me, but this alters everything, doesn't it?"

"I don't think we know what it means, Dara. If it's her, we've lost our opportunity to question her about what she wanted from Dad."

"Do you think I need to come home? How are the folks taking this bit of news?"

"Connor and I are here, and you and Brock can be back in a few hours. Right now, all we're doing is sitting around waiting for more information. I promise I'll keep you posted. I just wanted you to be aware, that's all."

****

Callie stood in Grace's kitchen waiting for her to take the bread out of the oven. "You must know something you're not telling me. How is this woman connected to my family? I have a right to know."

Grace focused on the kitchen timer. "I don't have any information that I can share with you. I have my orders. I can tell you that whatever is going on seems to have something to do with us. We have a plan, Callie. Just work our plan and the rest will fall in place. You'll see."

****

The locksmith changed the locks, and it didn't cost her a fortune. All that was left to do was to text Edward. Her conscience wouldn't let her move on without letting him know that their relationship was over. *How do I keep getting myself in these messes when it comes to men?* She sighed and began her text.

—*Edward, while we had some fun, it is obvious we*

133

aren't compatible.

It is better for us to walk away before we have too much more invested in this relationship.

Thanks for the good times. I wish you the best.

BTW, I've had the locks changed, so there's no need to return the key.—

For two seconds, she hesitated. Then pushed *send* before she could change her mind. Her next text was to Adalyn.

—Sis, locks are changed, and I just pushed send on a text of "sad" farewell to Edward. Anything new on the home front?—

Without a boyfriend, she was going to have lots of extra time. Her preparation for fall classes was complete, the apartment was clean, she hated shopping, and her girlfriends had left town for summer vacations. Was this a sign she should return to Shamrock Beach for the rest of the summer?

The knock on the door startled her out of her reverie and she was slow to respond.

"Who's there?"

"It's Edward. Open the door. We need to talk."

So much for text messages and sad farewells. When she opened the door, he barged in and pushed her aside.

"What is wrong with you?" she demanded.

"I don't like the way you assumed this relationship was over, Dara. I think you owe me more than a text message." He stumbled to the couch and sat down.

"You've had too much to drink, Edward. This is not a good time for a discussion about anything." She stood in the open doorway and didn't move. "It would be better if you left." Keeping her voice calm and level, she made sure she could exit the apartment if it became necessary.

"I'll decide if it's a good time. And it's not a good time." He raised his voice with every word. "You can't just walk away. I have plans for you."

"We'll find time to talk later. I'd like you to leave now." She raised her voice as she became apprehensive.

"You're a class act." He laughed and started toward her. "I don't like being pushed around. Not by you or anybody. I'm leaving, but I'll be back. Don't think you can mess up my plans and walk away. Your family can't control me."

Before he reached the doorway, he got close enough to punch her in the stomach and pummel her in the face several times. She stumbled and fell in a gasping heap to the hardwood floor. He turned and laughed. "That's a sample of how I talk, Dara."

Before she could get up off the floor, he had gotten in his car and driven away. She finally sat, breathless and in pain. Whatever was going on, she needed to get away from him. She crawled to the table and picked up her phone.

"Connor, it's Dara. I need a restraining order issued against Edward Jenkins and as soon as I can pack a bag I'm coming back to Shamrock Beach."

****

"Daddy, I don't know what to tell you. I've gone over everything in my mind and nothing that happened fits with the man I've been dating for the last several months. Yes, I did make the final break with him in a text message, but he's the one who really left the relationship. What did he think I'd do, welcome him back with open arms after he stranded me here? His coming with me was his idea as was his leaving without me." Dara's frustration echoed in her voice.

"Honey, I don't have any answers, either. Connor had the restraining order issued and if Edward comes anywhere near you, he'll be arrested. You did the right thing to come home. He didn't appear to be a violent man, so I think he probably already regrets what he did. You said you thought he'd been drinking."

Dara nodded and accepted her dad's hug. "I'm glad I can always come home."

Callie ran her hand softly along Dara's hair. "Sweetie, it's after midnight. Why don't you go upstairs and try to get a couple hours of sleep?" She tried to hide her concern for her daughter. "I think Adalyn is already asleep, but she won't mind being awakened. She tried to stay awake until you got here, but you know how she is about her beauty sleep. Or you can sleep in the boys' old room." She kissed Dara's cheek and whispered, "Your face will look better in the morning. You did the right thing. It is never okay for a man to hit you. Absolutely never."

After Dara climbed the stairs, Callie stood with her head bowed as tears flowed down her cheeks. "I prayed that neither of our girls would ever have to face violence like this. How do we protect them, Charlie? How do we keep them safe?"

"Let's call it a night. We can't do any more than we've done for now. Being angry wears me out." He slapped his hand on the table and stood. "Thank goodness that man is hundreds of miles away. I'd like to take him down a notch."

****

Out of habit, Dara tiptoed around the room she had always shared with her sister and decided she was too tired to do more than change out of her clothes.

Tomorrow she would think about moving to the other bedroom.

"Hey, sis," Adalyn turned over and whispered. "Do you want to talk about it?"

"In the morning. I'm physically and mentally exhausted." She stretched out on the bed and closed her eyes hoping sleep would keep her from thinking. The long drive had given her plenty of time to worry and relive the past few weeks. It was like a scene from a bad movie she couldn't erase from her mind. What had she done to deserve the way Edward had treated her?

It had started four months ago when she stopped in the off-campus Sweet Shop to grab a sandwich between classes. The place was packed with students and faculty, but she managed to find a table in one of the back corners.

She was going over notes for her afternoon class and eating lunch when he asked to share her table. After introductions, he seemed eager to talk, so she put the notebook in her backpack and gladly joined the conversation. An unusual move for her since she rarely allowed strangers to interrupt her reading, but he was easy to look at and even easier to talk to. She was sorry to end the conversation when she realized she was going to be late for class if she didn't leave.

"How does lunch tomorrow, same time, same place sound?" he called as she made her way to the restaurant's door.

He'd made it all so easy. Lunch led to dinners, to evenings at her place, and to giving him a key to her apartment. They started spending every weekend together. He fascinated her, he charmed her, he made her feel wanted, and often, adored. He was a professor of economics and had grown up in Tallahassee. At the time she didn't think she needed to know more.

Why didn't I ask more questions about his past and background? Why haven't I met his family or any of his friends? We dated the whole semester, and I don't really know anything about him. This is insane. I've got to get some sleep and stop trying to figure out how I'm going to answer these same questions when I go to the family interrogation breakfast.

****

Dara stood at the bathroom mirror and was horrified at the swelling of her eyes and the bruise that stretched across her cheek. She knew that Edward's punch had hurt, but she didn't think his hits had been hard enough to leave marks.

All she wanted to do was hide in the bedroom until they totally vanished. Her family was going to be incensed, and she was going to be on the defensive. Not to defend Edward, but to defend her ability to make good choices. She thought about trying to cover the bruising with heavy make-up, but Adalyn would ridicule that ploy, and her mom would freak out.

The only option was to face them with as much dignity as possible. She finished brushing her hair and practiced facial expressions she could use that might get her through the morning.

"What in the world happened to you?" Adalyn shrieked.

Dara had nearly knocked her over when she opened the bathroom door. "Sis, you scared me. I'm sorry. Did I hurt you?"

"Stop trying to change the subject. What happened to your face?"

"Meet me at the breakfast table. I don't want to tell this sordid tale more than once," she said over her shoulder as she headed down the stairs.

Well, if the best defense was a good offense according to the football experts, then she'd just go on the offensive and get it all over with. At least she was home and safe. She swung around the baluster at the foot of the staircase and put a bounce in her step.

"All right, bring on the interrogation so we can move on," Dara announced loudly as she entered the kitchen. "Connor, when did you decide to come to breakfast? Are you the head council for the prosecution this morning?"

"That's a warm and loving welcome." He stood as his sister moved to the table. "How 'bout I get *you* a cup of coffee and help you get your day started on a happier note."

Callie smiled at her youngest daughter. "Sweetie, none of us is trying to make things harder for you. Your brother is concerned for your welfare, just like the rest of us. Why don't you have your breakfast, answer a few questions, and then ask your brother and sister to leave you in peace."

As she hugged her mother, Dara looked over her shoulder and quietly apologized to her brother. "I'm sorry, Connor. Everything feels very heavy right now. I was expecting an inquisition this morning, so I came downstairs with a chip on my shoulder."

Connor gave her a smile and handed her a cup of coffee fixed just the way she liked it.

"Dara, here's what I told Connor and what he used to have the restraining order issued. The guy was drunk, angry, and upset that you broke off the relationship.

Right?" Charlie didn't raise his head from the newspaper he was reading. "You look gorgeous this morning, daughter. Even if the color of your make-up is an interesting shade of purple."

"Thanks for the encouragement and humor, Dad. That about sums it up, I guess. It's not like we had ever talked about a future together." Dara turned to her mother. "I'm sorry, Mom, I know you don't approve. Edward was one of those spring flings. He wasn't in the running for anything serious." She took a sip of coffee. "That's why I can't make sense out of any of this. I've never seen him drunk. I've never heard him raise his voice. And I've never been afraid of him until last night. Now he's made me very afraid."

"Don't start second-guessing yourself. You did the right thing. Even if this isn't the behavior you expected from Edward, the moment he hit you, the dynamics shifted." Connor touched Dara's arm and smiled. "Let me know if he tries to get in touch with you."

Turning to his father, he changed the subject. "Dad, I don't have any more news from Matt. I'll give him a call this morning to see if he has an update. I hate to eat and run, but I've got a full calendar. The new judge frowns if you're late to court." He laughed as he left the house.

"Sometimes I forget he's a real lawyer," Adalyn chimed as she entered the room. "Did I miss the main performance? Did Dara and Connor go to war before I got here?"

"No, Adalyn. I sounded off a bit, but Connor and I are fine."

"Dara, meet me in my office after breakfast. I have a couple of questions." Charlie pushed back his chair.

"Another great breakfast, honey. Now, I'll leave you ladies to solve the problems of the world."

As soon as the office door closed, Adalyn turned to her sister. "Okay, now answer my question. What happened to you? All I knew last night was you were upset and coming home."

"Edward barged into my apartment and punched me. What else do you want to know?" As she turned to face Adalyn, her mother got a good look at her face for the first time.

"Oh my. I didn't see how bad that bruise was last night. No wonder you wanted a restraining order. It's worse than I thought." Callie tried not to sound alarmed.

"Mom, I didn't mean to upset you."

"I'm trying to think what I should do for a bruise like that. Do I need to call Brock?"

"It looks worse than it feels. It'll fade in a day or two. Don't get him upset." Dara kept her voice level and worked hard to keep the tears welling in her eyes from spilling out. "It's the craziest thing and I can't explain it. I've gone over and over the last few months in my mind and I can't think of anything that I've done or said that would have caused Edward's behavior. I knew when he came in last night he'd been drinking, and he wasn't happy that I'd changed the locks on the doors, but I never thought he'd react the way he did."

"But he hit you, Dara. There must be more to it." Adalyn was adamant. "That can't be the whole story."

"Don't get dramatic on me, sis," Dara snapped. "The man is a jerk, and I didn't see it until he came with me for the retirement dinner. I misjudged and now he's out of my life. I'll give him a few days to cool down, then I'm going back to Tallahassee."

"It is a big deal, and you need to stop thinking he's going to let it go without another confrontation," Adalyn said quietly.

"Adalyn may be right. Find out what your father thinks before you make any decisions about when to go home." Callie looked closely at her daughter's face. "Your cheek is swollen, honey. Don't leave the table until I've gotten you an icepack."

"I'm here if you need to talk. I'm not trying to make things worse." Adalyn sipped the coffee that had gotten cold and smiled at her sister.

****

Icepack pressed against her face, Dara took a seat in her father's office. She sat quietly while he finished reading the paper he was holding, not eager to begin what she knew was going to be lecture.

"I'm sorry about what you experienced last night. Violence against you or any woman is so far beyond my thinking that I'm having difficulty processing it. I want you to know, I'll do anything to help make sure you are never in that position again."

"I know that, Daddy. I was so confused last night I didn't know where to turn. Coming home was the only thing I could think of."

"You made the right decision. Coming home and getting the restraining order were your best options for the moment. But you've got other things to decide now. Are you going to press charges against Edward?"

Dropping the icepack, she jumped to her feet. "That's crazy, Daddy. I don't want him to go to jail or anything like that. All I was thinking about last night was making sure he wouldn't hit me again, and I guess that's still where I am today."

"Sit down, and let's talk this through." He waited before he began again. "What do you know about this man? Do you have any ideas about his background?"

"I admit I didn't do a good job of finding out about him. He's an associate professor in the Economics Department. We like the same music, we used to laugh together, he likes the outdoors. That's about it." She hesitated. "I don't know anything about his family, and he never introduced me to any of his friends. Remember, I've only known him a couple of months. I thought all of that would come as time went on."

"Are you in love with him?"

"No, I just enjoyed his company. I wasn't planning a wedding."

"I had to ask. You and your siblings don't usually bring someone home for us to meet unless you're getting serious."

"He wanted to meet you and Mom. I didn't see anything strange about that when he asked, but now I'm not sure why it was so important to him."

"Connor has the restraining order in place. That's what he came over to tell us. But, with your permission, I'm going to do some investigating."

"It's over with Edward. I'll probably never even see him again. I don't want you to make a big fuss about this."

"It's not a big fuss. Chalk it up to my inquisitive mind and a father's need to know what sort of man makes a punching bag out of his daughter."

****

Connor took a deep breath and then looked his friend in the eye. "Matt. When you have time, I need you to do a background check on Edward Jenkins.

143

Remember, you met him the other night at dinner. He's an associate professor of economics at FSU, probably in his mid-forties. He and Dara were dating, in fact he came over here for Dad's party, but last night he decided to get rough with her. She thinks he'd been drinking, but whatever, she's got a nasty bruise across her cheek. A restraining order has been issued against him, but Dara doesn't want to press charges. Keep this between us, my good man. For the time being, this info is just for me."

"I'll do what I can. But I have a question for you." Matt cleared his throat. "Is there any reason why you hired extra security for your mom and didn't tell me?"

"What are you talking about? Why would I do that? And, what makes you think I did?"

"One of my men seems to think there is someone else tailing your mom. He's seen the same guy several times in the last few days, and every time it's always near your mom. Don't look at me like that. It's probably just a coincidence."

****

Dutifully carrying the icepack against her cheek, Dara followed Adalyn to the front porch and took a seat in one of the rockers that faced the house rather than the street. "Do you think I'm crazy, sis? I ran like a scared rabbit."

"I'm not your judge and jury. If you felt unsafe, you did the right thing." Adalyn sat down and tried to find somewhere to look besides her sister's swollen, bruised face. "I'm glad you're not trying to defend his actions. You know, if he hit you once, he's likely to do it again."

Ignoring Adalyn's last remark, Dara looked for something to talk about that would get her mind off her troubles. "I have things I wanted to do this summer. I certainly never thought about spending time hiding out at Mom and Dad's."

"Don't think of it as hiding out. Think of it as sacrificing yourself for the sanity of your older sister. I'm staying for a few more weeks and I need company. The family's great for a few days at a time, if you know what I mean, but my gut tells me this is not the time to leave. I've been watching Mom closely and something tells me she's not handling all this as well as she wants us to think. We need to offer her a distraction and, who knows, we might find time for the two of us to have some fun."

"You're right. I could use some time at the beach. I can't remember when we've had more than a few days together since you left home." Dara sighed.

"Moving to another subject, I haven't heard the name Paula mentioned lately. Wonder what's going on with that? Matt said they still don't have a positive identification on the woman they found in the river."

"What's your take on all of this? We do know she's not Dad's child, and since he's retired from the bench there's no reason to embarrass him or taint his reputation. And no one's trying to extort money from the family. What's to be gained by this woman accusing Dad?"

"I've worried about this until it's given me a headache. By the way, did you know that Dad's planning to go into private practice with Connor? I overheard a conversation he had with Mom. She's against it for at least a year, but he seems anxious to get back in the thick of it."

"Aren't they leaving for Ireland soon?"

"They're supposed to leave in two weeks. Mom's worried Dad will postpone the trip until this thing with Paula is resolved, so yesterday, to take her mind off of it,

I took her shopping for the trip." Adalyn settled deeper into the rocking chair and sighed. "I don't think Dad is the type to retire and that's a shame for Mom."

"Agreed. If he cancels the trip, we could take Mom to Ireland. Just the three of us. Now that I think of it, that would be a great get-away."

"Keep that thought, sis. But I'm hoping the trip goes as planned." Adalyn hesitated. "Dara, there's something going on with Mom. She's not acting like herself. I tried to get her to open up yesterday, but she's tighter than a clam. I've never known her to be so distracted and distant."

"Hey, good-looking." The words and wolf whistle that followed were very familiar.

They turned, even though they didn't need to see who was walking toward the porch. "You must be talking to me," responded Dara. "What's on your mind this morning, Matt?"

"I came to talk to your father, and I was hoping to catch your brother, but he's still in court. Guess I'll have to settle for two beautiful ladies instead." He laughed as he pulled a chair close to where they were sitting. "I've got some news about Paula, but I need to share it with the judge before it becomes public."

"That's not fair. You have to tell us now that you've mentioned it." Adalyn lowered her voice and batted her eyelashes.

"If I were a few years younger, I'd take you up on that look, Adalyn." Matt laughed as she swatted his arm.

"Honey, you're not old enough to know what you're missing," she bantered back.

"Seriously. I need to see your dad, then we can talk." He stood and walked to the door. "I will tell you, this may be good news. And, Dara, sorry about the bruises. The guy's a jerk."

****

"My case settled out of court so I'm free for the rest of the day," Connor shouted to his sisters as he jogged up the sidewalk to the house. "I got a text from Matt. Is he here?"

"Yeah. He's in with Dad." Adalyn looked up from her book. "Didn't know you could run if someone wasn't chasing you."

"Adalyn, don't you ever give it up?" He nodded in his sister's direction as he crossed the porch and disappeared in the house.

"Wonder what they'd do if we barged in on this top-secret meeting?" Dara asked.

"Let's find out." Adalyn jumped up and motioned for her sister to follow her.

Once inside, they walked silently to the door of their father's office. "Open the door," Adalyn whispered. "We can't hear a thing standing in the hall."

Dara didn't bother to knock. Instead, she firmly grabbed the doorknob and pushed. "You wouldn't mind if we joined you, right?"

Charlie looked at his daughters and laughed. "This isn't a gentleman's only meeting. Come in and take a seat. Matt has some news."

"It's good and bad, Judge. First, the body found in the river is not Paula. The young woman is a missing person from St. Augustine. Second, that means Paula is out there somewhere, and we're no closer to solving our mystery. We know she's no longer in Shamrock Beach, but she hasn't checked out of the hotel and her things are still in the room. My associate did find the papers we

147

needed, but they're just some additional photocopies. Nothing he found in the room is an original. She took her Paula McBride identification and didn't leave anything that might give us a lead to her real identity. We did get some distinct fingerprints that we can use. When she's been missing the required seventy-two hours, I can file a missing person's report. Then, the police will be able to use the prints to help us track her. Once we know who she is, we should be able to make some progress toward ending this saga."

Silence in the room made the squeak in Matt's chair sound like a loud whistle. Then, everyone began to talk at once, firing questions at Matt, expecting more information. Finally, Charlie stood up and scanned the room.

"Matt, I'm grateful for all the work you're doing, and I'm glad that wasn't Paula in the river. However, that woman belonged to a family somewhere, and I feel sorry for the news they'll be receiving." He paced around his desk, back and forth several times, before he spoke again. "Under the circumstances, the chief can have those prints run before the seventy-two hours. Let me give him a call. We've got to know who Paula really is before we can move forward."

"I agree, Judge. I can drop the evidence bag by the police station on my way back to Jacksonville."

Matt started to leave, but Connor stopped him at the door.

"Did your guys find anything in that hotel room that was suspicious? Anything that might give us a clue?"

"Not a thing. Her clothes were still in the suitcase; her toiletries were on the vanity in the bathroom. There were no medicine bottles, no books, or magazines. All the clothes had labels that could have come from anywhere. There was one piece of jewelry that seemed out of character. It's still in the suitcase. It's a small brooch that artistically resembles a shamrock."

"It's either a shamrock or it's not," Dara offered. "How can it be kind of like a shamrock?"

"Stay right there a minute, Matt." Charlie slipped out of the room, and they heard him close a door somewhere in the house.

When he returned, he handed Matt a small satin pouch. "See if this is what you're talking about?"

Matt pulled the strings at the top of the pouch and poured a small piece of jewelry into his hand. His eyes opened wide when he looked at the designer shamrock that he held. "Judge, this is exactly what it looks like. What is this?"

"Two years ago, I had a friend make up two brooches with emeralds from a beautiful bracelet that I inherited from my grandmother. I told him I wanted them to look like shamrocks with an artistic twist. Each brooch had three emeralds set in gold. Callie and I planned to give them to the girls on their fortieth birthdays. We kept them in Callie's jewelry box, but a few months ago when we were thinking ahead to Adalyn's birthday, we discovered that one of them was missing. To this day, we haven't been able to find it." Sadly, he turned to his daughters. "I always planned to have another one made, but just didn't get around to it.

"How in the world did that woman get hold of the brooch?" Matt asked.

At once, both girls grabbed his arm. "Let us see."

"Oh, Daddy. This is exquisite. I can tell it's a shamrock, but it's not a traditional look." Dara stared at the jewelry, captured by its beauty. Three emeralds surrounded by gold filigree, no bigger than a half dollar. "When this is over, may I have it?"

"When I have both brooches back where they belong, you and your sister will be given the gifts you were meant to receive." His eyes twinkled as he saw the pleasure in Adalyn and Dara's faces.

"We've got to figure out how the shamrock disappeared from this house and how we get it back." Connor scratched his chin and looked at Charlie. "Dad, after Matt leaves, we need to do some brainstorming. Maybe there's been a break-in…. We'll need Mom's help. Where is she, by the way?"

"I think she said something about going to the museum to see if everything was ready for the new exhibit."

****

"Grace, it's getting harder and harder for me to avoid questions I can't answer. Do you have any information that might help me? Who is Paula?"

"You're jumping ahead of yourself, Callie. Just stick to what you know, and you'll be okay."

"I know that's true, but nothing feels safe. What if we get a call to go to work? What do we do then? I'm under police protection for goodness sake. Nobody explained this protocol to me."

"If we get a call, we do what we've always done. You know that." Grace sighed. "They're doing everything possible to keep us safe. Let's take it one day at a time. You're worrying about tomorrow."

"Right. It's hard not to worry when all these unexplainable things are happening around me."

Grace laughed out loud. "You've always been able

to roll with the unexpected and unexplainable. The race is almost finished. Don't give up now."

"I guess if you can laugh about all this, I can, too."

"Keep me updated on what Connor and Matt find out."

Chapter Thirteen

Callie loved the smell and the ambience of the museum. From the moment she'd walked in the front door years ago, she knew she belonged. Every shelf, every display case, every table, and chair held a memory for her. These things were her memoir. Every corner chronicled a milestone of her life in Shamrock Beach. She could gather the dreams and disappointments of each stage of being a wife and mother as she walked from room to room and floor to floor. There was no need for a journal or diary, it was living history that surrounded her.

Life had been easy for her. She followed the rules, she knew who she was, and until a few weeks ago, she thought she knew who Charlie was. Now there were cracks in the façade of the house she had so carefully built. Her children had their own lives, and, fortunately, they shared much of it with her. But did she really know them? Why had Adalyn been married and divorced twice? Why had Dara and Connor never married? Were Brock and Marti happy together? She could put some of the puzzle pieces together, but there was so much she couldn't begin to know.

And none of her children knew who she really was. Were her lies and secrets as troubling as theirs? Were there events and issues in their lives that they prayed would never come back to haunt them?

She took a seat in the room that held the new exhibit.

Of course, there had been no need for her to come here and check on things. She was officially off the payroll and the new curator was a capable young woman who could run circles around her. Each display case looked inviting and exciting, each item arranged to capture the best light, each grouped in ways that told the most interesting stories. There was nothing for her to do, yet she lingered.

She could mull things over in this room without the prying, the questioning, the pitying looks from her daughters. Who was Paula McBride? What did this woman have to do with her family? What was really going on between Dara and Edward Jenkins? The more the questions rolled around in her head, the more she realized how many answers eluded her. She was a problem solver and usually she could fix things for herself, Charlie, and the children. That was her role, the place where she felt most comfortable and needed. She put her head in her hands and closed her eyes. There was no way she could fix any of this without making things more complicated. She didn't have enough information to work from and every issue seemed beyond her skill level.

"Callie, are you all right?" the new curator questioned gently.

"My goodness. I didn't hear you coming," Callie stammered and tried to gather her thoughts. "I'm just thinking about this wonderful new exhibit and what a powerful statement you've made with the displays." She smiled as she stood. "It's very impressive."

"That's a great compliment, coming from you. I'll be smiling all day on those words."

"A well-deserved compliment, my dear. You're

doing a grand job."

"I know you and Charlie want to travel, and I hear you're leaving for Ireland soon, but do you think you'd ever consider coming back to the museum on a part-time basis?"

"I'm surprised. Do you really need somebody?" She thought for a minute. "I'll think about it and let you know when our vacation is over. I hadn't given any thought to doing more than volunteering, but working a few hours a week might be what I need right now." She smiled. "The judge is considering going back to private practice." Callie waved good-bye as she strolled out of the room. "Yes, I just might take you up on that offer."

Her steps were lighter, and her smile broader as she made her way down the street toward home.

****

"I think we need to postpone our Ireland trip. We can always go later," Charlie said, knowing he was in for an argument.

"Fine, you stay here, and I'll ask Adalyn and Dara to go with me."

"Wait a minute. This was supposed to be our retirement celebration. Now you want to take our daughters?" His indignation grew stronger, and his voice got louder. "You'd really do that?"

"I've waited decades to take this trip. If you decide you don't want to go, so be it."

"You know I want to go. That's not fair."

"Every time we've planned this trip, something has come up and you've cancelled. Not this time. If you want to go, fine. If not, that's fine, too. But I'm going. There's nothing going on here that Connor and the girls can't handle, Charlie, and you know it. You very thoughtfully planned this trip so I could be back to help with the Museum Festival. If I don't go now, it may be months before I can go."

"We don't have any answers, Callie. Nobody knows what this Paula person is going to do next. And what about Dara? Aren't you concerned about her?"

"I'll ask Dara to stay here with Adalyn while we're gone. She'll be fine." Callie was determined and it showed in her stance and tone of voice.

"If Paula resurfaces, Connor and Matt will know how to handle it. That's all I'm going to say on the matter. Make up your mind and let me know whether to ask the girls or not."

"You drive a hard bargain."

****

"I've called this family meeting to finalize some plans your mother and I have made regarding our trip to Ireland. Try as I might, she will not allow me to postpone the trip," Charlie grumbled. "Brock, are you there? This Skype thing is a total mystery to me, so I hope you can hear me."

"Dad, if you'd look at the computer screen that Connor set up, you'd be able to see me. You can hear me, right?"

Charlie lowered his eyes to the screen that was set up near the middle of the table. "Will wonders never cease? Where are you, Brock? Looks like your office."

Everyone at the table shouted and waved at Brock. "All the way from Gainesville, I'm your number one son, sitting in my office, waiting to hear what's going on."

"We leave for our trip soon and we'll be gone two weeks. I've emailed each of you a copy of our itinerary, emergency contact numbers, all hotels, and our flight information. I have called our cell phone carrier and they have added Ireland, so, at great expense I might add, we will be able to receive your emergency calls." He picked up his list and checked off several items. "First, I've asked Adalyn and Dara to stay here until we return, just to keep an eye on the house."

"Dad means he's asked Adalyn to babysit me." Dara laughed. "He doesn't want me running back to Tallahassee in case Edward is still angry with me."

"However you want to look at it. I think you're better off staying here for a few more weeks."

Connor leaned forward and looked at his sister seated at the other end of the table. "I think all of us agree with Dad. And who else will water Mom's plants while they're gone?" he said with a wink.

"Second, if the Paula thing resurfaces while we're gone, Connor has our permission to handle it." He waited for Connor to nod. "Brock, if necessary, for any reason, you can be here in an hour or so to help out."

"Mom, did you have any input in this edict?" Adalyn got up and walked over to the chair where her mother sat quietly. "Daddy, why are you making such a big deal of this now?"

"I want to reassure your mom that we're really going."

****

"Good evening, Mrs. McBride. Are you planning to take a stroll?" The young officer stepped between Callie and the front gate. "I'll be happy to escort you."

She stepped back and took a deep breath. "I'm sorry. I didn't think we were still under protection."

"Oh, yes, ma'am. I'm supposed to stick close to anyone who comes out of the house. I can walk with you or follow behind. I don't want to upset you."

"No, no. Walk with me and tell me how your family is doing. I haven't seen your mother in weeks."

The young man walked beside Callie, his eyes searching even though he was trying to make light of the situation by telling her the highlights of his life in Shamrock Beach. Once they reached the church, he felt somewhat uncomfortable about what to do next.

"Mrs. McBride, there's no service going on at the church. Are you planning on going inside?"

"Does that seem strange to you?" She smiled at his confusion and patted his arm. "I was going to slip inside for a few moments of quiet. I'll be fine, so why don't you go on back to the house."

"Can't do that, ma'am. They told me to watch over you. But I think it will be okay for me to wait for you outside. I'll sit on that bench until you're ready to go home."

She was relieved and thanked him. It would have been unsettling to have the young police officer follow her into the church. "I won't be long."

Once inside the church, her mood began to mellow. The silence was what she needed most, and before the sound of her footsteps could shatter what she was feeling, she took a seat in a pew near the back. Closing her eyes, relaxing her shoulders, and taking a deep breath made her realize how uptight and distraught she had become over the past few days.

She'd worked hard to hide it from Charlie and the kids. But she didn't need to pretend in this sacred place where she could talk it over with God. Her breathing slowed and she let her mind wander.

When someone slipped into the pew next to her, she

jumped. "What? Oh, dear. I must have dozed off," she stammered before she turned to see who had intruded on her silence. "What are you doing here?" Her whisper resounded across the silence and uneasiness made her want to escape.

"I didn't mean to startle you. We've got to talk. You know, woman-to-woman." Paula's voice was steady, but her eyes reflected exhaustion.

"I have nothing to say to you. What you have done to my family is heartbreaking. What do you want from me?"

"Please believe me. I didn't want to hurt you or your husband." Her whispers sounded like the whimpering of a small animal. "I know who you are, and I know Grace. The same people who have been watching you are watching me, and I have to make my story look real, or bad things will happen to me, to you, and to her. You know that don't you?"

"How can I be sure of who you are? Who sent you?"

As footsteps approached, Paula jumped up and ran out the side exit of the church.

"Wait, come back. You didn't answer me." Callie stood to follow the woman when a hand on her arm stopped her from moving out of the pew.

"Mrs. McBride, are you all right? You were taking so long I came to check on you." The police officer looked around. "Who were you talking to? I didn't mean to interrupt."

Callie was shaking inside and grabbed the back of the pew to help steady herself. "It was just a friend who was late for an appointment. Will you walk me to my son's office?"

****

"Connor, I don't know what to think, and you're asking me questions a mile a minute." Callie leaned back in the chair and wondered why her first thought was to get to her son's office. "I've told you all I know. The woman wasn't with me more than five minutes. She said she wanted to talk woman-to-woman. Then, she said they were watching her."

"She didn't say who?" He sat back down and took out a yellow legal pad. "What did she look like? Was she disheveled or distraught? How was she dressed?" Without looking up, he continued questioning his mother.

"I'm going to close my eyes and see if that helps me remember." Sitting quietly, she tried to keep her thoughts focused on what had transpired in the church. "She had on dark slacks and a pinkish colored blouse. Her hair looked like always. I don't remember if she had on makeup or jewelry. I don't remember if she was carrying anything. You know, like a purse or cell phone. I never heard her approaching. One minute she was there and the next minute she jumped up and ran for the exit on the side of the church." Callie opened her eyes and looked out the window. She certainly couldn't tell him about Grace. Or why people would be after his mother and her friend, the housekeeper. But she could share what she was certain of. "Connor, I could sense she was afraid."

"How could you tell, in that short time, that she was afraid?"

"Her eyes. It was in her eyes. And I don't remember if she ever looked directly at me. But I saw it in her eyes."

"Okay, I believe you. We haven't seen her in days and all of a sudden, she shows up sitting next to you in the church. And she evaded your protection, too. Don't you think that's strange?"

"No stranger than anything else that's happened in the last month. Paula is still in Shamrock Beach. Or at least back in Shamrock Beach."

"Yes, but why wouldn't she go back to the hotel for her things? And where has she been since the night she got in the car with someone we haven't been able to identify?"

"I've told you all I can remember, and I can't begin to second guess or speculate on any of her actions."

"Are *you* afraid of her? Was there anything she said or did that made you uncomfortable?"

"Honey, that woman is in big trouble. Someone else is in control, and for some reason they are targeting our family. I'm scared of the situation, but I don't think I have anything to be afraid of from Paula. I know this might sound crazy, but this time when I saw her, there was something so familiar about her. I can't put my finger on it, or I'd describe it to you. Maybe it's just intuition." She stood up and walked over to her son. "Connor, I need to go home. The young policeman who is assigned as my keeper has been waiting patiently for me, and it is time for him to walk me home and move on to someone else." Kissing her son on the top of his head, she said her good-bye and walked to the door of the office.

"Mom, you are taking this seriously, aren't you? You know your security detail is there for a reason?"

"Yes. I won't try to outwit my protector. I promise."

****

Charlie met her as soon as she reached the front door. "Connor called and told me about your encounter with Paula. Are you all right?"

"I'm fine. I went to his office because it was closer than the house. I needed to relay the information before I forgot any details. I'm sure he filled you in on everything."

"Callie, I'm worried this isn't going to go away. We've got to find out why this woman is tying our family in knots, or I can't get on that plane for Ireland." He pulled her close. "You do understand, don't you?"

"Let's not discuss this right now. You're upset and I'm tired." She felt uncomfortable in his arms and wiggled away. "I need a cup of tea and something to think about beside a woman named Paula. Where are the girls?"

"They're waiting for you in the kitchen, and if I know them, the tea is probably steeping as we speak." He grabbed her hand. "Don't shut me out, please. We need to talk until the pieces of this puzzle and our relationship are back together."

"I know, Charlie. I know." She sighed and walked into the kitchen. She knew he was disappointed, and she felt his eyes on her as she walked away. His declaration was something she couldn't deal with now. Maybe later she would be able to think more clearly, but not now. She heard the girls talking and laughing before she reached the kitchen door and knew it was what she needed to take her mind off the last hour.

"We've fixed you a cup of tea, and Miss Grace made scones this morning. I've warmed one for you and I'll put out some of your special blackberry compote. You look like you need a treat." Adalyn busied herself in the kitchen, afraid if she looked at her mother she would begin to unravel. "Here, Dara, take this tea to the table and I'll finish with the scone. Have a seat, Mom."

"Girls, I'm fine. You don't need to make a fuss over me. I'll answer your questions after I've had a minute to catch my breath."

"This isn't an inquisition. You don't need to do anything but drink your tea and enjoy that scone. Adalyn, please warm-up one of those for me while you're at it. My mouth is watering already," Dara said. "Miss Grace makes the best scones ever. When the kitchen smells like this, I don't know why I think I can resist."

"You'll have to let us know how Miss Grace's scones compare to the ones you'll find in Ireland. I bet hers will win." Adalyn placed the plate in front of her mother and turned back to the microwave to warm two more scones. "I can't let the two of you enjoy this treat without me."

"Both of you are trying hard to dance around me." Callie almost smiled. "You know Paula was in the church and she talked to me. I can tell you, she's scared of something. She told me she had to make us believe her story or bad things would happen." She took a sip of the hot tea before she continued. "Then, we were interrupted by Larry Denton; you know he's my bodyguard. Before I could stop her, she ran out the side door of the church."

"The only way she knew you were going to be in the church this afternoon is if someone is watching you. Or she is watching you. This is crazy." Dara placed a pad of paper on the table and jotted notes. "Did you get any strange vibes from her?"

"Dara, why are you taking notes? The woman is scared and that's all I know. Don't ask me to think beyond that right now."

"Sorry. You know I think better when I write things

down."

"The worst part of the day is now your father says there's no way we can go to Ireland." And going to Ireland might be the perfect solution for everyone. By the time she returned, the trial would be starting, she would testify, and her real life could go on. Her family and Grace would be safe, and Charlie would be none the wiser about her secrets. She sighed in resignation.

"Well, we'll have to change his mind about that. Right?"

****

Callie slipped off her shoes as she settled into her bedroom chair. Although the curtains were open wide inviting the late afternoon sun, a strange coolness floated across her shoulders causing her to shiver. Before she could reach for the summer blanket that was folded at the end of the bed, the sensation had passed.

That's like my life. In the heat of the moment, mysterious flashes of cold bring shivers and memories that come unbidden. When she closed her eyes, all she could see was Paula's face.

"Callie, wake up. If you sleep much longer, you won't be able to sleep tonight."

Charlie's voice sounded distant, like in a fog, and she tried to think why he would be so far away.

"Callie, I know you hear me."

The dream overshadowed her effort to respond to Charlie's voice. In one afternoon, her past had crashed into the present with the force of a hurricane, and she knew if she opened her eyes, the world would never be the same.

"Go away, Charlie. I need to rest for a few minutes more."

"Honey, you've been asleep for several hours. It's not like you. You never take naps." He smiled and gently touched her arm. "The girls are worried and sent me to check on you."

"Not yet. Go away." But she managed to open her eyes.

"Are you sick? What's going on?" A frown crossed his face. "The girls fixed dinner and it's on the table. We're waiting for you." He turned toward the door and started to walk away. "Wash your face and let's go eat."

"You all eat without me. I'm not hungry."

"Okay, but don't be surprised when they come in here and try to drag you to the table."

He closed the bedroom door and, once again, the memories surrounded her like a silken web. She was caught in a web of her own making; this time there was no spider tediously spinning and creating. This web belonged entirely to her.

Chapter Fourteen

Adalyn slowly opened the bedroom door and tiptoed to where her mother slept. It was peaceful in the room, but the look on Callie's face was anything but serene. Gently, she touched her mother's arm. "Mom, you need to wake up and let me bring you something to eat. Or get in the bed." She shook Callie's arm and waited until her eyes fluttered open. "You're going to get a crick in your neck from sleeping in this chair. The best thing would be if you joined us in the dining room."

"Sweetheart, you all need to stop fussing over me. I'm fine." Callie yawned as she spoke to her daughter. "Really, I just needed a short nap."

"If that's all it is, then you're going to come to dinner, right?"

"Will that make everyone stop worrying about me?" Her voice held an edge that alarmed Adalyn.

"Are you sure you feel all right? It's not like you to nap in the afternoon or be so touchy."

"I've got a lot on my mind, and I just wanted a few minutes to myself."

"That's all well and good, Mom, but you've been in here with the door closed for about three hours. Connor is here, Dara cooked, and it's my job to bring you back to the real world."

Adalyn laughed and hoped a bit of humor would stir Callie to action. "You'll hurt my reputation as the queen if you don't come to dinner. The peons in this family think I always get my way, remember?"

"Oh dear, it would upset the natural order of things if I didn't follow your every command." A slight touch of sarcasm rolled off Callie's tongue as she allowed Adalyn to pull her out of the chair. "Thank you for coming to my rescue."

"I'm going to ignore the jabs, Mrs. McBride, as long as you wash the sleep out of your eyes and run a brush through your hair. I'll go warn the others of your good mood while you pretty up."

"Stop. I'm sorry I seem so out of sorts. It's been crazy around here the past few weeks and you caught the brunt of my frustration. I'm awake now, and I promise to be my old self by the time I get to the dining room."

"I love you no matter your mood." She wrapped her arms around her mother and gave her a squeeze. "You're entitled to feel your feelings." Smiling, she kissed the top of her mother's head and turned to leave the room. "I'll let everyone know the conversation at the table has to be happy. No mention of you-know-who. Will that help?"

"Yes, darling, it will. Thank you."

****

When Callie entered the dining room everyone was eating, and Charlie was holding court with one of his stories. She slipped into her chair just as the mashed potatoes were passing by. It almost felt normal, and she smiled.

"I missed the platter of chicken, so please pass it back around. And the rolls, and the butter, and whatever's in the blue bowl. Sorry to interrupt your story, Charlie. Please go on."

Charlie lifted his head and smiled at his wife. "It's

probably one you've heard a hundred times, so be prepared to be bored."

Life around the table ebbed and flowed. Food passed, her children laughed, and Charlie's hands moved back and forth as he illustrated the points of his story. *This beautiful family is why I did what I did. This justifies the lies, the secrets.* She wanted to frame the moment and make it last.

The truth shall set me free, yes, probably free from moments like this one. If she confessed to her family, moments like this one might never come again. Her story was hers to tell and she knew that it was time to tell Charlie part of it. It was the part that would probably destroy their marriage. Now she understood her exhaustion.

Connor and Adalyn volunteered to clean the kitchen, and Dara moved to the porch to make a few phone calls.

"Looks like it's just you and me, Charlie. Would you take a walk to the beach with me? I promise we won't be gone long." She smiled. "Do you think we can lose our police escort for a few minutes?"

"It might be possible if we slip out the back door." He grinned mischievously.

Twilight on the east coast was her favorite time. There was usually a gentle breeze, and the colors of sunset gave a rosy glow to the clouds and the rolling waves. Day was transitioning into night, but it seemed to want another minute of glory. As they crested the dunes, the salt spray felt cool on her face, and she wished she could bottle it for later when things heated up between them.

"There's an empty bench if you want to sit for a little

bit." Charlie held on to her elbow and steered her through the sand. "This is the life, isn't it, Callie? You and me sitting on Shamrock Beach watching the seagulls catch their dinner, listening to the waves break."

"This is what you always planned for us, isn't it? A gentle life that followed tradition and made sense to the world."

"Is that bad? We've been happy here, haven't we?" He turned to look her in the eyes. "Have you waited all these years to tell me this isn't what you wanted, too?"

"Oh no, Charlie. We shared the same dream, we followed our plan, and we made a good life for us and our family. I didn't mean to imply something different." She closed her eyes and continued. "But we each made sacrifices to achieve this life. We made decisions we thought were right at the time."

"Where are you going with this? Is there something you need to say?"

She turned to look at the horizon but kept hold of his hand. "I made a decision a long time ago that I didn't include you in, and, yet, it was one that we should have made together. I have regretted it for years, but I hid it in my heart because I thought I would never have to tell you about it. This is the hardest thing I've ever had to do. You are going to hate me when I tell you what I've hidden from you for more than forty-five years."

His voice was quiet. "Don't stop there, Callie. Just tell me what you think you did that was so horrible."

"It started the night you asked me to marry you. Remember, we were on Cedar Key, and it was the first time we made love. Something, by the way, I've never regretted. It was the perfect night and my love for you deepened to a dimension I didn't know was possible."

"Oh, honey, you're right. It was the perfect night. Every now and then, I remember, and I fall in love with you all over again. What could possibly have happened that night that will change my mind?" He reached over and put his arm around her, but she moved away.

"Don't, please. Let me finish. I don't want to feel you pull away when you hear the rest of the story." She took another deep breath. "Remember how I tried to avoid making love with you? I wanted you so much, but I also wanted to keep my vow to wait until we were married. Both meant so much to me." She sighed. "I guess you meant more. I got pregnant that night. We made a baby, Charlie, and I didn't tell you about it."

For a long moment he was as still as a statue. Then, he bolted up and stomped away from the bench. Never turning to look at her, he growled, "Are you telling me you had an abortion?"

"I could never have done that." A weariness overtook her, and her shoulders sagged. "I carried the baby to term and gave her up for adoption."

"How is that possible? How could you have kept that a secret? Why would you do that?" He walked a few more steps away from her but didn't turn around. "Why?" he shouted.

"I thought it would ruin our plans, and your parents never would have accepted me or the baby. If you remember, I was at school working on my thesis, and I kept making excuses when you wanted to come to Gainesville. She was born the week before Christmas. I never even saw her."

Once she finished, the tears began to roll silently as she felt the space between them expand. She whispered, "I'm so sorry, Charlie. I'm so sorry."

"Why now? Why did you wait all these years and decide to tell me now?" He slowly turned around, but he made no move toward her.

"Over the past weeks, I've found myself wondering if Paula could be our daughter. The DNA test might be wrong. When she sat beside me today in the church, something snapped inside me, and I knew I had to tell you. I've been sick with worry since I left the church. What if she's our daughter? What if she needs our help? What if I've ruined our marriage and destroyed your trust in me when she needs us?" She stood and took a step in his direction, but he stepped away and held his hands in front of him to halt her motion.

"Not yet. Don't you dare try to touch me until I've had some time to digest this. You broke us even before we were us, and for the life of me, I don't know why. You didn't trust me." He began walking down the beach faster and faster, the distance between them growing with each step. His anger tinted the air many shades of red.

She stood and watched his body disappear in the shadows. The body that had been her comfort, her lifeline, her fortress. As her tears dried, a hardness formed around her that felt impenetrable. Perhaps God was giving her protection against the onslaught that was to come, a way to keep her from shattering into a million little pieces.

She had never felt so alone, not even the night their baby was born. Turning to walk home, she wondered how much longer she would be able to call it her home. Shamrock Beach belonged to Charlie. No matter how long she had lived here, this was his town.

Out of the corner of her eye she caught a slight

movement. Someone was watching her, but she was too distraught to care.

****

"Where's Dad?" Connor questioned as soon as Callie walked in the door. "I thought you all were going for a walk together."

"Change of plans. Your dad wanted to walk farther than I wanted to go. I'm sure he'll be back soon. Where are your sisters?"

"I think they're in the kitchen making us a surprise. With their combined domestic talents, this ought to be interesting." He smiled to himself. "I can remember them feeding me mud pies."

"You were an easy target for them. It's a wonder you didn't spend your childhood in the emergency room." She sat down on the couch next to him and took his hand. "I love you, Connor."

"I love you, too, Mom. I guess I don't say it often enough."

"I think I'll go pester your sisters. Hopefully, your dad will be back soon."

At eleven o'clock, she began to worry. Charlie still wasn't home. Connor had gone, the girls were watching television, and she had gotten ready for bed even though she knew she wouldn't sleep until he was home.

"I'm going to fix me a cup of Chamomile tea. Anyone else interested?" she called out to her daughters as she passed through the den on her way to the kitchen.

"Sounds good," Adalyn and Dara chimed.

"Are any of Grace's scones left? I could go for a part of one," Dara said.

By the time she had heated the water for tea and cut the remaining scones in half, the girls had joined her in the kitchen. "Did Dad say where he was going? It's not like him to walk this late." A note of concern crept into Adalyn's voice. "You all aren't fighting, are you?"

"Maybe he stopped off at the hotel for a drink. If one of his pals is there, he will talk all night. You know Daddy. Stop worrying, Adalyn, he's got a security detail following him around. They'd let us know if something happened," Dara said.

"Well, if he's not here in the next hour," Adalyn said. "I'm going to get in the car and go look for him."

"Did either of you try his phone?"

"Mom, his phone is on the table by his chair. He doesn't have it with him."

"All right, now I agree with you. If he's not home soon, we'll start looking."

They sat around the table making small talk, trying not to look at the clock. "Time's up. I can't sit here another minute," Adalyn announced. "Let me borrow your car, Mom."

"My purse is on the dresser in my room. The keys are in there." She stood up and started out of the kitchen when she heard the front door open.

"Mom, I need a little help," Connor called and the three of them went running. At the door, Connor was holding his father under the arms, trying to keep him from falling.

"What in the world happened? What's wrong?"

"I believe it's called excessive celebrating or too much to drink. After I left here, I decided to stop by the hotel to have a drink and your husband was at the bar entertaining everyone with stories of the good ole days in Shamrock Beach. It took me a while to drag him away and I mean that literally. I had to drag him out of the bar."

A look of astonishment crossed his face. "I don't ever remember him having too much to drink and, let me tell you, tonight he was not happy to see me. Once I got there, the bartender knew he'd better stop serving Dad anything else. But it was apparently too late. When I walked over to him, he fell off the barstool and would have cracked his head if I hadn't caught him."

"Help me get him to bed, Connor, before that happens here. We'll let him sleep it off." Callie's relief at knowing he was home masked her concern. Like the kids, she had never seen him drunk. "Boy, is he going to be sorry in the morning."

Connor helped her get him on the bed. They took his shoes off and pulled a trash can next to his head in case he got sick. Before they could turn out the light, Charlie was snoring like a freight train.

"Thanks for your help. Tomorrow's going to be rough for him, so I'll sleep in one of the beds upstairs. Even without a hangover, he's going to be embarrassed that his son had to practically carry him home."

"I won't tell if you all won't." He smiled at his mother and sisters. "It's late and I have a busy day tomorrow. Call me if you need me." Blowing them a kiss, he headed out the door before they could begin asking questions. He didn't want them to know he and the security detail had pulled his dad out of an argument that seemed headed for a fist fight.

****

How did I get in my own bed? Charlie's head was killing him, his mouth was dry, and he still had on yesterday's clothes. *Oh, dear Lord, what did I do? I don't remember where I was or even why I had so much to drink.* Sitting up very carefully was harder than he thought it was going to be. He was dizzy and his eyes wouldn't stay focused. Somehow, he needed to make it to the bathroom before his bladder burst. Where was Callie, anyway?

Carefully, he got out of bed, each new step more tentative than the last one. It seemed to take him hours to get from the bed to the bathroom and into the shower. As the warm water flowed over him, he began to remember. Anger flashed, but his head hurt too much for him to hang on to any emotion. He needed to dry off and find an aspirin and a cup of coffee. Then, maybe he would be able to think rationally. But, at this moment, even thinking hurt his head.

He managed to get dressed and make his way to the kitchen. If he was fortunate, no one else would be around. But his luck ran out when he stepped into the room and found Callie, Connor, and the girls staring at him. "Is there a cup of coffee left in that pot?" he croaked and stumbled to his chair.

Callie didn't say a word as she poured the coffee and brought it to him.

"You look rough around the edges, Dad. That must have been some walk," Adalyn teased him.

Charlie glared at her as he took a sip of coffee. "I don't need your smart mouth this morning."

"Dad, you missed morning. It's two in the afternoon," Connor offered as he observed his father's misery and stifled a laugh. "You really tied one on last night."

"I need some quiet. Why don't you all go on about your business." Charlie's mood was not improving. "Could someone get me a couple of aspirin, please?"

Dara set the bottle of aspirin in front of him and left

the room in disgust. Callie and Adalyn decided to follow her to avoid a confrontation.

"We need to talk. You've got some fences to mend after the scene you caused last night. When you're ready to talk about it, I'll be glad to fill in the pieces you don't remember." Connor stood up from the table and started for the back door. "I made up a story to tell Mom and the girls. I didn't tell them what was going on when I walked in the bar, so it can remain between us. But, if I were you, I'd be making a few calls as soon as you feel more human."

"It was that bad? You said calls. How many people did I insult?"

"You and Booker Donaldson almost came to blows, and when several of your friends tried to defuse the argument, you turned on them. It was not pretty and, most likely, everyone in town has heard about it."

"Booker is my friend. What in the world would I be arguing with him about?"

"I wasn't there for the start of it, but from what I could piece together, he was giving you grief about Paula. It really heated up when he accused you of cheating on Mom."

"Then you should have let me knock his block off." Charlie put his head in his hands. "Is that what everyone thinks? Does this town think I cheated on your mother?" The coffee and aspirin were not working. His head continued to pound, and he could feel his son's eyes locked on him. "What are you waiting on? Is there more to this story?"

"I've never seen you drunk, and I've always been proud of how you handle conflict. This goes deeper than Booker accusing you of cheating. What's really going on? Was it something between you and Mom?"

"I can't talk about it now. Maybe later." Charlie stood up and started to walk away. Something made him change his mind and he turned around. "It's a story you'll hear sooner or later. It's not very pretty."

Connor was surprised by his father's tone of voice and the look of anguish on his face.

****

He was stretched out across the bed when he heard her footsteps. He kept his eyes on the ceiling and waited to see if she was there to talk to him or if she needed something from the closet or chest of drawers.

"I need to know what you want me to do. I don't want to pack a bag and leave without telling our kids why I'm going. I thought we could talk about this, but you don't seem ready to hear anything else I might have to say."

"I heard everything you said. What else is there to say? The bottom line is always about trust and, plain and simple, you didn't trust me." His head still pounded, but he knew he couldn't ignore her. "I find it laughable that you're the one who felt so betrayed just a few weeks ago. You were ready to believe that I had cheated on you. You have a trust problem, Callie, and I never thought that would happen to us."

"You're right. I made a selfish decision because I was afraid that you, your parents, and this town would never have accepted me if the truth was known. Our future was planned, and your mind was made up about living here. Your roots are here, you are everyone's favorite son, and no matter what, no one would have changed their opinion of you. But I would have been the girl without morals who got pregnant to catch you."

"Is that what you think? How could you have judged us so harshly?" His words were clipped and angry.

"You have no idea what it was like in the beginning. I was the outsider who stole you away from Celeste Jolson. It took me years to be a part of this community. But I did it, Charlie, by being the perfect wife and mother, by working hard at the museum, by volunteering at the school, by being at the church every time the doors were open." Her words were spoken without bitterness or regret. Just the relief of finally saying them. "I wanted to fit in, to have our life here, but it wasn't without fear and insecurity especially in the early days. Now, please answer my question. What do you want me to do?"

He swung his legs around and sat up. "You're full of surprises. Everything you've said to me feels life-altering, and now you want an immediate response. In all our years together, I've never gotten one hint that you have lived a life of resentment and pretense."

"Resentment and pretense, really?" She wiped her sweaty hands on her sleeves and took a breath. "I have no regrets about our marriage or living here with you. From my first visit to Shamrock Beach, I knew what it was going to be like. I made a choice that gave us a chance to have the life we've built here. Can't you understand that? I love you and I loved you then. I had to make a choice that nearly killed me in order for us to have what we have." Her composure melted and salty tears slid down her cheeks. "I knew you would be upset, but I never expected you to get drunk and act so out of character." She fought hard to regain her composure before her tears turned to sobs and her legs buckled. "I'll pack a bag and be gone in a few minutes. You tell the kids whatever you want." She walked to her closet and

177

opened the door. As she reached for her overnight bag, she felt his hands on her shoulders.

"Don't go. Don't walk away from us again. Trust me this time to work through it with you. I loved you then, I love you now. But I am stunned." He didn't let go and she didn't move. "Give me some time to digest everything, and I promise you we will talk. We'll figure out what to tell the kids." His tone softened and he gently squeezed her shoulders. "We can get through this."

Pulling gently away from his touch, she avoided looking him in the eyes. "Thank you," she whispered and left the room.

****

The day dragged on, and Charlie was still behind the closed door of the bedroom. The girls avoided asking questions and kept their conversation as light as possible. Callie kept busy with the laundry, dusting, making grocery lists, and redoing tasks she had done the day before.

When she felt tears gathering once again, she left the kitchen and walked to the backyard. Even with rain clouds building all around her, she jerked on her gardening gloves and large straw hat and began pulling weeds.

"What in the world is going on between Mom and Dad?" Dara looked at her sister and shook her head. "They've had their share of arguments, but I can't remember anything like this. Dad getting drunk and disorderly and Mom showing signs of hyperactivity. They're wrecking my whole idea of the perfect parents."

"Well, nobody is perfect, I guess, but they sure made it look that way. It's hard to be a casual observer. I want to barge into the bedroom and demand answers. Can you imagine what a scene like that would cause?" Adalyn tried to laugh, but it was more like a fake cough. "I've been married and done my share of yelling and fighting, but it's hard to watch them act like this."

"Things around here are getting weirder by the day. They left the house all lovey-dovey, and a short walk turns them into people I don't recognize." She grabbed her purse off the counter and started for the door. "I'm going to walk to the bakery and indulge myself in a sugar fest. Do you want to come with me? I mean, do you want to tag along with our police escort?"

"I can hear a red velvet cupcake calling my name. Let's go."

As soon as he heard the front door close, Charlie walked out of the bedroom and began looking for Callie. From the kitchen window he spotted her kneeling in the flower beds pulling weeds. Her straw hat blocked her face, but her movements echoed her sadness and broke his anger into little pieces that shattered all around him.

Somehow, we've got to fix this. She's my life. He braced his hands on the counter and took a deep breath. *Callie, how can we let this unravel everything we've built together? I'm angry, and it's going to take me some time to tamp it down, but I'll do it. There's no way we're going to let this break us. I promise.*

****

For the rest of the afternoon, the dance continued. If Callie was in the kitchen, Charlie went in the den. There were no words, no eye contact, nothing but awkward silence. Dara and Adalyn called to let them know they'd decided to have dinner in town, and Callie put the leftovers back in the refrigerator. She didn't have the energy to face Charlie over the dinner table. If he wanted to eat, he could make himself a sandwich. She picked up a book and headed for the swing on the front porch.

At ten o'clock, she opened the bedroom door, wondering if she would be acknowledged or ignored. "I need to take a shower and get ready for bed." As she walked through the room she didn't glance at the chair where Charlie sat reading. He kept his eyes on the book and made no attempt to speak.

After her shower and night-time routine, she pulled down the covers and got into bed. It had been ages since she and Charlie had gone to bed with tension and conflict brewing. Thoughts raced and emotions flooded her mind, and she knew she would never get to sleep or find any rest if they didn't begin to find resolution. She sat up and drew her knees to her chest.

"Charlie, we've got to talk. I can't handle the tension."

"All right, if you want to talk, we'll talk." His words were soft, but there was no tenderness. "I've given this a lot of thought and you need to let me say what I need to say without interrupting me." He hesitated as he closed his book and placed it on the night table. "First, there is no way Paula can be our daughter. The DNA results would have been different if she was. So, get that idea out of your head. Second, it's going to take some time for me to accept that we have a daughter out there somewhere that I wasn't made aware of. Third, we need to go back to square one and discuss your deception and why you excluded me from something that very definitely included me. And fourth, how in the world did you hide a pregnancy from me, your family, and our friends."

"You sound like an attorney, not a husband. But at

least you're talking to me." She was surprised at the strength she heard in her voice and the feelings of love she still felt for this man she had wounded so deeply. "My only defense is that I was young. I thought I was making the right decision for me and for us. I didn't want a rushed wedding that would ignite the gossip mill in this town, and I was immature enough to think I couldn't stand up to our parents' disapproval. I was deeply ashamed that I had let my guard down for one night and so I was going to pay the consequences. The whole world was going to know what we had done." She raised her eyes and looked directly at his face. "We weren't ready to be parents and I wanted to give us a chance to be a couple before we became a family. It all sounds hollow now that I have the maturity to understand what love really means."

"You were ashamed of our love making?" he said, his anguish evident.

"I was raised on values that made me a slut if I gave in to my desires. There had been some casual kissing before, then you came along and lit a fire inside me. For two years, I said 'no' to temptation even when I wanted you with every fiber of my being. I struggled until that night when logic and values no longer seemed to matter. You kissed me until the only thing that mattered was you."

He walked over to the bed and took her in his arms. "Oh, Callie, why didn't you tell me these things then? I knew you wanted to wait, but I didn't realize the depth of your commitment. That night, all I could think about was how much I loved you and wanted you." He held her even more tenderly. "I'm sorry you felt pressured." He moved so he could see her face. "When I think back, making love to you for the first time is one of the most precious moments of our life together. How could something so beautiful have hurt you so deeply?"

She shook her head slowly. Now she had started, the words wouldn't stop. "Once I discovered I was pregnant, I wanted to die. My shame almost destroyed me. When I finally decided to get help, a wonderful woman counseled me. She suggested I think seriously about adoption and helped me find the resources I needed to get through it. At first, she wanted me to tell you, but I convinced her that wasn't an option. She made me believe I could finish my degree, talk my mother and sister into planning our wedding, and avoid seeing you until after the baby was born. And with some major finagling, it worked. I watched my weight, exercised, took my vitamins, saw the doctor on a regular basis. And my new friend was there when our daughter was born. She'd found a couple who had tried for years to have a child and helped me see they would provide a loving, secure home for our baby." She closed her eyes and tiredness overwhelmed her. "I cried for months after that. Even on our honeymoon there were moments when I felt the emptiness."

"I can't believe you went through this alone and I never had a clue. You've always been the calm, loving woman of my dreams. You've hidden your pain well." He let go of her and moved to his side of the bed. "Okay, but why Paula? The DNA results should have proven to you that she isn't the one you've been longing for."

"When she was sitting next to me in the church, something about her grabbed my heart and it won't let go. She made me remember what I've tried for years to come to terms with, and I knew I had to tell you. I realized that only the secrets can hurt us, and I suddenly saw clearly that my secret—not yours—was what threatened to destroy us. But maybe, just maybe, our daughter is out there somewhere needing our help. Just like Paula is reaching out for help, Charlie, our daughter may be reaching out to someone for help, also."

"There is something dark and sinister about this mess we've been dealing with for the last month. Now I think someone out there thinks they can destroy us by using Paula. We need to tell our children. They can't be blindsided by this." He pulled the covers up and turned on his side to face her. He groaned. "Nothing in this family is ever easy. How do you want to handle it?"

"I'll call Brock in the morning and see if he can come for lunch on Saturday. He won't like it when I ask him to come alone, but this is not a time for me to be distracted by our grandchildren." She took a breath. She was ready to take care of business. "If he can't make it or can't come alone, we'll tell the others and fill him in later. Does that work for you?"

He yawned. "No more secrets. I never want to go through another twenty-four hours like this."

She used her most charming smile and batted her eyelashes. "Where would the mystery go if you knew all my secrets?"

****

When everyone had finished lunch, Callie stood and asked for quiet. "I have something to tell you that will most likely change your opinion of who I am. Please understand this is hard for me and will be hard on you, but that's not what's important right now. The important thing is I love your father with all my heart, and I love each of you more than you can imagine." She looked around the table and prayed the love she felt would still be flowing toward her when she finished her story. "Once upon a time, I fell in love with your father. Head over heels, passionately in love, and we had a three-year courtship that tested my resolve to remain a virgin until marriage."

"Oh boy, too much information, Mom. Do we really have to go there?" Connor's face was flushed, and he looked to see if his siblings were as uncomfortable as he was.

"Buck up, Connor." Adalyn grabbed her brother's hand. "Let Mom finish this."

"The times were very different. Sex before marriage and to have a child out of wedlock was frowned upon. Especially in a town like Shamrock Beach." She closed her eyes and prayed for the strength to continue. "On the weekend before your dad graduated from law school, I let desire overrule logic and your father and I made love." She paused to let her children take a breath. "The result of that one night of passion was a baby that I gave up for adoption. Don't look at your father that way, Dara. He didn't know any of this until two days ago. He is as hurt and shocked as you are."

"I'm a doctor, and I can't begin to imagine how you could be pregnant and Dad not know." Brock's astonishment reflected the thoughts of his sisters, Callie would bet.

"Yeah, Mom. How did you finish your degree, stay in Gainesville, and not let on that a baby was on the way? What were you thinking?" Dara stood up and began to pace the room.

"Please sit back down and I'll try to explain." Callie was baffled by the attitude of her children. "You all seem more interested in the fact that I managed to accomplish this than you are in the fact that I hurt your father deeply and you have a sister out there somewhere that you didn't know about."

"Oh, lord. Are you trying to tell us Paula is really our sister?" Adalyn was incredulous.

"That's not possible." Connor pounded the table with his fist. "The DNA test says that's impossible. Dad is not Paula's father. Don't go there, Adalyn."

"All of you, stop this and let your mother go on." Charlie assumed his role as head of the family and stared down his children. "We're only telling you this because we don't want this information to be used against your mother or any of us by the people who are attacking our family. This is not easy, and the sooner she can finish, the better."

"I didn't want a rushed wedding that would start the whispers around town, and I wasn't ready to be a mother. I made a decision I felt was best and I've regretted it all these years. Our baby was placed with a loving family, and I've had no contact with her since she was born. Seeing Paula in the church—feeling her fear—somehow convinced me to finally tell your father and you."

Exhaustion hit her and she sat down. "I'm sorry that I kept this secret from your dad all these years. I was raised in a strict family, and we just tried not to disappoint my father, or make him angry. I was too young to understand trust and the true meaning of love. After a hard-fought battle with himself, your father has forgiven me. I hope you can find it in your hearts to do the same."

Adalyn and Dara rushed to her side. "Mom, you did what you thought you had to do. There's no reason to ask for our forgiveness." Adalyn hugged her mother with one hand and motioned to her brothers to join her with the other.

"Okay, family. If there are any more secrets we need to be told, do it now while my heart can take it." Brock sat back down and shook his head. "I thought this was going to be a quiet lunch away from my kids. Boy, was I wrong." He turned to his mother. "I still can't believe you pulled this off. I'd almost admire you if I wasn't so blown away."

"Okay, we're all in shock and have a thousand questions, but we need to think about this from a different perspective. As a son, I'm in a daze and I will probably never get past the fact that my parents had sex five times instead of four. But my attorney mind has taken over and I want to find out why Paula met Mom in the church. She leaves town without taking any of her things and shows up in the church at the same time as Mom. The officer with Mom didn't see Paula, so she snuck in past him. Isn't anyone else in the family curious about that?"

"Can't you stop being an attorney for a few minutes? Mom has bared her soul, dropped a bomb on Dad and us, and all you can think about is this Paula thing." Dara nodded her head and tried to stare down her brother. "Geeze, Connor, where is your heart?"

"Calm down, Dara," Charlie said. "Your brother has a valid point. We're all reeling from your mother's story, but this 'Paula thing' as you call it is getting more sinister by the minute, and we can't lose sight of the danger we all might be in because of it. Your mom understands, and it's the reason she decided her story needed to come from her. Don't you understand there is some outside force that is trying to destroy this family?" His voice wasn't soft and tender. "If I can put all of this aside until we are out from under Paula, then I expect all of you to do the same."

Dara looked at her siblings for support but realized if it came to a vote, she would lose. "I yield to the majority. But, Mom, I want you to know I'm hurting with you."

Everyone at the table began talking at once. Each one tried to let Callie know they loved her and felt her pain. "Forgive us, Mom," Connor said. "None of us is trying to minimize what you're going through. I know for me, the shock hasn't worn off and my way of handling it is to get busy."

"Kids, I don't want to stop progress on the issue of Paula, but I wanted you to hear this from me. I wanted you to know why your father went crazy the other night and I wanted you to see how hurtful it is to keep secrets in a family."

Callie looked at her children and wished time would reverse itself. She wished it was an hour ago before her children knew this part of her sad truth. She wished it was years ago before all the secrets really began. "One day, when the timing is right, we can talk more about my story." She reached for Charlie's hand. "For now, all you need to understand is your father loves me and has forgiven me. And that I have always loved him with all my heart."

"This is not for discussion outside the family, except for your wife, Brock." Charlie let go of Callie's hand and stood up. "Brock and Connor, let's take a walk."

****

"I imagine you have questions. Most of them are

probably the same ones I had when I got calm enough to think. I was angry, angrier than I care to admit." Charlie cleared his throat noisily and looked straight ahead. "Getting drunk and making a public spectacle of myself was not a good choice. I'm sorry if I embarrassed you and the family."

"Yeah, I've got lots of questions and my first one makes me angry at you. For crying out loud, Dad, why didn't you use protection? I have a hard time with that little omission." Brock's face was red, his hands were on his hips, and the level of his voice had risen with each word.

"I planned to, Brock. The heat of the moment took over and I forgot all about it." Charlie hated to admit this part to his sons. "I know, I lectured you both so much on this issue that it embarrasses me to admit I'm the one who forgot."

Connor began to whistle, trying to cover up his discomfort. "This is not a conversation I ever wanted to be a part of, but here I am listening to my dad tell me he forgot to use a condom the first time he had sex with my mother. Don't you agree, Brock?" He shook his head and tried not to look at his brother. "Dad, why did Mom feel she couldn't trust you? I'm sure you would have married her if you'd known. Right?"

"Different times, boys. I know you can't understand how it was in the late 1960s. There was the Hippie thing and free love, but not in small town America. Shamrock Beach was steeped in a moral code that said sex outside of marriage was a sin and our parents would have been unforgiving. And your mother wasn't raised in a home where trust was part of the equation. Her father was a strict man who ruled by intimidation. When your mother said her own shame made her feel like dying, she wasn't kidding. She understood what she would have faced if we had eloped and everyone in town knew she was pregnant."

The three stood still and looked at each other in silence.

"I can't walk in Mom's shoes, then or now, but I'll try harder to see this from her point of view. I know I'd be devastated if my wife kept this kind of news a secret." Brock threw his arm around his dad's shoulder. "But in my heart of hearts I know the two of you could have found a way to make it work."

"I have another question." Connor hesitated and stumbled over his next words. "Does Mom really think Paula might be this daughter?"

"Son, she knows it isn't possible. Maybe it's wishful thinking. I don't know, but her encounter with Paula triggered something and she is convinced there is a connection."

Chapter Fifteen

Long shadows fell across the back yard as day turned to night. The sun was finally setting on an unusual day and Adalyn was relieved it was ending. She had been brooding and pensive since her mother's lunch-time confession and needed time to let it all soak in. The sea oats blowing across the dunes caught her eye and she began to sway in time with them.

That's what life is like. We just blow with the wind, waiting in between the stillness and the storms. Out of fear, she never allowed her reflections to go too deep. She could maintain control of her life if she lived on the surface. Fighting her way up in the entertainment world and two marriages ending in divorce had taught her that lesson the hard way. Yet, tonight, she was having trouble remaining on the surface.

It was hard for her to imagine the truth of her mother's story. Callie wasn't a saint, but she had held her place on a high pedestal as long as Adalyn could remember. Besides, children rarely question their mother's virginity, in fact, most can't believe their parents ever had sex. For her to imagine passion between her parents was so far-fetched she almost laughed out loud.

But, today, Callie confessed she had struggled to resist temptation even though she had an aching desire for Charlie. Then she admitted that passion had overruled her logic and she had surrendered.

That part of the story altered the way Adalyn looked at her parents. Not in a judgmental way, but in a human way. *My parents are real people after all.*

The other part of the story caused her to look below the surface at who she had always believed she was. As the first born, she had enjoyed using that position to manipulate her siblings, and she felt it gave her special status with her parents. Today that had changed. Would the family look at her differently? Would her role as the older sister be diminished by the fact that *she* had an older sister?

And who was the usurper, this mysterious new member of the family? Where did she live? How had she functioned in the world? What did she do? Would they ever know her?

Adalyn was uncomfortable with her feelings and her questions. She didn't want any of it to be real. Leaning back in the chair, she realized her whole body was responding with exhaustion, but she was too tired to get up and go inside. The sun had set, the night air was cool, and if she closed her eyes, sleep might produce memory loss. Sleeping on the back porch was not ideal but going inside might mean conversation or interaction with a family member.

Later, as the night air became damper, going inside became the better option. Quietly, she opened the back door and gently walked through the kitchen to the stairs. No one else was around. Everyone, like her, had sought solitude.

****

"Where have you been hiding, sis? I've been waiting to talk to you." Dara was curled up on the bed with a

191

book and didn't raise her eyes from the page.

"I don't feel like talking. I need a shower and two days of sleep."

"We need to talk. I'll never be able to sleep if I don't get some of these thoughts out of my head."

"It can wait 'til morning. I'm exhausted emotionally and physically."

Dara's mouth was forming a reply as she watched her sister disappear into the bathroom and soon heard the sound of the shower. In her frazzled state of mind, she worked hard not to react to the rejection she felt. She needed Adalyn. She had always needed Adalyn as a sounding board, a confidant, a shoulder to lean on and sometimes to cry on.

Tonight, she needed to tell her how sad she felt for their mother and how worried she was about their parents. Would this new wrinkle damage their parents' relationship, and what role did she and her siblings play in this new scenario? And, like her mother, she couldn't get Paula out of her mind. The timing of her mother's confession was bizarre. Why now? Did Paula say something threatening to her that she wasn't telling them?

While she waited for Adalyn, she went back over everything she could remember from lunch. Was there a hidden meaning in her mother's words? What exactly had Connor's reaction been? Did her father seem too removed from it all? Something wasn't adding up and she was going crazy trying to figure out what it was.

When she heard the shower turn off, she walked to the bathroom door and started voicing her concerns. She was startled when the door flew open.

"What is wrong with you?" Adalyn hissed. "Don't

you think Mom and Dad can hear you?" She grabbed a towel and vigorously rubbed her wet hair. "I told you I don't want to talk to you, but I never imagined you would try to tell the whole neighborhood what you're thinking."

"Aren't you worried? You're acting like none of this matters."

"Good grief. You wear me out." Shrugging her shoulders, she wrapped the towel turban-style around her wet hair and moved past her sister to the bed. "You have until my hair dries and then I'm going to sleep. So, start talking."

For the next thirty minutes, Dara talked. She voiced all her questions and concerns and waited for her sister to respond. Adalyn finished rubbing her hair with the towel in silence.

A frown crossed her face when she finally spoke. "You're right. And how did that beautiful brooch go missing? Did Mom give it to someone or has someone been in the house and gone through her things? We're missing something and, in the morning, we need to talk to Connor." She walked to the bathroom to hang up the towel. "But, tonight, I need sleep, so don't say another word."

****

"Marti, I've told you all I know. Believe me, I was blown away and I still can't wrap my head around the logistics. How did my mother hide her pregnancy?" He settled in the bed next to his wife with more questions than answers rolling around in his mind.

"Brock, that's the least of what you should be worried about. She's not the first one to do that." She snuggled closer to him. "Think what it cost your mom emotionally to first, give up a child, and second, to stand in front of her grown children and tell them about it. My heart is breaking for her."

"On the drive back home, she's all I could think about. Part of me feels sorry for her and part of me keeps wondering what else she's not telling us. And, before you say anything, you know I adore her and nothing she tells me will ever make me feel differently."

Brock's world had been shaken by his mother's confession and he needed Marti's arms around him. "Honey, you don't have any deep, dark secrets, do you?"

Her lips softly touched his cheek, and she tightened her hold on him. "I did buy a new coat yesterday that I wasn't going to tell you about."

Laughing quietly, Brock turned and pulled his wife into an embrace meant to let her know a new coat wasn't on his mind. "I love you, Marti. Help me forget this unbelievable day."

****

Connor paced. He walked from his front door to his back door, turned around, and retraced his steps. There were legal ramifications that needed to be explored; there were unanswered questions. After lunch and the walk with his dad, he was convinced that a new piece of a puzzle was falling into place, but he couldn't figure out which piece it was.

Why had Paula appeared at the church? Why was her initial attack directed at his father, and why was her strategy changing? Why was she targeting his mother? He thought he understood his dad's reaction to his mother's story, although getting sloppy drunk was not his father's usual style. But if he had been in his father's shoes, Connor knew he would have reacted the very same way.

On the after-lunch walk, he tried to pose some questions even though he wasn't thinking clearly. His words generated questions, not answers, from his father. He stopped pacing and thought about the process he followed in his law practice. Whenever he had a difficult case, he researched every aspect until the answer he needed became apparent. He looked at evidence, he looked at precedence, he talked with trusted colleagues, and he drew conclusions based on everything he had discovered. He used his mind. But this was different, this was personal, and his heart was more invested than his mind.

Before he walked the soles off his shoes, he picked up his phone and called Matt. "Hey, man, are you still in town? I need to talk."

Within a few minutes, Matt was at his door.

"This better be good. I was watching a killer movie with my folks, and Mom had just popped me a big bowl of caramel corn."

"Why didn't you bring it with you?"

"There are some things a man doesn't share, my friend. Now, what couldn't wait until tomorrow?"

The event of the day unfolded as Connor brought Matt up to date. Hoping for a breakthrough as he talked, he tried not to leave out any details. He wanted Matt to hear logic, not emotion. "I thought I grew up in a very normal family, don't you agree? Can you believe the last few weeks? I can't."

"In my opinion, Adalyn's producer must be secretly filming all this for next season's show. You are living the perfect soap opera. Your wholesome, pillar of the community Mom is full of surprises, but I never figured her for something like this. The family must have been blindsided." Matt punched Connor in the shoulder. "Now would you get me a beer. I need to do some serious thinking."

Connor popped the tops off two beers and sat down across from Matt. "I've looked at this from so many angles, it's beginning to hurt my brain."

"You need to chill. You won't find answers when you're wound so tight." Matt took a long swig of his beer, leaned back, and stared at the ceiling. "We're missing the connections. I always look for the connections, and there's a broken link somewhere. Nothing happens by chance, and I'd be willing to bet all these bits and pieces belong together. Is Paula driving this train or is something even more sinister going on that we haven't uncovered yet?"

"All evening I've been wondering if Paula knows my mom's secret." He stood up and started pacing again. "But what would be the advantage? It's a personal issue between my parents. Right?"

"I confess. I sort of let my guard down about Paula. After she disappeared, we tried for days to find her, and when it seemed she wasn't a threat, I told my people to back off but keep a watchful eye out for her." He finished the beer and stood up. "We'll be more vigilant now that she's made another appearance. You know I talk to the front desk people at the hotel every day; she hasn't been back for her things." It was Matt's turn to pace. "Someone is watching your mother very closely if Paula showed up at the church." He pulled out his cell phone and began texting.

"What are you doing?"

"As of right now, my people are back on duty and I'm texting the sheriff to make sure he keeps surveillance tight at your house. I'm asking him to step things up a notch around your mom. All I told them was new information had come to light that prompted us to make the request." Matt turned and started for the door.

"You headed back to your folks?"

"Not right away. I think I'll take a little walk around town." He watched as Connor stood up. "You're not invited. There are some people I need to talk to, and you don't need to know who they are. I'll call you if I have any new information. By the way, I can't find a thing on Edward. He's as squeaky clean as they come. But I'll keep looking."

****

Charlie watched his wife reading in her favorite chair, a sight he knew he'd never grow tired of. But he still had questions, so he decided to ask them quietly. "In all the confusion, I didn't ask you about the woman in Gainesville who helped you. How did you find her? Did you go to a counseling office or church?"

"Actually, she found me when I went to the infirmary," she said, looking at him. "I can't remember if she was sick or on staff. Maybe the university hired her to work with young women who found themselves in my predicament." She went back to reading. "I don't remember all the details. Her name was Martha something."

"Have you ever gotten back in touch with her to try and find our daughter?"

Again, she stopped reading and looked at him. "I signed papers. I wasn't even allowed to see her, though they did tell me that she was healthy. Why would I try to find her?"

"She'd be older than Adalyn, so we wouldn't be

breaking any agreements if we tried to find her now. We should think about it."

"I think about it every day and I don't think it's a good idea. If she wanted to find us, she'd have done so by now. She may not know she's adopted, and we could turn her world upside down." She walked over and put her hand on his shoulder. "I'm sorry. We have to let it go."

He reached over and placed his hand over hers. "Maybe you're right. I wouldn't want to do anything that would hurt her. But now that I know about her, I can't get her out of my mind."

"Here's a question to take your mind off this. Are we going to Ireland, or not?"

"I told you the other day that I cancelled our trip. But really, I postponed our trip for six months. I worked with the travel agent to change our plans without losing any of our money."

Sadness welled up inside her and she snatched her hand from his shoulder like she was being burned. "You didn't tell me you cancelled the trip. You simply said we shouldn't go." Her shoulders slumped and she felt defeated. "What has happened to us, Charlie? We used to be on the same page." As she walked away, she mumbled, "I'm going for a walk."

Instead of walking, she got in her car and drove to Grace's house. Grace would tell her what she should do. Callie used every bit of her training to confuse and lose the car that was following her.

She wasn't prepared for her trip to Grace's house to be in some police or detective's report.

Chapter Sixteen

Grace stood at the window and watched Callie approach the house, even though she had warned her to stay away. She didn't know what was wrong, but her instincts told her to be ready for a heavy-duty visit. Callie wasn't one to bring drama into everything, and she was usually cool-headed. Nevertheless, her body language suggested a high level of anxiety. Grace would have to handle her very carefully.

More than forty years ago, she'd been introduced to Callie, and the two of them had been taking care of each other ever since. Twice a week, she helped in the McBride house doing household chores, preparing for special occasions like the judge's retirement celebration, and long ago, raising the children. Working together had melded into a friendship with professional boundaries. It would be interesting to see why Callie was so upset today.

"Come in, Callie," Grace said as she led her friend to the room she used as her office. "You look like somebody did you wrong."

"Grace, I'm scared. You know about Paula meeting me at the church, and how that prompted me to tell the family about the baby that was adopted. But what do we do about the people watching me? How can I protect my family?"

"Sit down and stop that fretting. There isn't anything

so bad it can't be fixed."

"We thought this Paula thing had something to do with Charlie, not with me. Now it seems I'm the target, and my family is going to begin asking questions I don't have the freedom to answer. The implications are more serious than we first thought."

"I'm looking into it, and right now I don't have anything new to tell you. No message has come from our people that even hints at you being compromised. I haven't put all the pieces together and I can't reassure you that Paula doesn't fit into the scenario. This is not the time for you to lose your cool. Your family is too smart. If they see you faltering, they're going to get in the way."

"I over-reacted. I should never have told them about the baby." Callie knew Grace would agree with her. "The encounter with Paula brought up all the guilt I haven't faced in years, and I got the sense that she knew all my secrets. Grace, I didn't want her to be the one to tell Charlie about our daughter, so I decided it was time for me to tell him."

"I'd have recommended against that, and it would be used against me, but it's too late to cry over spilled milk." Grace's expression hardened "You can't let your emotions get to you like this again. You do understand, don't you? You've held it together for over forty years, why come apart now? In just a few weeks our most important work is finished. We can't let anything interfere with that. Did you tell him what we know about your daughter?"

"No. If I'd done that, he would know more than I can tell him now. Unless something goes wrong in the next few weeks, my family will never know the true story. I won't betray us."

"I know and I believe you."

"What do I do now? I've never felt this unstable. Am I in real danger?" Callie's calm demeanor was crumbling. The secrets were finally catching up with her, and it was going to lead to a disaster if she couldn't stop the momentum.

"You're strong and you've always faced the challenges with determination and grit. I'm counting on you to stop this nonsense. You know these hard days will be over in a few weeks. We have a job to finish and then we can rest." Grace turned away and walked toward her front door. "Now go home and find something to do so you won't overthink everything. There's always danger in what we do. You have always known that, and you know they've got us covered."

"Knowing it doesn't make it any easier. It used to, but now it doesn't."

"I'll be at your house early in the morning to start the laundry. Those girls of yours sure do pile up a bunch of dirty clothes." Smiling at Callie, she gave her a reassuring hug and gently pushed her out the door.

Once she was sure Callie was in her car and pulling out of the driveway, she walked to the back bedroom and opened the door.

"Our friend is starting to fall apart. I think I managed to stop the damage, but we've got to keep a closer watch on her. We must protect her from them—and from herself."

****

"Mom, I've been thinking about your cancelled trip and wondering if you'd like to take a girls' trip to New York. I need to check on things, and it would be fun to have you go with me. I'm even thinking of asking Dara." Adalyn grabbed her mother around the waist and gave her a hug. "We won't be gone for more than three days. It's not Ireland, but it's a whole lot better than sitting in this house staring at the walls."

Pulling away, Callie wondered if a short trip might be the answer she'd been looking for. "Let me check with your dad. If he agrees, then ask Dara if she wants to go with us." For the first time in the past few days, she felt a slight smile begin to form. Charlie wouldn't have any objections and, after today, she knew Grace would think the trip was a good idea.

"Great. I'll make arrangements for us to leave day after tomorrow. And, Mom, I've already talked to Dad about this, and he says for us to have fun." Adalyn laughed when she saw the surprise on her mother's face. "You are so predictable."

****

Grace stood at the bottom of the stairs and shouted to Adalyn and Dara, "If you've got anything white that needs to go in this load of laundry, you'd better get it to me now. I'm not doing a special load for one white blouse, you hear me?"

She'd been doing laundry all morning, checking on Callie whenever she could. It was evident the trip to New York had changed Callie's mood. In all the years they had worked together, she'd never had to worry about her, but she had concerns now.

"Grace, have you seen a blue and white striped blouse by any chance? I thought it was in the closet, but I can't find it," Callie called down the hall. "I wanted to take it with me to New York."

Grace walked to the bedroom door and shook her

202

head. "Gracious, Callie, that blouse is right there on the bed beside your suitcase. Slow down and you'll be able to find everything you're looking for."

"You think this trip is a good idea, right? It will take my mind off all the nonsense we've been dealing with for the past several months and, best of all, it'll give me fun time with my girls." Callie folded the blouse and placed it in the suitcase. "I know I've worried you, but I'm really all right. I haven't forgotten who I am."

"You've never let me down." Grace knew better than anyone how important that was to Callie. And she knew why. She looked at her friend intently for a few seconds, then smiled. "We've depended on each other for so long, I knew you were doing better than you gave yourself credit for. This is a good time for you to get away. We'd already planned time off because of the Ireland trip, so nothing really changes." She reached for Callie's hand and gave it a squeeze. "Go and have fun and when you come home, we'll move on." She released her hand. "Everything's okay, my friend."

"Thanks, Grace. You always know what to say to make me feel better."

"By the way, what are your flight numbers?"

Grace had to make sure the protection team was on the same plane.

****

"Dad, how're you doing? It isn't often you're by yourself." Connor laughed as he walked into a kitchen where dishes were piled up in the sink. "You do have a dishwasher, or don't you know how to operate it?"

"Very funny, young man." Charlie looked embarrassed as he got up from the table and started to put the dirty dishes in the dishwasher. "I was waiting until I had enough dishes to make a full load."

"Sure, Dad. Whatever you say." Connor laughed and took a seat at the table. "I stopped by to see if you wanted to go to dinner with me. There are a few things I need to get your opinion on. We haven't had time to talk in several days and Matt has some new information he wants to share with us."

"Where are you thinking of going for dinner? I've got two or three casseroles in the fridge and freezer that your mother is expecting me to eat while she's gone. Call Matt and tell him to come here. I know there's a chicken pot pie in the fridge somewhere and it'll feed all three of us."

"Good idea. Matt will love that," Connor yelled over his shoulder as he let the kitchen screen door slam. "I'll be back in about an hour."

Charlie made a salad and put the pot pie in the oven to warm, glad to have something to do while he waited for Connor and Matt to show up. He was surprised how lonely the house was without Callie and how much he missed her. It had been a long time since he'd been all alone. Usually there was someone around to keep him company.

Being alone had given him too much time to think. The issue with Paula that had not been resolved, the idea that he and Callie had a child that he hadn't known about, the postponed trip to Ireland, and Dara's trouble with Edward crowded his mind.

Plus, he had to decide when he was going back into private practice. If the past few weeks had taught him anything, it was he didn't do well when he had too much time to think about his own life. He was much better at thinking about the lives and problems of others. He could always find case law and precedence for the problems that were presented in his courtroom. It wasn't that easy to solve the things that happened in his own house.

On top of everything else, Callie wasn't acting like herself. There was an undercurrent he couldn't identify but he'd swear it was fear. He couldn't put it into words, but something was different. Or maybe he was looking at her differently because of the secret she'd kept from him for decades. How could he not have known she was pregnant? Were there other things she'd hidden from him? Did he really know who she was? He always thought he knew her and how she would react in any given situation. She was organized, methodical, caring, and honest. Or was she? Maybe all that was just an act when he was around.

When he looked down at the cutting board, he realized he'd chopped up more vegetables than he'd planned for the salad. He scraped everything in the bowl and laughed. There wasn't any room for the lettuce. The timer buzzed on the oven, and he grabbed a potholder. He had done his part for this dinner. It was time for Connor and Matt to walk in the door.

****

"Judge, that was a great dinner. I didn't know you had such excellent culinary skills." Matt placed his napkin on the table and let out a sigh. "I'm stuffed."

"There's always room for Grace's pound cake, Matt. And while I appreciate your compliments, you know all I did was chop some veggies and put the pot pie in the oven. If you had to depend on me for dinner, it would have been a grilled cheese or peanut butter and jelly sandwich."

"If you insist. I'll have a slice of that cake." Matt

smiled as he watched Charlie cut him a generous piece. "I have a report on Paula that I hope answers a few more questions. She's been seen in the area on several occasions and one of my guys got a license tag number from a car she was seen driving. I ran the tag, and the car was registered to a woman named Martha Lawrence who lives in Gainesville. I've run that name through several data bases and come up with nothing. So, one of my team is sitting in front of her house as we speak. That's all I have right now, but we're checking every angle I can think of."

Charlie put down the knife he was using to cut the cake and stared at Matt. "Let me get this straight. The car Paula was seen driving is registered to a woman named Martha who lives in Gainesville?"

"Yes, sir, and hopefully, before too much longer, I'll have more than a name and address."

"That's strange. In the last few days, I've heard that name somewhere, but I can't remember where." Charlie frowned and shook his head. "It probably has no connection. When it comes to me, I'll let you know."

"Dad, we know Paula got in touch with Mom. Has she tried to contact you?" Connor was browsing the file folder Matt had placed on the table. "We seem to be going around in circles, but every little thing we find out gets us closer to understanding who Paula is and what she wants with our family."

"Connor, I'd tell you if I'd heard from her. Once she embarrassed me in front of my family, she's let me be. I wish we knew why she wanted to speak to your mother." He picked up his fork and started eating his dessert. "Grace knows how to make pound cake taste like a little bit of heaven, doesn't she, boys?"

****

"Have we ever had a slumber party, Mom? You know, just the three of us?" Dara laughed. "We had to come all the way to New York for this to happen. By the way, Adalyn, your apartment is gorgeous."

"We've had fun, haven't we? Thanks, girls, for including me in this trip." Callie was finding it hard to keep her eyes open. "I've enjoyed every minute of our New York adventure, but I'm exhausted. I think I'm going to bed."

"Wait, Mom. Can't you stay awake a little longer? We never have time to talk. You know, girl-to-girl," Adalyn persisted. "I have things I've wanted to talk to you about."

Callie forced herself to breath normally and sat back down into the comfortable chair near the window. She smiled at her daughter. "Go ahead, Adalyn, I'm listening. Is everything okay?"

"Yes, I'm fine, but with all that's happened recently, I've wondered about you and Dad. You know, things like how did you meet? How, with your high moral code, did you end up having sex before marriage? And I'm dumbfounded that you were able to keep a pregnancy a secret from him. Do you feel like you can talk to me and Dara about it?"

Callie leaned back in the chair and closed her eyes. "Your first question is easy. We met when your dad stumbled over me while I was studying."

Dara laughed. "You're kidding. How did he manage to do that?"

"It was a beautiful day. I was stretched out on the Green at the university, and he wasn't watching where he was going. He literally fell over me. It was not a pretty picture." She laughed.

"How have we missed hearing about this before now? That's a vision I will hold onto forever. Dear ole Dad losing his dignity over a girl."

"You can ask him for his version of the story when you see him. My books and papers went everywhere, my skirt and legs had dirt and grass all over." Callie smiled. "He was so cute I couldn't stay mad long, and he offered to buy me lunch. The rest is history. Your second question may take more than just a few minutes to answer." Memories of a weekend away flooded over her and she wondered how she could help her daughters understand. "When your dad proposed and gave me a ring, all my walls came tumbling down. It seemed so natural for us to celebrate by making love." A silent tear fell across her cheek. "It changed my life. I realized how much I loved your father and how much I was going to miss him when he left school and I had to stay in Gainesville for another year. It was a year of being busy for both of us. He would be taking the bar exam and getting settled in the law firm; I'd be finishing my thesis, doing an internship at the museum in Washington, DC, and graduating. Then, I had to add making wedding plans. It seemed manageable until I found out I was pregnant."

"I can see how you were overwhelmed, but people had to know you were expecting. It's not usually something you can hide," Dara replied.

"Today, with cell phones and the internet, it wouldn't be easy. In the 1960s, it was easier." She took a breath. "Your grandmother agreed to do most of the wedding planning and didn't seem upset when I couldn't go to Atlanta for fittings and wedding parties in the fall.

I kept postponing things until late spring using my studies as an excuse. Then I met a woman who helped me work out a plan. Every time your dad wanted to come to Gainesville, I found a reason to stall. Over that summer and fall, my new friend helped me find financial help and an agency to handle an adoption." Callie began to cry harder. "It made sense to me at the time."

"Oh, Mom. I didn't mean to make you cry. I'm sorry." Adalyn grabbed her mother's hand and tried to console her.

"It's okay, honey." Callie wiped away the tears. "I thought adoption was the best solution to my problem. I knew your dad would want to get married right away if I told him. It would have changed his careful plans for his career, and he would never have considered what the consequences would be for me if I moved to Shamrock Beach a fallen lady."

"A what? A fallen lady? Are you kidding?" Dara gasped.

"You wouldn't understand. Shamrock was a conservative community, and your dad was one of the 'golden boys.' I would never have been accepted, and his parents would never have approved of me. I thought I was doing the right thing for both of us, but in hindsight, I hurt everybody: your dad, myself, and our daughter."

Adalyn and Dara rushed over to hug their mother. "Mom, don't cry anymore. Dara and I appreciate you for telling us your story. Please, forgive yourself for making an impossible choice."

Callie stood up and forced a smile at her daughters. "Thanks for asking your questions and letting me explain. I think it helped me to finally be able to talk about a painful time in my life. But, if you don't mind, I

really need to get some sleep."
****

Three days later, the limo pulled up in front of the house and three very tired travelers looked at each other as if trying to decide whether to move from their comfortable seats.

"Mom, when the driver opens the door, tell him we'd like to sleep in the car." Dara looked from her mother to her sister and tried not to laugh. "We look like we've been on a three-day bender. Dad's going to think we're bad influences on you. But didn't we have fun?"

"I can't believe we crammed so much into such a short trip. I'm worn out." Callie moved a few inches and tried to pick up her purse. "Girls, as much as I don't want it to end, we are home and we've got to get out of this car. I'm going to move and so are you."

The driver opened the door and took Callie's hand to help her. "Ladies, it has been my pleasure to drive you home. I'll make sure your luggage is at the door, and then I'll head back to Jacksonville."

"Thank you, Tom. I'll call you in a week or so when I need to head back to New York." Adalyn slowly emerged from the car and walked with her mother to the house. "I'm glad the agency always sends Tom to drive me. He's a good driver and seems like a good man." She had started up the front steps when the door flew open, and her father almost knocked her over.

"I am so glad you're home." Charlie grabbed Adalyn to keep her from losing her balance. "Sorry, sweetheart, I didn't hurt you, did I? I heard your voices and wanted to welcome you all home." He pulled Callie into his arms and hugged her tightly. "I missed you."

"Honey, we had such a good time. But it's good to

be home." Callie pulled away and walked into the house. "Grace must have been here today to help you clean up the place." She laughed as she gazed around the room.

"She did not." He was indignant. "I'm a very neat person."

"Dad, sometimes you really are funny." Dara kissed her father's cheek and headed for the stairs. "Let's talk tomorrow. All I want to do is take a hot shower and jump in bed."

"I'm right behind you, Dara. And don't you even think about using all the hot water," Adalyn called after her sister. "I'll get my suitcase in the morning. Good night."

Charlie watched his daughters climb the stairs and then turned to look at his wife. "I know you had a good time and needed time away, but I really missed you." He wanted to hug her and not let go. "Everything that's happened over the last couple of weeks has frayed all our nerves, but, Callie, we're fine. No matter what, we're fine and I'm glad you're home."

Later that night, Callie laid her head on Charlie's shoulder and wondered what she'd do without this man she had loved for more than forty years. When she was lying secure in his arms, all her worries seemed far away. He was her safe harbor even when she knew there were storms up ahead. She longed to believe that everything was fine, just as he had said.

****

The alarm from the bedside clock shattered the silence, waking Charlie and Callie from the security of their sleep. "Good grief, turn that screeching thing off." Callie rolled over in the darkness, momentarily forgetting where she was. "It has to be the middle of the night."

Charlie reached over and hit the snooze button. "It's five thirty. I'm meeting Parker at six thirty to go fishing. Go back to sleep."

"You're going fishing with the new judge? Why?" By now Callie was awake enough to think. "You and Parker aren't fishing buddies."

"We could be. He asked, and I said I'd go." He headed for the bathroom. "He must have something up his sleeve if he wants to talk to me. Maybe he needs my advice on something." Shaking his head, he started to close the door. "He's only been on the bench for a few weeks. There's a lot to learn about being a judge."

"Who are you trying to convince, me or you?" She sat up and pulled herself out from under the covers. "Please don't let him yank you back into something you just left. Remember, you are retired." The bathroom door closed, and she knew he'd decided not to listen.

She found her slippers and robe, rubbed the sleep from her eyes, and went to the kitchen. Another day had started at Shamrock Beach.

Flipping the light switch, she was startled to see Dara sitting at the table nursing a cup of coffee. "Good morning, Mom. You're up early."

"It's not even six o'clock. How long have you been sitting in the dark?" Placing her hand on her daughter's shoulder, she gave her a little squeeze. "Glad you put the coffee on, thanks."

"I'm having trouble sleeping. I think I miss my own bed."

Callie poured herself a cup and waited for Dara to continue.

"It's time for me to go back to Tallahassee." She

looked at her mother defensively. "Before you start lecturing me, just listen. The restraining order is still in effect, the locks have been changed, and I'm way behind on a project I wanted to finish before the next semester begins."

"It's not a good idea. You have no way of knowing what Edward's capable of or why he came after you like he did." Her voice became shriller. "You live alone, for heaven's sake. It's not a good idea."

"I hear your concern and, believe me, I've thought about the reasons I shouldn't be returning. Please try to understand I need to go home. I have several neighbors that I trust enough to tell them what happened. They'll look out for me."

"Don't you think you should talk to Connor or your father before you make a decision?"

"I'll tell them my plans tonight at dinner. They'll give me a hard time, but my mind is made up."

"When are you thinking of leaving?" Callie stopped to think. "Perhaps Adalyn would go with you for a couple of days."

"Mother, stop. I've been rooming with my sister long enough and it's getting old. Remember, I've been on my own for a long time." She looked at her mother's frown and smiled. "Don't suggest it to her, please. Besides, she's been talking about going back to New York in a week or two."

"Okay, okay. But if you don't bring it up at dinner, I will." She opened the refrigerator and pulled out eggs and sausage. "After breakfast I need to go to the museum. I promised I'd help with some new items that need to be displayed. Do you have plans for the day?"

"Adalyn and I are going to the beach. We both need

a bit of sun."

****

When Callie left the museum, she walked toward the familiar car that was parked on the side street. It had been parked in that spot on the second Wednesday of every month for as long as she could remember. The passenger window was rolled down and, without saying a word to the driver, she dropped the envelope on the front seat and continued her walk home. It was always the same, nothing changed but the make and model of the car. She sighed and picked up her walking pace; after all, she had dinner to prepare and the young man who was tailing her needed the exercise.

****

Everyone was talking at once as the bowls and platter were being passed around the table. Charlie and Connor were holding court on some legal issue, Adalyn and Dara were discussing whether to drive to Jacksonville to do some shopping, and Callie was wishing Brock was with them. She was her happiest when all the children were seated at their places in the dining room. Until this summer, the occasions were few when it happened. Someone was always traveling or too busy at work or had some other reason for not being in Shamrock Beach. She studied each face, wondering how they had grown up so fast. The years had gotten away from her, and she didn't feel old enough for them be as old as they were.

"Mom, did you hear me?" Connor's voice abruptly ended her daydreaming.

"I'm sorry. I must have been a hundred miles away. What did you say?"

"Pass the rolls and the butter, please."

She laughed at the tone of her son's voice. "That was earthshaking. I'm sorry I missed it the first time."

Everyone chimed in, teasing Connor about using his attorney voice at the family dining table. "Dear family, you think you're funny, but seriously, I would like to have a roll and some butter." After Callie handed him the requested items, she patted his hand.

"Thanks, Mom. What were you thinking about so hard?"

"Just enjoying the company and wondering how I've stayed so young while you all have gotten older. Don't you feel the same way, Charlie?"

"Your mother is right. We haven't aged at all." His laughter was contagious and soon everyone at the table had joined in.

Dara tapped her glass with her fork. "Could I please have the attention of everyone, old and young? I have an announcement to make." She waited until they had gotten quiet and put down their forks. "I'm going home tomorrow."

"Whoa, daughter of mine, not so fast." Charlie almost jumped out of his chair. "That's not in the plan. You can't go back to Tallahassee until we know what's going on with Edward."

"I need to go home, and I'll take all the necessary precautions to be safe." She looked around the table. "Would somebody take my side? Adalyn, Connor? Won't you give me some help? It's time for me to go home."

"Would you give me a day or two to have Matt look into what's going on now with Edward? If he gives a thumbs up, then I'll vote for you to go home." Connor's voice softened. "Maybe you've forgotten, but I still remember what you looked like the night you came home. That's not going to happen to you again if I can help it."

He walked around to the back of his sister's chair and gave her a hug. "I promise I'll call Matt after dinner, and he can have some of his people back on the case by tomorrow. We backed off when you went to New York. Surely, you can put up with Adalyn for a few more days."

"Connor is right. Give him a few days to see if Matt can get us some information. If Matt feels you can go home safely, then I'll have no objections." Charlie looked relieved and nodded at Callie.

"I know you have my best interest at heart, but you all can be so aggravating." She turned to her mother. "What was it you were just saying about us being so old?"

Chapter Seventeen

Matt hung up the phone and looked at Connor. "Don Glider has had Edward under surveillance since this ugly business began. He just told me that the guy goes by Dara's place and her office at least once a day. He seems to be looking for her car. He parks down the street, sits for twenty minutes or so, and then drives off. He does the same at her office. Don has never seen him get out of his car or go close enough to break the restraining order. If I were you, I'd tell Dara to wait a few more days. Don is going to try to talk to Edward tomorrow. He'll remind him of the order and let him know he's being watched. Then, we'll see what happens." Matt closed the folder he was holding and waited for Connor to reply.

"I don't feel good about this. I know it could be a coincidence that he's on campus near her office, but why is he in Dara's neighborhood?"

"Maybe we'll have a better handle on this after Don talks to him. I've told Don to call the Leon County Sheriff's Office if the guy gets even an inch closer than the order allows. It makes me nervous that Edward is hanging around, but so far, he hasn't done anything that we can use against him."

"If he's within sight of her place, isn't that stalking?" Connor asked. "Changing the subject, do you have anything new on Paula?"

"No, she's disappeared again. She's like a mirage.

You think you see her, but when you get close, she's not there. I've got two people trying to find her. She'll surface again."

"Anything on this Martha Lawrence?"

"Another mystery. No one has seen her, but the neighbors say that periodically someone stays at the house for a day or two. It's been well maintained. The yard is mowed, and the electricity and water have never been turned off. Those bills are paid automatically every month by a Martha Lawrence, but so far, I can't trace her. I think that's a bogus name and the place might be a short time rental. The neighbors made sure to let Don know there's never been any trouble there. In a town like Gainesville, that means it's not being rented to college kids."

"I'll be glad when all the puzzle pieces come together. I'm tired of thinking about Paula and Edward. I feel like my family *is* living one of Adalyn's soap opera plots."

"You want to go back to small-town boring? This is the most excitement Shamrock Beach has had since we were teenagers." Matt gathered his folders and walked toward the door. "By the way, my mother said to thank you for giving me work that brings me back here so often. She's seen more of me the past few weeks than she has in the past few years."

After Matt left, Connor tried to concentrate on his work, but he kept mulling over everything related to what was happening with his family. Why did Paula claim she was his father's daughter and why did she confront his mother at the church? Who was Martha Lawrence and how was all this connected? What was Edward's story? *Why is all of this happening now?*

The ringing of the phone brought a halt to those thoughts. "Yes, this is Connor McBride. How may I help you?" He listened carefully to the person on the other end of the line. She didn't have to identify herself. He recognized her voice immediately. "I'll be glad to meet you. Name a time and place."

After it had gotten dark, he drove down to a little-used part of the beach where he saw the parked car. He pulled alongside and turned off his engine. Within minutes the passenger door opened, and she slid next to him.

"It's been a while, Paula. I was hoping you had moved on to bigger and better things."

"I've only got a few minutes, and this isn't a social call. I trust you, and I need your help. It's urgent or I wouldn't ask."

"I'm probably the last person you should trust or ask for help. There's this little matter of you trying to destroy my family." His hands gripped the steering wheel. "I'm usually good at digging down through a person's layers to find the truth, but you have baffled me. I can't figure your angle or your motive. All I know is you have embarrassed my father and alarmed my mother. You've used up all my good graces and here you are asking for my help. What gives with you, sweetheart?"

"First, I had to prove my loyalty to someone—a very dangerous someone—by humiliating your father. I hadn't planned to do it so publicly and I regret that part. Second, you need to know everything I've done had the same goal. I needed to get to your mother. You see, I know her better than you do, even though I've only just met her." She let that sink in before she spoke again. "Your mom is in trouble with a certain group of people and, if they can't be stopped, the outcome is not going to be pretty. You've been warned, and you need to protect her."

She opened the car door and started to get out, but Connor grabbed her arm and held tight. "Oh no you don't. You're not going to drop your warning on me and then take off. I want to know what you're talking about, and I want to know now." His voice hardened and the hold on her arm strengthened. "Turn back around, close the door, and start talking."

"I can't stay. They're constantly watching me. and if they find me talking to you, they'll probably kill me. Let go, you're hurting me. I've taken a huge risk coming here, but I wanted you to help me by protecting your mother."

"Callie McBride is a small-town museum curator, wife, and mother. What in the world are you talking about? By the way, who are you and why should I believe you? I need some answers."

"Your mother is part of an agency that's about to unravel a big criminal operation, and there's a group of people that will stop at nothing to make sure that doesn't happen." She pulled hard to untangle his grip on her arm. "I'm on your side. Now let go of me. Tell your friend, that nice detective, to back off me and Martha Lawrence or it may get even more dangerous." She struggled free of his hold and moved out of the car. "I'll be in touch."

Connor was angry and dumbfounded as he watched her drive away. Who was she, and more importantly, who was his mother? He pulled out his phone and dialed Matt's number. "Where are you?"

"I'm about three hundred yards from you, parked behind the dune. What's next?"

"Go ahead and leave. I'll wait a few minutes before I head back to town. Go to your folks' house and then walk to the park. I'll meet you there."

His head hurt as he tried to wade through what he'd just heard. It wasn't logical. Why would anyone go after his father to get to his mother? His mother involved with some governmental agency was beyond belief—wasn't it?

The moon was coming up beyond the breakers, its white light catching the top of each rolling wave. Before he met with Paula, he was riding the crest, feeling free, it was exhilarating. Then he lost his balance, crashed to the shore, left dazed and alone with his fears. His body tensed as he started the car and tried to shake away his imaginings. His life had gone from small-town boring to crazy as quickly as the ocean's waves ebbed and flowed.

****

"Matt, call your dogs off Paula and Martha Lawrence, but stay as vigilant as you can. If what she told me tonight is legitimate, this thing is bigger and more dangerous than we ever thought." He leaned back against the park bench and turned his gaze to the sky. "I don't know what to think or even how to approach it. I don't trust that woman, and yet, if my mom's in trouble, she must be protected." In a few minutes, he told Matt what Paula had said and then quietly waited for his friend to respond. "Well, what do you think? It's not like you to just sit there."

"Man, if I didn't know you better, I'd think you were crazy. What do you want me to say?" He folded his hands behind his head. "To think your mother is messed up in something covert is like trying to imagine my mother as Wonder Woman. You know I told you last week that I thought someone was tailing your mom, but I couldn't wrap my head around it until now."

"That confirms it. Paula didn't sound like she was making this stuff up, but I'm not sure what her game is or who's side she's on. What do I do now? Confront my mother, send her away, call in the National Guard to protect her? I'm not ready for her to be someone other than who she's always been. What if this nonsense is true?"

"One thing is for sure. We can't ignore it. I think you need to go have a talk with your mom. Give her a chance to deny everything, and then I'll go back to tailing Paula."

****

"Where are Dad and my sisters this evening? Don't tell me they talked him into going shopping?"

"Goodness no. Your dad is at the Rotary meeting and your sisters went to the movie. They asked me to go, but I'm in the middle of a good book that has to go back to the library in two days." She noted her place with a bookmark and looked up at her son. "I've always got time for you, Connor. Would you like a drink or some dessert?"

"No thanks. I'm headed back to the office to finish something I need for court tomorrow. Thought I'd stop in for a chat."

"Okay. Is there something specific that you wanted to chat about?"

"Have you ever had another job? Did you ever work for the government? Where did you work when you were in college or before you and Dad started the family?"

Callie smiled to hide her fear. "Where did all this come from? You know I've been the museum curator in

Shamrock since your dad and I got married. Now I've gone from fulltime employee to parttime volunteer. That's been my job. Why are you asking?" She got up and walked across the room before she turned around and faced Connor. "Honey, again, why are you asking?"

"Matt and I were talking about our parents at dinner tonight and it hit me that there are so many things I probably don't know about you and Dad. After the bombshell you dropped last week, it made me think."

"You know I've often felt the same way about my parents. Yes, they were my parents, but maybe I don't know who they were outside of that role. Thank you for asking, Connor. Any time you want to know something about my life beyond being your mother, just let me know."

"If you'd had the opportunity to be something besides a museum curator, what would you have chosen?"

"I can't think of a thing I'd rather be than who I am. Wife, mother, curator. It's been a full life." She smiled lovingly as she relaxed. "Once upon a time, I thought a big city museum would be exciting. That changed when I met your dad."

"By the way, have you ever met a woman named Martha Lawrence who lives in Gainesville?"

"That name doesn't ring a bell. Should I know her?"

"That's the name and address of the person on the registration for Paula's car. Right now, that's all Matt knows. Have you seen or heard from Paula again? You'd tell me, wouldn't you?" He kept his eyes on her face.

"Of course, I'd let you know. Is there a reason for your questions?" Callie looked perplexed and sat down next to him. "I still worry about that young woman. She seemed so afraid when she talked to me at the church. I pray she's all right."

"Mom, we're all worried. About Paula, about you, about Dara." He reached for her hand. "Dara can't go back to Tallahassee right now. It seems Edward is spending time every day parked down the block from her place and her office. One of Matt's guys is going to try and find out why. Until we know more, she has to stay here." He stood up and kissed his mom on the top of her head. "I'll stop by tomorrow after court to talk to Dara."

His hand was on the door when his thoughts made him stop. *Everything about her looks the same. The serene smile, the adoring way she looks at me, the blue eyes that always seem to take in the whole world, the gentle spirit that is always willing to give a helping hand. All my life I've felt her protection, known her motive for everything, and counted on her predictability. Or do I only know what she wanted to reveal? Is my mother a figment of my imagination?*

He tried to regain his composure and struggled to find his voice. Clearing his throat, he turned the knob on the door and called over his shoulder, "Mom, you remember the sheriff's detail is still here, don't you? Anywhere you want to go, they go with you. No exceptions."

"You all won't let me forget, and I'm obeying all the rules." She shrugged. "This family thinks I'm two years old."

"You've got that right." He sniggered. "Lock the door when I leave."

Callie waited ten minutes before she picked up the phone. "Grace, are you coming over tomorrow? I've just had a strange visit from Connor that we need to talk about."

****

Finding Grace in the laundry room folding clothes, Callie slipped in beside her and grabbed a towel to fold. "My son was asking all kinds of questions last night," she whispered. "He wanted to know if I'd ever worked for the government or thought about being something other than a museum curator. He was fishing, Grace, and I don't know why."

"Did he talk in specifics or was he just being nosy? You know, sometimes our kids wake up and see us as human beings. They get curious about who we are. Don't you think it was that kind of conversation?"

"It didn't feel that way. He said my true confession about the baby made him realize he didn't know much about my life before I became his mother."

"See? What did I just say? He told you why he was asking the questions. Stop making something out of nothing."

"I think you're wrong." She placed the folded towel on the stack and waited. The silence caused her to wonder if she had been heard.

When Grace finally spoke there was a hardness to her voice that was meant to leave no doubts in Callie's mind. "Don't you do or say anything that'll back us into a corner."

Callie needed to tell her the rest. It was maybe the most important information. "He also asked me if I knew a woman named Martha Lawrence who lives in Gainesville."

Grace looked up in alarm. "Oh, lordy. Why in the name of heaven did he ask you that? What did you tell him?"

"I was startled, but I don't think I let it show. Apparently, Matt was able to trace the tag on a car that Paula was seen driving and it's registered to Martha."

"Did he say anything else?"

"Just that Matt didn't have any other information about this woman. You and I both know that Matt will keep digging until he finds something, and then what do we do?"

Grace shook her head. "I've got to do some thinking."

****

Matt was sound asleep when Connor called. "Last night when I questioned my mom, she denied everything without blinking. Nothing I said caused her to miss a beat. She's either a great actress, highly skilled at defusing anything that gets too close, or she doesn't have a clue."

"I'll take that for now. Something fishy is going on and we wasted a lot of time focusing on your dad. Keep your eyes and ears open, I'll do the rest." Matt turned the speaker off and put his phone back on the nightstand.

He tried to go back to sleep, but after tossing and turning for a few minutes, he got out of bed and walked to the kitchen. He started to boil water for hot chocolate when he remembered he was at his parents' house, and they were sleeping. He opened the refrigerator and settled for a bottle of ginger ale.

We're missing some crucial pieces and I've got to figure out where to start looking. Thoughts swirled in his head, bumping into each other, yet not connected. He reached for the paper his mom used to write her grocery list on and began making notes on everything that had happened since the night of the judge's retirement dinner.

When he ran out of space, he went back to the top of the page looking for a clue that might give meaning to something else he'd written. He grabbed another piece of the paper and made several columns. Each column was headed with a name: *Judge, Mrs. McBride, Paula, Martha*. He thought about it for a few minutes, then decided to add a column for *Edward*. His gut feeling kept telling him that somehow the guy was involved.

Question one, who are these people? Question two, what the heck is really going on? And at this hour of the morning, why do I even care? He had long ago finished the ginger ale and knew if he didn't try to get a few hours of sleep, he would regret it. He carried the two pages with him to the bedroom and hoped he could find answers in his dreams.

****

Walking from one corner of the room to the other, counting out loud the number of steps she was taking, wasn't helping Grace decide. There was so much to consider, so many issues within issues, and none of it was easy. She crossed the room again before she picked up her phone and called her contact. Three rings, she hung up and called again. This time the call was answered, and she put the caller on speaker.

"This better be important. Do you have any idea what time it is?"

"They've traced the license tag on the car and know it's registered to Martha Lawrence in Gainesville. The house is already under surveillance. Just thought you'd be interested."

"It didn't take them as long as I'd hoped it would. They have no idea it's a safe house, do they?"

"Not to my knowledge. There's nobody in the house right now. There hasn't been any activity there for several weeks, but the group we've been watching may be ready to move in the next couple of days. What should I do?"

"Tell our people to stay clear of Gainesville. If the house is under surveillance, a good detective will know exactly what's going on the minute a van arrives. He'll call local law enforcement and there'll be too many questions. If you have word that something is happening, you snatch those kids and take them to Shamrock. I'll make sure that house is ready when you need it."

"We have a rescued group coming from Jacksonville, three girls and one boy. They're in bad shape. At least three of them need detox and medical attention before we can move them on to the center. We'll pick them up tonight from Duval County and take them to Shamrock. I don't have information about another drop being made any time soon."

"That's good. I'll call one of our doctors. He knows the code. You and Callie need to be at the house when he arrives. Is there anything else?"

"Not until I know what's going on in Gainesville."

"How's Callie? Is everything under control?"

"She's doing better. Her son and his detective friend are getting nosy, but she defused it. She'll be ready when we need to make our move. Connor and Matt traced the car, but the mob's our main worry right now. Mario's people are still watching Callie."

"I know. That's why I sent Paula. She'll be at your house a few more days."

"That's good, but she needs to change cars."

"Look out your window, Grace. That change has

already been made. She'll be heading back to Tallahassee. Edward's having her watched, but I don't think he knows she's staying at your house. Paula's pretty slippery." After a few seconds the call abruptly ended.

Grace glanced at the clock and groaned. No wonder she was exhausted. Yawning, she turned off the light and made her way down the hall to her bedroom. In four hours, the alarm would ring, but four hours would be good enough. Now that she had a plan, she could get some sleep.

****

Meet me at the house ASAP. Doctor on the way. Callie read the text on her phone and called over her shoulder, "Charlie, I'm going to the museum for a few hours, then I have some errands to run. Why don't you ask your daughters to go to lunch with you?"

She didn't have time to worry about the deputy assigned to watch her, but he couldn't follow where she needed to go. She parked in the back of the museum and walked around to the front entrance. Once she was inside and could see the deputy trying to look inconspicuous in the exhibition hall, she ducked around a corner and ran out the back door. When she was sure she wasn't being followed, she drove out of the parking lot.

As she drove out of town, she wondered how much longer she was going to be able to allude her protector and her family. She'd worked smart for over forty years, and no one was the wiser. But now that Charlie was home all the time and the trust issue exposed between them, she wasn't sure she could finish up the next few weeks. With so many people around the house it was becoming harder for her to leave, and Connor's suspicions made her nervous.

The safe house was thirty miles west of town and usually took her about forty minutes, yet, today, the drive seemed to be so much longer. It was giving her too much time to think. *Human trafficking in the State of Florida was a filthy business that brought in millions of dollars. It was upsetting to think that people were being bought and sold everyday by immoral criminals who worked for the mobsters and drug cartels. A human life had a value from fifty to over a thousand dollars depending on the market: Prostitution, forced labor, domestic servitude, sexual enslavement. Sometimes the victims were killed to sell their organs for big profit.*

Task Forces from many agencies worked in cooperation to stop the flow, but it was an uphill battle. Poverty, unemployment, and life under dictatorships contributed to the willingness of adults and teenagers to listen to the promises of a better life that often led to them becoming victims. Children were being sold by parents who were desperate, or they were kidnapped off the streets and sold to the highest bidder to fulfill the sexual desires of depraved men and women.

The movement of people through Florida was primarily a result of its proximity to port cities in South and Central America, but the state was also a haven for runaway teenagers who were easy prey for the traffickers.

Callie didn't know who was waiting for her at the safe house. Even though her work was usually with children and teenagers, every now and then she helped adults. Her responsibility at the safe house was to evaluate the victims and make recommendations for their next step. Short-term medical assistance was given, intake counseling was offered, and food, baths, and clean clothes were provided. The victims were given a secure place to rest and adjust before their long re-entry to a normal life began.

Many years ago, she had worked in victim rescue, but she was not able to save them all. A few minutes too late was all it took to watch lives whisked away in innocuous vans that would make them vanish. She always did her best, but it wasn't always enough.

But as her own family demands grew, she became a victim advocate and intake counselor. Once she moved from rescue to the safe house, she no longer considered her work dangerous—heartbreaking and secretive, but not dangerous. During a rescue, the trafficker was determined to protect his investment, and anything could happen. The safe house was secured through the cooperative work of nonprofit, state, and federal agencies. There was no watchful eye on her or those inside the house, but a fail-safe existed if she needed help.

Before she turned off the highway onto a dirt road, she made sure she wasn't being followed. Then she drove to the gated driveway and used the remote she carried in her purse to gain access to the property. As she approached the house, the first thing she noticed was the vehicle parked in front and assumed the doctor had arrived before her. She got out of the car and walked slowly toward the front porch. Before she reached the first step, the door opened, and her son Brock stood before her with a shocked look that probably mirrored her own.

"My God, Mom, what are you doing here?"

When she recovered from the surprise, she replied,

"I could ask you the same thing, but since you're a doctor, I know why you're here. The short story is I'm the intake counselor you've been waiting for, and we have work to do. Grace should be arriving at any minute, and I'd like to have as much of my work finished as possible. Shall we begin?"

She walked past him and entered the house, leaving him with his mouth hanging open.

No one was in the living room and the house was very quiet. "What's going on, Brock? Where is everybody?"

"We've got some serious problems here. The housemother is in the back bedroom with the two younger girls, there's a teenage girl in the front bedroom who has an acute drug withdrawal issue that I've given meds to, and there's a young boy in the bedroom at the end of the hall with critical physical injuries. I've finally gotten him settled down. Since I can't call an ambulance for the boy, I was waiting for intake so I can transport him to the hospital in Gainesville. Looks like someone has been using him as a punching bag for years." He sat down to recover from his shock. "Did you say Grace was on her way here? Our Miss Grace?"

"Yes, our friend, Grace." Her determination to maintain a professional stance was wavering. Having Brock here was the last thing she expected. "Why are you here, Brock? Isn't this out of your district?"

"The doctor who is on call for this house had an emergency, so I was next on the list. It's a little over an hour drive for me. Mom, we need to make this as quick as possible, that boy is in serious trouble." He stood and walked down the hall. "If you'll start with him, I can leave for the hospital as soon as the federal agent arrives." He stopped and turned back to his mother. "Please don't tell me Miss Grace is the federal agent in charge of this region." He closed his eyes and shook his head. "I'm trying hard to digest this. You and Miss Grace have just about knocked the wind out of my sails."

"We'll talk later, honey. Neither of us knew you were the on-call doctor. First things first. Let me talk to the young man."

The room was dark and the figure on the bed looked too small to be a teenager. As she got closer, she could see that his face had deep lacerations and one eye was swollen shut. His hair was matted with dried blood. With one hand, he held an ice pack, the other hung useless at his side. "The doctor is going to make sure you have the care you need, but I have to ask you a few questions." Her voice was gentle and soothing. "Do you think you can answer a few questions for me?"

The young man moaned when he tried to move his head. Callie could tell this was not going to be easy. "Can you tell me your name and where you used to live?"

****

Grace was standing in the doorway when Callie turned to let the boy rest. "Didn't we get a big surprise today?" She made a huffing sound as she walked away from the bedroom. "I've got to talk to Brock and then he can take this poor boy to the University Hospital."

"Oh, Grace, he's so young and has probably seen horrible things. My heart is breaking," Callie said as the door was closed gently.

Grace stood tall when she addressed the man she had helped raise. "Brock, I know you have many questions, and your mother and I will try to answer as many as we can. You know, of course, that you may not discuss who we are or what you've witnessed in this house. I don't know what you know about our operation, and I won't be able to go into details with you. Your oath as a doctor is as valid with us as it is with your patients."

"Miss Grace, I've worked at the Gainesville house for almost three years. I understand the need for secrecy and discretion. What I don't understand is you and my mom."

Grace nodded. "First, why are you here today?"

"The doctor who usually comes to this house wasn't available and I was called to cover for him. I carry a cell phone that only rings when I'm needed. I do know the routine and I have a security clearance. It's been explained to me how much danger these victims are in once they are brought back to the outside. I know their captors fear they'll tell what they know and become witnesses against them in court." He ran his hand through his hair, shaking his head. "Both of you have been in the house around me for three years and you had no idea I was involved, exactly like I had no idea that you and Mom were involved." He smiled. "I'm still not sure this isn't a dream."

He looked at his mother as she joined them. "Too bad I'm not in elementary school. I'd be the most popular kid in school if I told everyone at 'show and tell' that my mother and our housekeeper are really involved in covert operations." He noticed that his mom and Grace didn't smile back at him. "Okay, enough of my bad humor. I really need to get Ralph to Gainesville, but while his medication is taking effect, you and Mom can do some explaining."

Grace sat down and motioned for them to do the same. "I work with the FBI out of their field office in

Miami. Before the formation of the Crimes Against Children and Human Trafficking program, I worked for a small nonprofit in Gainesville that did victim rescue and recovery work. I recruited your mother and we've been a team for more than forty years. The nonprofit was assimilated into the multi-agency program years ago and my team was assigned to the FBI. Your security clearance doesn't give you access to any more information than what I've told you. Sorry, but you'll have to trust that your mother and I have been well trained, and we know how to do our job. We know how to keep secrets. Do you understand, Brock?" She waited for his nod before she continued. "You may not question me or your mother, and for heaven's sake, you can't share any of this with your wife or your family. I guess if you've been on board for three years, you know how to keep secrets, too."

"Brock, how much does Marti know?" Callie asked.

"She knows I do some pro bono work for the hospital, and she doesn't ask questions." He stood. "I've got to see about getting Ralph to the hospital. I may need your help."

It took the three of them and the house mother to move the injured teen to Brock's van. With every step they took, Ralph groaned and winced. He cried out in pain as he was lifted onto the pallet that took up most of the space in the back of the van.

"I'm sorry, Buddy. I wish I could give you something more to make this easier." Brock shook his head as he strapped Ralph in place. "Until the blood work is done, and we know what drugs you have in your system, I can't give you anything that might complicate your other injuries."

Brock closed the back door of the van, hugged his mother and Grace, and started the engine.

"Wait, Brock." Callie walked over to the van and whispered to her son, "I'll get to Gainesville as quickly as I can, and we'll talk." She backed up and watched as he drove away.

"Small world, my friend. Small world." Grace put her arm around Callie. "We'll process this later. We have work to do. You talk to the older girl, and I'll touch base with the housemother about when and how we can get all the girls moved to the center. I should be finished by the time you're ready to talk to the younger girls."

"Brock said the teenager is heavily drugged. I may not be able to get much information from her today." They entered the house and went in different directions.

****

"There was a time when I didn't know how much evil existed in the world. Then Grace recruited me to work with her. In turn, she found financial resources to get me through that first pregnancy and took care of the adoption process. I never dreamed I'd be involved in this work beyond my college days. It drew me in and has never let me go." Callie stood in the lobby of the University Hospital and talked quietly with her son. "I've seen horrendous things. They haunt me and make me want to do more."

"I understand, Mom, I feel the same way. It's still a shock. I would never have suspected you or Grace. Never in a million years. You're a much better actress than Adalyn. Now I know where her talent comes from." His smile was gentle and full of love. "One more question. How have you kept this from Dad?"

"Honey, the same way you keep your part in this

from Marti. It's not a full-time job, as you know. We don't get rescue victims on a regular basis. When you kids were younger, it was almost impossible to do the work I needed to do, so they gave me more courier work and less field work. One of my contacts left messages at the museum for me to pass on. As each of you began school, I was able to increase my involvement as an intake counselor. I hadn't decided what I'd do when Grace retires until your father wasn't reelected. His retirement really forced my hand and I've submitted my retirement papers. Remember, Grace is five years older than I am and she's beginning to make noises about moving closer to one of her kids. What will I do when she moves to Oregon?" She sighed. "I guess I'll cross that bridge when I have to."

"Do you have any idea how much danger you could be in? The guys who traffic these kids are not playing games."

"That's part of the job. I can share this much with you, and it should answer a few of your questions. Grace and I are part of an investigation that's going to court shortly. It's a big case against one of the kingpins. You've probably read about it in the papers. We have been subpoenaed to testify, but they take precautions to protect us. Most of the time we do recorded depositions rather than appear in court. The court is careful with our identity. One time, I sat behind a screen and entered and left the court through the judges' chamber. I was nervous, but I got through it." She watched a scowl cross her son's face. "Don't worry about me. I'm small potatoes to these people. Grace would be more of a target than I am."

"Mom, don't tell me you have anything to do with

the Mario Villa case? My worry alert just went to the top of the chart. That guy is ruthless."

"You know you can't ask me that. Now, for a few more weeks try to pretend we didn't have this conversation and for heaven's sake, stop worrying. When the time comes, our testimonies will be done via video and our identity will be protected."

"I've never been as shocked as I was when I walked out on the porch, and you were walking up those steps. Thanks for driving to Gainesville and talking to me. You've eased my mind somewhat, but don't tell me not to worry. You and Grace will need protection for some time to come. You do understand it won't end with the trial."

"Maybe it won't be as bad as you think. Honey, it's my turn with a question. How did you get involved?"

"Three years ago, law enforcement brought a ten-year-old girl to the hospital who had been so severely abused we weren't able to save her. It tore me up, Mom. I couldn't get her out of my mind. I called the officer who brought her in and asked him a lot of questions. He told me she was a rescue victim they had found in an alley; no identification and they couldn't match her to any missing children in the area. She was one of the nameless humans who are trafficked every day. That's when I asked if there was a way for me to help. I went through the training and have been working at safe houses in my area ever since."

"I'm so proud of you. I knew you were a good doctor and I've watched you mature as a husband and father. Today you showed me your heart and soul." She gave him a hug. "Now I've got to go home. I've overstayed my time at the museum." They shared a laugh and, as

Callie walked away, she heard her son whisper.

"Mom, I'm proud of you, too. Be careful."

****

The man in the black pickup truck grabbed his cell phone and called his boss. "Hey, I've tracked the lady in question. It looks like she's leaving Gainesville and is on her way back to Shamrock Beach. There are a couple of very lonely stretches of highway with little or no traffic. I think this is my chance. Do you want me to take it?"

****

She was on a curvy section of highway that meandered on the edge of the state forest when the black pickup truck barreled up next to her car and, before she could put the pieces together, he ran her off the road. Her car rolled in the ditch and the last thing she remembered was the impact of the airbag as it inflated.

"Mrs. McBride, hello? Can you hear me? I'm trying to open the door to get you out. You need help. Oh, Lord, you've got to help me." He'd been assigned to follow her, to protect her. But he wasn't equipped to prevent this accident.

Someone is calling me. I need to open my eyes, but all I want to do is sleep. Why do they want me to wake up?

****

The man continued to pull frantically on the car door that was bent out of shape from the crash. He feared the lady inside was dead when she didn't move or respond to his calls. Even though the EMTs were on their way, he continued his efforts to get inside the car. There had to be some way he could help her. As he was about to break the window with a hammer he found in his truck, he heard the sirens in the distance and saw another car stop behind his truck.

"Oh no. What happened? What can I do to help?" the lady called to him as she made her way from the road to the ditch where the car lay on its side. "Do you think she's alive?"

"I can't tell. She's not moving." He was panting from the energy he'd expended trying to open the car door. "The emergency people are on their way."

The EMTs and fire truck arrived and began to work on getting into the car. Within minutes, Callie was on a gurney that was being placed in the ambulance.

"Do you all know this woman?" one of the firemen called out.

"No, sir," the two bystanders responded.

"Find her purse or get me the car's registration if you can. Something that has a name on it."

As they started back down the embankment, two policemen arrived, and one yelled for them to wait. "I'll handle it. Don't touch anything and don't go anywhere. I'll need a statement from both of you."

One policeman retrieved the car's registration, and the other went back to his squad car to run the license tag number. "Her name is Callie Elizabeth McBride and she's from Shamrock Beach. I bet she's Judge McBride's wife."

He turned to the EMT. "Take her to Putnam County Medical Center. I'll radio ahead for them to have the helicopter ready. She needs to be airlifted to Orange Park Trauma as soon as they make sure she's stable."

The wail of the siren ricocheted off the trees and could be heard long after the ambulance was out of sight. "I need a statement from the two of you. Tell me everything you know."

The lady wrung her hands and answered softly, "I got here a minute or two before the ambulance. When I saw this man's truck pulled off the road I slowed down. That's when I saw the car in the ditch and offered to help."

"I came on this accident right after it happened. I was coming down the road when an oversized, black pickup truck zoomed by me going close to a hundred. It almost ran *me* down. When I came around the curve in the road, I saw the truck run this car into the ditch. I called 911 and did my best to get that lady out, but I couldn't open the door. This nice lady stopped to help about the time the EMTs got here. That's all I know."

"Did you see the tag on the truck?"

"No, sir. It was going too fast for me to see. I couldn't even see who was driving. Must have tinted windows or something."

"Thanks. When we've filled out these accident reports, you're free to go. But you'll probably be contacted at some later date, so make sure you give me a number where you can be reached."

The man waited until he was back in his truck to call his supervisor. "There's been a terrible accident and the lady is seriously injured. I was following her when a black pickup truck came roaring out of nowhere and hit her full force. Her car flew off the road and rolled down the embankment. I heard them say they'll airlift her to Orange Park. I didn't get a tag number or see the driver." He inhaled and exhaled heavily.

"It's bad, Martha. Very bad. I had to lie to the police officer, so you might have to cover me if they find out who I am."

Chapter Eighteen

"Oh, what a beautiful morning. It's great to be alive." Adalyn bounced into the kitchen and poured herself a cup of steaming hot coffee.

"What are you so cheerful about? You'd think you had a new boyfriend or were on drugs." Dara was puzzled. It was not like Adalyn to be so wide awake so early.

"You are such a grouch all the time, Dara. Can't you just look out the window and appreciate how glorious it is? God has given us another day in paradise: sunshine, blue sky, and that great big ocean to enjoy."

"You're right, and about noon, I'll be able to agree with you."

"What's got you so down today?"

"Connor called and told me I can't go home. Seems Edward has been on my street and near my office every day since I left town. One of Matt's guys is going to have a talk with him. You know, to remind him there is a restraining order against him. Maybe then he'll take the hint and go away." She pouted. "All I want to do is go home."

Adalyn walked over and gave her a hug. "Sweetheart, I'm sorry. Let's make the best of a bad thing and head for the beach. We can do some people watching, grab a chili dog from the food truck, and put our toes in the water. What do you say?"

"I'm not in the mood." It was almost a whisper as she continued to pout.

Adalyn began tickling her without mercy and soon Dara had fallen off the chair and was rolling on the floor. "Stop, stop or I'll tell Daddy you're the one who took his car and ruined the floorboard with rotten eggs you were going to throw at Ben Hardy's house."

"Oh no you won't, because you know I have stories I could tell on you." She got up off her knees and walked away leaving her sister to recover on the cold, tile floor. "Did that help improve your sullen mood?"

"You are the meanest sister that ever lived." Dara's laugh came from deep inside and soon both were giggling like schoolgirls. "I'm psychologically warped growing up in this house."

"You've got that right. Now what would you like to do today to get us out of this chamber of horrors?"

"I want to walk into town and get Millie to cut my hair short. Maybe highlight it or something wild."

"Call and see if you can get an appointment today. I wouldn't miss this for the world. You have never worn your hair short."

The jangle of the house phone cut short their conversation. "I'll get it," Dara offered. "Why in the world do Mom and Dad still have a land line? It is so old fashioned. Hello. Yes, this is the McBride residence." When she hung up the phone, her voice shook and her knees buckled. "Adalyn, there's been an accident. Mom's been airlifted to the trauma unit at Orange Park Medical. You call Dad's cell, I'll call Connor. We can call Brock from the car. We've got to go," Dara called over her shoulder as she ran upstairs to get her purse and car keys.

"I think Dad went to Connor's office. I'll tell them to meet us at the hospital." Adalyn pulled out her phone and dialed her brother's number.

****

The clicking noise of their shoes as they walked to the ICU sounded like rifle shots in a tunnel. Adalyn turned to Dara. "Try walking a bit softer. Your shoes are getting on my nerves."

"I thought the noise was coming from your heavy footsteps. Nothing matters but us getting to Mom."

"You're right. I'm sorry—I'm edgy."

"We should be there. The lady at the desk said it was down this hall and to the left."

As they came closer to the double doors of the ICU, Dara stopped. "She's going to be all right, isn't she?"

Adalyn grabbed her sister's hand and squeezed. "She doesn't have a choice, does she? We need her too much. I've been praying since the phone call, and I know in my heart that she's going to be fine. Now put on a smile and let's go through those doors holding on to every bit of faith we can."

Once inside the ICU waiting area, a nurse stopped them. "How may I help you?"

"We're here to see Mrs. McBride. Callie McBride. We're her daughters."

"I'm sorry, but you'll have to wait. There's a room across this hall for family members. I'll let the team know you're here and a doctor will see you soon." She pointed the way and continued down the hall.

They had just seated themselves in the room when they heard their dad's voice asking questions.

"I need to know about my wife." Charlie's voice had a frantic edge. "Where is she and what's going on?"

"A doctor is with her. That's all I know at this moment. He'll be here to talk with you as soon as he can. I know it isn't easy, but you'll have to wait here."

Connor took his dad's arm. "Come on. They'll come to this waiting room when they have something to tell us. Look, Adalyn and Dara are already here."

Reluctantly, Charlie allowed his son to walk him into the room.

"Oh, Daddy. I'm so glad you're here. They haven't told us anything." Adalyn moved from one side of the room to the other to sit by him. "This is rough on us so I can imagine how you must feel. She'll be okay. I just know it."

"Do you know what happened? Why was she over there anyway? I thought she was at the museum," Connor said.

"We don't have any answers. She did say she was going to run some errands after she left the museum. Do any of you have an idea why she was nearly fifty miles from home?" Charlie was talking a mile-a-minute.

"Dad, take a breath. None of us has answers to your questions. Lean back and take a couple of deep breaths." Adalyn took hold of his hand and forced herself to breathe deeply. It wouldn't help for them to continue to let their anxiety show. "Dara and I have been praying, and it's helping us stay calm. I'd gladly pray with you if you'd like me to."

Charlie looked at his daughter as if he'd never seen her before. "You've been praying?" He hesitated. "Why didn't I think of that?"

The four of them huddled together, each with their own silent thoughts, and waited.

Nearly thirty minutes passed before a doctor walked

into the room. Charlie stood up and confronted him. "What can you tell me about my wife? She's all right, isn't she? Just tell me something."

"Are you Mr. McBride?"

"Yes, I am. And these are my children."

"I'm Dr. Davis. I'm an internist and I'll be handling your wife's care. You need to know she's in critical condition. She lost a lot of blood and has several broken bones that are going to require setting and physical therapy. Our primary concern is internal bleeding that we can only stop through surgery. She's being prepped now, and the surgical team is waiting for her in the OR. As soon as she's in recovery, I'll come back with an update, and answer your questions."

Before they could ask him anything else, he was gone.

****

Brock was breathless as he raced down the hospital corridor. It had only been a couple of hours since he'd seen his mother and he knew he would have to be careful. His family would be asking a hundred questions that he knew the answers to but couldn't divulge. Under stress it would be easy to slip and reveal their secrets.

As he drove to Orange Park from Gainesville, his thoughts had raced, and his tension mounted. This was no accident. His mother must know the identity of the trafficking kingpin, and her court testimony was going to be important in convicting the devil who had inflicted so much harm.

The work he did was insignificant compared to what his mother and Grace had been doing for years. How could he help protect them? How would he answer his family's questions?

He stopped to catch his breath as he approached the waiting room. From the doorway he could observe the family and his eyes quickly scanned the small area. His father was sitting alone on the far side of the room. His head was resting against the wall behind the chair, eyes wide open, staring at the ceiling. Brock was stunned by how old he appeared. Gone was the look of vigor and vitality Brock had always associated with him. He was filled with a sadness that was hard to put into words.

Adalyn, Connor, and Dara were deep in conversation. Their voices and motions were more subdued than he could ever remember. Their usual banter and easy comradery had been replaced by the sad looks of worry and concern. His heart swelled with love as he felt the tears collecting in his eyes. This was his family minus the one person who was its warmth and compassion.

Dara raised her head and saw her brother standing in the hallway. She stood and walked toward him with her arms open for his hug. "I'm glad you're here." His arms closed around her, and their embrace invited her tears to begin flowing. "They haven't told us much." She pulled away and looked into his eyes. "She's critical. That's all we know."

He pulled away from her, nodded to his brother and sister, and took the chair next to his father. Charlie didn't move or acknowledge him. "Hey, Dad. I got here as soon as I could. I'm here if you need me for anything."

Slowly, Charlie lifted his head and looked at his oldest son. "What was she doing over here? Why was she on the road between Gainesville and Palatka? What errands would bring her here? I don't understand," he mumbled and lowered his head. "I don't understand."

"Dad, I don't have answers for you, but I can find out if there's an update on her condition." He stood to leave but turned around. "Keep praying. All of you, just keep praying."

He had gotten to the door when Grace ran into the room almost knocking him down. "Oh, lordy! How is she? What happened?"

BOOK THREE

*"It takes courage to love, but pain through love
is the purifying fire which those who
love generously know."*
~ *Eleanor Roosevelt*

Chapter Nineteen

"Mrs. McBride is in recovery. Her condition is still critical, and I don't have a prognosis. The next twelve hours will be crucial. Because she's in ICU, visitations will be limited to one person for ten minutes per hour." The doctor looked at Charlie. "I'm sorry, Judge. I wish I had more to tell you. Your wife is in the fight of her life, and I promise I'll do everything I can to help her win this battle. Sir, you will be the first to see her. The touch of your hand and the sound of your voice may give her the strength and fortitude she needs."

As the doctor turned to leave, he gave Brock a nod to follow him. The two men moved down the corridor a distance, then stopped to speak quietly.

"Brock, I'm sorry to report your mother is still very unstable. We have stopped the internal bleeding, which is a good sign, but her blood pressure is still fluctuating. Her spleen, liver, and kidneys were impacted in the crash, and we're monitoring her carefully to determine the extent of the damage. The imploding of the airbags broke several ribs, fractured her collarbone, and caused bruising around her face and eyes. There were some minor lacerations and one gash on her head that has been repaired. The next twelve hours will tell us what our next steps should be. I wish I had better news for you."

"Leon, I haven't seen you since medical school. I thought you were practicing in New Orleans." Brock shook hands with his colleague and felt some of the tension in his shoulders relax. "Mom is in good hands if you're in charge of her care. Have you got time for my questions?"

The doctor handed him the chart and they began discussing the results of her tests and possible treatment options. After Brock was satisfied, he nodded. "When did you decide to come back to this area?"

"I made up my mind last year. I grew up around here and knew it'd be a better place to raise my kids. It was a choice between Bourbon Street or green fields and lakes. Can you blame me? I'm headed to ICU if you'd like to go with me."

They started walking down the long corridor toward the nurse's station. "Ask your family to move over to this waiting room. It won't be long before they'll allow your dad a short visit."

"Thanks, Leon." Brock turned to the wall of glass windows that separated the hallway from the ICU and looked at his mother. She was bandaged and hooked to several monitors. IV lines were connected to her arms and the bruises on her face were prominent. He felt hollow and helpless. His medical degree was suddenly useless.

He was a doctor, highly trained, but nothing could prepare him for the shock of seeing his mother so tiny and frail and damaged. He closed his eyes and whispered a prayer. When he was sure he had his emotions under control, he turned and walked to the area where his family was waiting, knowing he had to find words to cushion the shock that awaited them.

He looked up to see Grace standing outside the waiting room. "Brock, tell me the truth. How bad is she?"

"Miss Grace, I won't lie to you. Right now, it's a waiting game. She has some serious damage to her internal organs that complicate her recovery. It's touch and go. But she has strength and good health on her side."

"Plus, the Good Lord. Don't forget that, son."

Brock nodded and let himself be folded into her ample arms. "She'll be fine. I just know she'll be fine," he mumbled.

"I agree," Grace whispered. She took a step back and looked him in the eyes. "You know the danger she's in. This was not a hit-and-run accident. Her deposition next month will make a difference in the DA's case. You know we must protect her. A security detail has been assigned to the hospital and is already in place. Unfortunately, the man who was right behind her when this happened couldn't have done a thing to prevent it."

"Dad is already asking questions. He wants to know why she was over here. What do I tell him?"

"I've taken care of that. I told him she went to Gainesville to see about collaborating on a project with the History Museum." She hesitated before continuing. "You do know she stopped at the museum before she met you? Your mom is good at covering all her bases."

He smiled tenderly at the woman who was still holding on to his shoulders. "It's going to take me the rest of my life to figure out who you and my mother really are. You do know that don't you?"

Grace laughed. "Boy, you don't have that many years left in your life. Your mama and I wear so many different faces it would take you a hundred years to figure it all out. We're just like you, Brock, just like you."

****

In the distance she heard a steady beeping. In the silence of the night, it was out of place. But Callie couldn't be late. She had no time for the anomalies. She'd been late before with disastrous results. She tried to wake up but the darkness wouldn't go away.

Waiting was not something she did well. She tried not to fidget, tried to be patient, tried to think of something to take her mind off the reason for the wait. She had volunteered to be here, crouched behind a hedge, and waiting was part of the job. There was nothing for her to do but settle down and continue her vigil.

The darkness crept around her like a monster from under the bed, and the Florida humidity was worse than a puppy's slobbery kisses. The unfamiliar night sounds heightened her senses, and she curled her arms tighter around her body for protection. Taking a deep breath, she fought against her instincts to flee.

Another hour went by. She stretched her arms, wiggled her toes, silently recited every song lyric she could remember, and even tried counting backward from one thousand. Her eyes had begun to droop when a movement on the other side of the hedge startled her, causing her to lose her balance.

When she righted herself and looked between the thin branches, she realized an unmarked delivery van was driving closer to the abandoned house. With a

252

swiftness that defied time, two men jumped from the front seat and opened the cargo doors. Each man reached in and picked up an oblong, blanketed bundle, one smaller than the other, and carried it into the house. From the size of the blanket, she knew each one carried a child, most likely a female somewhere around the age of ten. She couldn't be positive of the gender because in this business boys were a desired commodity, also.

For several minutes, she continued to sit in the shadows and tried to detect movement in or around the house. She listened for the cry of a child awakening from a drug-induced sleep and tried not to cry herself. The job she had been assigned was not finished, and tears would only get in her way.

Without warning, the door to the house flew open and the two men emerged empty handed. They ran to the van and quickly drove away. This wasn't the usual pattern. Had something gone wrong?

As she was preparing to leave the cover of the shadows, a large, black Cadillac turned onto the street and moved slowly toward the abandoned house. The car had no lights, but she could see the glow of a cigarette coming from the back seat. As the car came closer, she stepped back into the bushes and fought to control the trembling that had started in her hands. Never had she felt fearful, but this was different, and she was afraid of what she was seeing.

A tall, thin man, dressed in a dark suit, stepped from the driver's seat and walked quickly to the house. Within minutes he emerged with two groggy little girls who limply leaned into him for support. Their hands were tied, and they had no shoes.

The man in the back seat opened his door and the

253

children were thrust into the car. In less than ten minutes, the car had arrived and been driven away. And two beautiful little girls would never be heard from again. They would never see their parents, never go to school, never again be innocent.

This was the first time she'd witnessed the transfer of children to the terrible fate that awaited them. Usually, she had time to report the drop so the agency could make a rescue, but things had accelerated, and she'd failed to save these children.

She patted her swollen belly and vowed this would never happen to her child. From now on she would fight harder, work smarter. She would do everything in her power to save the next child and the next one and the next one.

****

He lingered in the shadows of the dimly lit corridor, waiting for the chaos of the shift change. Then he would make his move. All he had to do was change the settings on a machine or two and it would be over. He watched each person who entered the corridor and tried to determine who was assigned to watch her. He couldn't afford to get caught.

****

Brock had gone back to Gainesville, Adalyn and Dara had returned to Shamrock Beach. In the quiet of the waiting room, Charlie's light snores seemed to be rebounding from wall to wall. He stretched out on the small sofa when they had finally persuaded him to get a little sleep. He knew it was going to be a long night.

Connor had a good view of the ICU nurses' station, but he couldn't see the glass windows that partitioned the patient area. Every fifteen minutes he walked from the waiting area past those windows and back to his chair.

"Just checking," he told his father. "I'm walking off some of my nervous energy." He had taken the first watch, and Matt would be there before midnight to relieve him. At least he would be able to get a few hours' sleep, even if he was sitting up in one of those uncomfortable chairs.

The shift change would happen in less than an hour, and activity around him was beginning to increase as out-going staff executed their final duties before the handoff. There was a flurry of movement done in a hushed manner. The beeps and whines of the machines were still the dominant noise.

Connor stood outside the glass windows and watched as the nurses and technicians checked his mother's monitors and changed the IV bags dripping the needed medications into her veins. She looked small and lifeless.

There was no color to give vitality to the area where she was lying. White linens, white walls, white bandages, and her white skin made Connor wish for a box of crayons. He'd color some life back into the scene. Maybe blue walls, green sheets, red blanket, pink cheeks. He smiled at his musings and leaned his head on the glass. *Oh, Mom, please be okay. This family can't function without you. I left my crayons at home. You'll have to do this by yourself.*

The late shift started to arrive. Voices grew louder as instructions and orders were discussed and reviewed. The commotion at the nurses' station was probably quiet, but his ears had grown accustomed to subdued conversation and the repetitious harmony of the machines. He focused his attention on his mother and blocked out as much noise as he could.

"I'm sorry, sir. You're going to have to move back to the waiting area." The request being made by the burly man didn't register at first, and Connor continued to lean against the glass.

"Hey, buddy. Did you hear me? I said you need to move."

The tone of the man's voice jarred Connor and he took a step back. Just as he raised his head to get a good look at the person who was speaking, the man shoved him.

"Whoa. I'm going. There's no need to push me." The man was dressed in street clothes, no scrubs, no uniform, no identification badge. "Excuse me. Are you security or what?"

"I'm night security and you need to move away from this area. Weren't you told to stay in the waiting room unless someone on staff was with you? Now, don't make trouble. Go back and take a seat down the hall."

"Okay. I'm going." Connor started to move slowly down the corridor. He'd keep his guard up because something didn't feel right. Just as he turned away from the glass, something hit him across the back of the head, and he fell to the floor.

Alarms and bells began sounding from the hall where he had been standing, but he was too fuzzy to understand what was happening. Within a few seconds his mind began to function, and he knew there were people running around him. Someone shouted orders to find security and a Code Blue was being announced over the hospital PA system.

"What's going on?" he whispered as he struggled to get up. Then someone was bending over him.

"Are you okay? How did you fall?" Before he could respond, the nurse was checking his pulse.

"I've got to get up. Someone has done something to my mother. Help me get up. I've got to catch him."

Once he was on his feet, he tried to run toward the hospital exit. His head hurt and his legs didn't want to hold him. When he slumped against the wall, the nurse grabbed him to prevent another fall. "You need to sit down, and I'll get someone to come see about you. The emergency response team is with your mother."

Charlie, rubbing the sleep from his eyes, grabbed Connor's sleeve as he passed him in the hall. "What's happening? Are you okay? Is your mother all right?"

"There's a Code Blue and everyone is rushing to Mom's cubicle. They've asked me to move out of their way. Come on, let's step away. They'll let us know something when they can." Connor straightened up and held on to his dad's arm.

Minutes passed slowly as the two of them walked back to the waiting area. Then, as quickly as it began, the commotion died down and quiet was restored. Before Connor could move away, the charge nurse was standing beside him, looking at his father. "We have a problem. I've called for night security." She stopped and looked back down the corridor. "I don't want to frighten you, but someone just tampered with your wife's machines and pulled out her IV."

"Why would someone do that?" Charlie shouted. "Is she all right? What's going on? Someone tell me something."

Connor spoke quietly, "Calm down, Dad."

"I'm not going to calm down until I get some answers. The two of you move out of my way. Someone in this hospital is going to give me some answers."

"Stop." Connor ran behind his father and grabbed his arm. "You're not helping the situation. Please sit down until I find out what's going on." He turned to the nurse. "You may have to give him something. I've never seen him this agitated."

"I thought you were the one I was supposed to take a look at, not your father."

"I took a fall, but I'm better. He's the one who needs help."

"You have quite a knot on the back of your head." The nurse ran her hand across his head. "Your pupils are dilated. You might have a concussion, so I'll get a doctor to come check you out. Stay right here."

As the nurse hurried away, a uniformed policeman ran into the room and asked for Connor. "I need for you to come with me."

Connor stood up slowly and started to follow when Charlie ran up behind him and took hold of the officer's arm. "Tell me what's going on. Why do you want to see my son? What happened to my wife?"

"Judge McBride, someone will be here to talk with you in a few minutes. But I need for your son to come with me. He'll be right back."

The nurse came in with a glass of water and a pill for Charlie. "I want you to take this. It'll help. Believe me, all of us wish we could take one of these, too. You're going to be asked some questions and they need you to be calm, okay? This won't make you sleepy or anything. It'll just take the edge off for a while."

****

"Officer, what's going on?"

"Someone named Matt Granger needs to talk to you

without your father being around."

When they walked out the front door of the hospital, Connor could see Matt in the parking lot talking to several people. As he got closer, he shook his head and wondered if he was hallucinating.

The woman Matt was talking to was Paula, and leaning against a squad car was the night security guard who had rudely ordered him to leave the ICU.

"I know you're wondering what I'm doing here and, if you'll give me a minute, I'll explain everything." Paula continued her conversation with Matt and another man that Connor assumed was a police detective.

His patience was wearing thin when the detective turned to him. "Did you have a recent conversation with the man leaning against my car?"

"Yes." Connor told the detective what happened. "I think he's also responsible for the massive lump that's forming on the back of my head and my possible concussion. What's going on?"

"We have reason to believe this man is responsible for the Code Blue. We think he unplugged the machines in your mother's cubicle and pulled out her IV. He's not hospital security. This young lady tripped him as he was trying to leave the vicinity. I'll need your written statement, so don't leave the parking lot. Right now, my men will escort this one to the county jail."

The officer walked over to the car, read the man his Miranda Rights, and gave the orders for him to be taken away.

When he came back to where Connor, Paula, and Matt were standing, he addressed Paula. "Okay, where were we? You said you were walking toward the front door when this man ran out the door and almost knocked you down. You tripped him, pulled out a gun that you have a concealed permit for, and held it on him while this man, Matt Granger, called 911. Is that correct?"

"Yes, those are the basics, Officer."

"Why would you trip him and hold him at gunpoint?"

"I had a previous encounter with the man, and he threatened me. When I saw him running out of the hospital my instincts kicked in," Paula answered.

"Sir, I'm a private investigator and I've been following this man because he fits the profile of the person who may have been involved in a hit-and-run accident," Matt interjected, drawing attention away from Paula.

"I need to see photo IDs for all of you, and you'll have to sign statements. I'll let someone higher up the chain than I am figure this out."

The officer collected the IDs and headed to his car. "This will take a minute. Don't go anywhere."

Connor rubbed the back of his head and yawned. "This is giving me a headache." He turned to Paula. "You are planning on giving me an explanation, right?"

"I can't discuss everything with you or that officer, but both of you need to know that I'm one of the good guys. This isn't the time or place for true confessions." She smiled at the surprised looks on the faces of the two men. "Matt, I know you've worked hard to pigeonhole me, and I've done everything to stifle you and your team. I have good reasons." She looked directly at Connor.

"I warned you earlier. Your mother and Grace Samuels are in danger, and I'm part of a team trying to keep them safe. Although I don't know how we could have prevented her accident, I should have been able to stop that man from doing what he did just now. Our man was behind Callie on the road and did everything he could to help. If he hadn't been there, they would probably still be searching for her."

"This is crazy. You told me that my mom and, now you're adding our housekeeper, are in danger and you want me to believe that you're acting in official capacity to protect them. I don't know who you are, but you have a lot of explaining to do."

Paula reached inside her jacket and withdrew her badge. "My name is Paula Felton and I'm a field agent for the FBI. That's all you need to know currently. A highly trained security team is on the way to Orange Park, and we are doubling protection for your mother and Grace. The man that was assigned to hospital watch is in worse shape than you, Connor. He was hit on the head before you were but was able to radio me to be on the lookout. That's how I knew to trip the guy. Things have accelerated at such a fast pace, I need backup." She turned to Matt as she started to walk away. "Thanks for stepping in for me just now."

"Wait a minute, lady. You can't walk away and leave us with so many unanswered questions. Why should I believe you're not trying to destroy my family?" Connor's anger spilled out, and he needed more than he was getting from Paula.

"One simple reason. It was part of my job."

"Really? Your job was to ruin my father's reputation? How dare you," he shouted.

"When the time is right, you'll understand it all. I promise." Her voice was calm, and her words were measured. "Little white lies were necessary."

"Connor, you're tired and you have a nasty looking

bump on your head, but you've got to calm down." Matt tried to defuse Connor's anger. He moved closer to his friend and took hold of his shoulder. "Use your energy to help, not hinder. Your dad is relying on you. You need to reassure him the police have the person in custody who unplugged the machines, and they are working to find a motive. If I understand what Paula is saying, we can't mention seeing her tonight."

"The surveillance you've done over the past weeks has helped me do my job, Matt." She smiled. "You are hard to shake. I've had to work hard to stay one step ahead of you." She turned to Connor. "He's right. I wasn't here tonight."

****

"What is going on, Connor?" Charlie began firing questions at his son as soon as he came into the room. "Why did they want to see you? Who wanted to see you?"

"Slow down. Matt was in the parking lot when the man they believe is responsible for unplugging those machines left the building. The police got the call from the hospital and, together with Matt, they were able to apprehend the man. They needed me to answer some questions because this guy is the same one who made me leave the ICU just before the incident. He was impersonating a night security guard." He sat down beside his father and took a deep breath. "The police are going to put their own security outside the ICU to make sure nothing like this happens again."

"Why would someone do this to your mother? She has no enemies." Charlie dropped his head into his hands. "It's all so confusing."

Connor could tell the anti-anxiety pill the nurse had

given his father was beginning to take effect. "Why don't you stretch out on that couch? Matt is here to give us some relief and he'll answer any questions that come up."

After he got Charlie settled on the couch, he walked to the hallway where Matt was talking with the charge nurse. "Is my mother going to be okay?"

"There was no damage done. Thank goodness the monitor has alarms. The team was there so fast, nothing happened because of the disconnect." She patted Connor's arm. "Nothing happened, okay?"

"Thanks. I appreciate all that's being done for her."

The nurse nodded her head and started walking away. "Why don't the two of you go to the lounge and get a cup of coffee? The night shift has probably put on a fresh pot." She stopped and turned to look at the ICU. "I see the police security is here and, I assure you, Mr. McBride, my staff will be extra vigilant from now on."

"Matt, a cup of coffee sounds great. It'll give us a chance to talk."

When they entered the lounge, it was empty, and the smell of fresh brewed coffee was inviting. Matt poured two cups and handed one to Connor. "Those chairs don't look too uncomfortable. Sit down and we'll talk."

"What do you make of all this? First, my mom doesn't usually go off and not tell someone where she's going and how did she lose the security that was assigned to her? Then, she gets sideswiped and pushed off the road in a hit-and-run accident. She's in critical condition and some idiot unplugs her. On top of that, Paula shows up." Connor was talking faster and faster and his hands were moving back and forth like he was conducting an orchestra.

"Whoa, buddy. One thing at a time." Matt took a sip of coffee. "I have no idea why your mom was two counties away from home. You told me over the phone that Grace said your mom had been asked to pick up something at the museum in Gainesville. That makes sense." He continued sipping the hot coffee. "Now, to all the parts that don't make sense. Paula is FBI, your mom and Grace are in danger, and the stunt about Paula and your dad was simply subterfuge. The puzzle pieces are flying off the table. Did Grace go home after she left the hospital?"

"That's where she said she was going. Why?"

"We didn't ask Paula, but if Grace is in danger, shouldn't she have protection, too?" Matt pulled out his phone and made a call.

He looked over at Connor. "Do you know her house number?"

"Yeah. It's 1505. White house, navy blue shutters, on the corner. You know if they had someone on my mom, she probably has a detail on her, too."

Matt relayed the information and ended the call. "You're right, but I want some double coverage considering what just happened. I'm sorry I didn't think to do that sooner. Where were we on all your questions?"

"Why is the FBI interested in Mom and Grace? What could a small-town museum curator and housekeeper be mixed up in?"

"I don't have a clue. You can bet I'm going to find out."

"Is there some way you can get in touch with Paula? She needs to know that you've sent someone to check on Grace. We wouldn't want the FBI to think your man is one of the bad guys."

"She gave me an emergency-only phone number. Let me see if I can get her to answer my call." Matt listened as the phone rang and rang. "It's gone to voice mail." He waited for the beep. "It's Granger. One of my guys is on his way to keep an eye on the other lady's house. Call him Sam."

"I need to go check on my dad." Connor tossed his coffee cup in the trash can and started walking out of the room. "Guess you are taking back the offer to relieve me."

"People to see and places to go, my friend. I'll be in touch. Hang in there."

****

When Connor returned to the waiting room, he was surprised to see Adalyn and Dara whispering quietly on the far side of the room. "Shhh, Dad's asleep." Dara held her finger up to her mouth then motioned to the couch.

He crossed the room and sat down. "Why are you guys at the hospital? I thought you wouldn't be back before daylight."

"We couldn't sleep. We're here if you want to run home. You still have time for a nap and shower if you want," Adalyn offered.

"My adrenaline is flowing. I'd never be able to sleep."

"Has something happened to Mom? We got here right before you walked in, so we haven't checked in at the nurses' station." Dara struggled to find the words and looked at her brother for some reassurance.

Connor told them about the Code Blue but left out the part about Paula. He'd tell them about her when he had more information, more answers.

"That's horrible. Who would do that to her?" Dara

exclaimed.

"The police and Matt are searching for a motive. It's all too confusing." Before he could say more, his brother, Brock, walked into the room.

"Couldn't sleep." He looked haggard. "I've had an emergency at my hospital. When I finished, I thought I'd drive over and check on Mom before I went home." He took a seat next to his brother. "You all look more conspiratorial than usual. What's going on?"

"I know you just sat down but come take a walk with me." Connor stood up and motioned for Brock to follow him. As they walked down the silent corridor, he told his brother about the events of the evening. "The nurse told us the monitor alarm allowed the staff to get to her before damage was done. We can be grateful for that."

"My God. Will this day ever end? I need to talk to the nurse." Brock started to walk away. "Wait, if you got hit over the head has anyone checked to see if you have a concussion?"

"Yeah. The nurse said my eyes were dilated and told me to stay still."

"You might want to listen to what she said. I'll check you out when I get back."

"Wait, there's more. I haven't shared this with Dad or the girls, but you need to know." He relayed the rest of the story, including the part about Paula. Connor could see the color draining from Brock's face as he listened.

"Are you telling me that Paula told you she's with the FBI and that Mom and Grace are in danger? And you believed her? Connor, you may be playing into her hand. Did you consider that?"

"That's the gist of what she told the police and me and Matt, and I believe her. She's got the badges to prove

266

it. She tackled the guy that pulled the plug and held him at gunpoint until the police arrived. Pretty crazy, huh?" He looked at his brother and saw from his expression there was something he wasn't telling. "What do you know that you're not telling me?"

"Nothing. I think I'm in shock. I've got to process this and I'm too tired to do it now. Let me go to the nurses' station and then we can talk."

"Fine. There's fresh coffee in the lounge if you think that'll help." He could see tension knots in his brother's neck as he walked away. *What is going on with him?*

Brock waited until he turned the corner before he pulled out his phone and made a call. "Dr. Brock McBride here, I've just been told my mother, Callie McBride, and Grace Samuels are in more danger than I was led to believe. Apparently, my mother's accident wasn't an accident. What information do you have on this? Is Paula Felton on our team?"

When Brock returned to the waiting room, his dad was awake, and a family conference was underway. As tired as he was, he was hesitant to enter the room. He wished he could leave before any of them took notice of him.

"Did you find out anything new?" Adalyn asked.

"No, I think you all know the latest."

"Who in this room has any idea of what's going on?" Dara demanded. "Surely someone in this room knows something. Brock? Connor?"

Connor spoke directly to Dara. "I've told you what I know. The police are interrogating the suspect and will report to us when they have anything definitive to tell us. They assigned a security detail to both the ICU and Mom." He turned to Charlie. "With your permission, I'll have Matt put some of his people to work on this."

"His help is always appreciated. Tell him to send me the bill." Charlie spoke more assuredly as he struggled to wake up. "Do any of you know if there's coffee around here? Whatever that nurse gave me has made me groggy."

"Come on. It's after six o'clock. I think the cafeteria should be open." Adalyn took her father's arm and walked him out of the room. She stopped at the door and called over her shoulder, "Anybody else want to join us?"

Dara glanced at the others. "I think I'll go with them. Will you all be here when we come back?"

"Sis, I'm going home. I've been up all night and my work starts again at nine o'clock. If I hustle, I'll have time for a shower," Brock replied. "Connor, you'll give me a call if you need me or something changes."

When everyone was gone, Connor and Brock stared at each other, their shoulders drooping.

Finally, Brock broke the silence. "Where do we go from here? How do we explain all of this to the family? I've gone over and over everything, and to be honest, I'm stumped by most of it."

"There is one person we know who may have some of the answers we need. Matt is on his way to meet with that person." He held his nose and laughed. "If I were you, I'd go home and take that shower."

Brock huffed as he backed away. "I'll go by the cafeteria and let them know I'll be back later. Then it's home for a shower, since you think I need one." He raised his arms. "I can't smell a thing."

"You're the only one." Connor chuckled. He could still get a rise out of his brother. "I've got to go by the office to clear my calendar. It's a good thing I don't have court today. Then, I'll be here until I know Mom is out of the woods."

They walked out the door and turned in different directions.

****

"Miss Grace, this is more than a friendly visit. I'm worried about you. You know what happened at the hospital last night and you've seen the security outside your house, but there are some things you might not know."

"Matt, my worries are about Callie. I don't understand why everyone is worried about me."

"What's your connection to the mysterious Paula?" He waited for her reaction, but her expression didn't change. "The person who told the world she's Paula McBride showed up at the hospital last night in time to catch the guy suspected of unplugging Callie's machines and IV. She introduced herself to me and Connor as Paula Felton, FBI agent. You can imagine our surprise."

"Goodness, this story is taking some strange turns, isn't it? Why do you think I know this lady?"

"Come on, Miss Grace. There's more than meets the eye in this so-called story. Paula is the one who told us you and Mrs. McBride are in danger, and I'm the one who put a watchdog at your front door." Matt needed Grace to answer his questions. He studied her and knew it wasn't going to be easy.

"She must have me confused with someone else. I don't know her, but I did lay eyes on her at the judge's retirement dinner." Grace walked toward the kitchen. "Come with me. I've got some hot biscuits in the kitchen. You look like you might need to eat."

"I'd never pass up one of your biscuits. How about a cup of coffee to go with it?"

Grace set a plate of biscuits, the butter dish, and a bowl of blackberry jam on the table and motioned for Matt to sit down. She poured two cups of coffee and brought them to the table. "I've known you all your life, Matt Granger, and I've never told you a lie. Have I?" She watched him shake his head. "You can trust me, can't you?"

This time, he nodded.

"Well, then, you gonna need to trust me right now."

"I can do that even though I think you have information I need to know." He was trying hard to break though the high wall that separated them. "Miss Grace, I'm going to keep you and Mrs. McBride safe. This trust thing goes two ways."

"Right. For now, that's all I've got to say." She picked up a biscuit and began to butter it. "Callie's safe, Matt, and so am I. Trust me on that."

He finished the biscuit, grateful to have something in his stomach. He hadn't taken time to have breakfast this morning. "You do understand that my team is digging deep, and we'll get to the bottom of this. You could save me a lot of trouble and money by telling me what you know."

"What fun would that be, Matt?" She patted his hand and gave him a big smile. "Now finish up and be on your way. I got things to do." She left the table and wrapped several biscuits in a large napkin that she handed to him. "You tell that man outside my door to enjoy these while he's watching after me."

Reluctantly, Matt accepted the food and hugged her good-bye. "You know I'm going to keep trying to get you to talk to me."

The house was too quiet, and she thought about turning on the radio. No, the quiet would help her do some thinking. She sank into her favorite chair in the living room. Keeping her eyes on the man sitting on her front porch, she tried to figure out how to escape his scrutiny. She had talked to Adalyn earlier and knew there was no change in Callie's condition, so going to the hospital would not help.

She needed to talk to Martha or Paula, and neither of them were answering their phones. It wasn't a good idea for Brock to go to either the safe house near Shamrock Beach or the one in Gainesville. She had called him earlier to let him know the housemother and the three victims were safe in a new location. Her checklist had been completed.

She closed her eyes and began to quietly hum one of her favorite hymns. All that was left to do now was wait and have some faith.

****

Charlie was fully awake, waiting for them to let him see Callie. It had been hours since his last visit to the ICU and he was worried. He wanted to hold her hand and tell her she was going to pull through. They were a team, he and his Callie. She needed to know he was close by.

"What are you thinking?" Adalyn pulled her chair closer and waited for him to respond.

"Honey, I wonder when they're going to let me see your mother. It's been a while since we've had an update on her condition. I've been back and forth to the nurses' station and the answer is always the same. They're running tests. I'm going to call Brock and see about having her transferred to the hospital at the university.

Your mother needs specialized care, and I don't think it's available here." He shook free of her hand and headed for the door.

"Daddy, please come back and sit down. Brock will be here soon, and he's been checking with her doctors on a regular basis. You know he would have her moved if he thought it best." She watched the indecision cross his face.

"Have you heard anything more from the police? Adalyn, call Connor and tell him we need to talk. I'm not going to leave this room until I've seen Callie and have some answers, so your brother needs to come back here."

An hour passed before one of the staff walked into the room. "Judge McBride, if you'll follow me, you can go in to see your wife." The nurse smiled at Charlie. "She's awake and asking for you. Don't expect too much, but I think a short visit will do you both some good."

He smiled at his daughters as he walked away. "This is what I've been praying for, girls. Did you hear the nurse? Your mom's awake."

"Ladies, why don't you come with us. You can stand at the window, and I'll have her turn her head so she can see you. Sometimes a wave and a smile are almost as good as a hug."

*****

Charlie looked tenderly at his wife and squeezed her hand. "Oh, Callie, I'm so sorry this happened to you. Help the doctors and nurses fight for you, sweetheart. I love you and want you home."

She blinked her eyes, and he felt a slight pressure as she tried to squeeze back. "All the kids have been coming and going since this happened. Grace has been here and so has Matt. They're all praying you'll be better soon." He wanted her to hear his voice and feel the love he was sending. If he could keep talking to her, he knew it would make a difference.

"Brock is staying in touch with the doctors and staff, Connor and Matt are busy tracking down who did this to you, and…"

Suddenly, she pulled her hand away and opened her eyes wider.

"What? Callie, what's wrong?"

Something had changed. She looked frightened. He brushed his hand gently across her forehead. "Callie, it's all right. I'm here." He reached for the call button and rang for the nurse as her agitation increased. "Callie, I'm right here. You're fine, sweetheart." His stomach began to churn, but he kept his voice soft. What could he do to calm her?

He felt the nurse's presence before he saw her. She rushed past him and began checking monitors. Over her shoulder, she whispered, "Judge, you'll have to leave now. I'll take care of her." The woman assured him and motioned for him to leave. "She'll be all right. I think seeing you was too much excitement for her."

"Daddy, what happened?" Dara rushed over to the doorway of the ICU. "We saw Mom react. What were you saying to her that was so upsetting?"

He was bewildered and didn't have an answer. He was shaking his head and looking toward the nurse. "I don't know. I was telling her what you all were doing when everything changed."

"Can you remember exactly what you said?" Adalyn joined in. "Were you telling her something specific? Think, Daddy. It might be important."

"I told her Brock was keeping track of her medical progress."

"What else? Did you tell her anything else?"

"I think I'd started telling her that Connor and Matt were trying to find out who ran her off the road." He paused. "That's it. That's when she changed. Why would that upset her?"

"It doesn't add up unless her accident wasn't an accident and the unplugging of the machines wasn't random." Dara shuttered as she said the words and watched her father's face lose all color.

"Oh, dear God. I need to sit down," Charlie mumbled. "We need some answers from Connor and Matt."

Dara held on to her father's arm as they walked away from the ICU. She knew her father was tired and anxious. He also needed a diversion. "I bet you're hungry. Do you want to get something to eat?"

"I can't leave until I know she's okay. If you'll go to the cafeteria and bring me something, I'd appreciate it. Maybe a cup of coffee and a muffin."

"I'll be right back. Adalyn, are you coming with me?"

"Sure. I need to walk around some. Daddy, will you be okay?"

"Just let me sit here. I'll be all right."

"Okay, but after the nurse lets us know how Mom is, I think you should go home and take a shower. You'll feel so much better. Dara and I will call you if anything changes."

Charlie started to protest but Adalyn interrupted him. "Be reasonable. It'll only take you a couple of hours to drive home and shower. You've been here all night and at this point all we can do is wait. Getting away from the hospital for a little while will make the time go by faster."

Chapter Twenty

The work was getting more dangerous, and Grace wondered how much longer she'd be able to manage. Her age was starting to slow her down. The years had been gratifying but there was still so much to be done. As soon as one trafficking operation was broken up, another appeared, and it had become more sordid.

The newest statistics proved it was a lucrative and expanding business. Every year more than a million children, women, and men were sold for hundreds or thousands of dollars each. The United Nations estimated that worldwide, the "businesses" brought in close to $32 billion annually. If there was a demand, someone would step up to fill it. Agriculture needed forced labor, the wealthy wanted free servants, and immoral people wanted the innocent to satisfy their sexual fantasies.

Human trafficking in the state of Florida seemed never ending. Port cities, international airports, and major highways made the state ideal for moving people, mostly from South and Central American countries. Yet, the crime didn't get much public attention and very few cases ever reached the courts.

This time was going to be different. The FBI and Homeland Security had an iron-clad case against the leader of one of the biggest trafficking organizations that operated in Florida. The testimonies she and Callie were going to give in court would ensure that many in the operation would go to jail for a long time.

They had years of information on rescued victims, and Callie had witnessed a murder that occurred when a transaction had gone bad. She was vital to the prosecution, and as the court date drew nearer the threats against her had now progressed from words to actions.

Grace thought back to the day she first met Callie. They were both at the infirmary on the campus of the University of Florida. She was there to see a doctor about an ear infection, when she noticed a very pregnant Callie crying quietly in the opposite corner of the room.

As she watched, she assumed the poor girl was simply one more victim of a college boy's irresponsibility. She approached her, thinking she could offer a few words of support and comfort. As they talked, she was drawn in by Callie's intellect and sensibility. The young woman didn't need comfort, she had a plan, but she needed money to help her actualize it.

Meeting for coffee soon became an everyday occurrence for them. They talked values and beliefs and causes. Slowly, Grace introduced the topic of human trafficking and gauged the impact her words had on Callie.

After a month, she introduced her to Martha from the FBI field office in Miami, and together they recruited Callie as an intake counselor in the human trafficking division. In exchange for the work she did while still at the university, the division paid for Callie's medical expenses and arranged for the adoption of her baby.

Grace thought Callie would resign once she married, but the work became so important to Callie she decided to continue on a part-time basis. Over the years, as the workload intensified, they became a team, and the agency moved Grace to Shamrock Beach. For forty years they'd worked side by side and she didn't think anyone, including Charlie, had suspected.

They were no longer involved in the dangerous part of rescue; they were the follow-up team. They set up safe houses, trained housemothers, worked with carefully selected doctors who volunteered their time, and searched for the resources needed to help rehabilitate victims.

The hardest part of their work was witnessing the impact that drugs, forced labor, and sexual abuse had on the victims. Every victim served a master and, in the process, had become what Grace called a "shadow person." Most were able to be rehabilitated, yet there were some who couldn't function outside their addiction to drugs and sex.

When she and Callie came face-to-face with a "shadow person," it was so heartbreaking they had to rely on their friendship and their faith to keep them from falling into despair.

I can't let my feelings of fear get the best of me. I've got work to do. God's going to take care of Callie. I need Martha's help to deal with Callie's family.

Two phone calls later she had meetings set up with Martha and Brock. All the years of secrecy were coming unraveled; it was good that she and Callie planned to retire. That part was inevitable and acceptable, they had talked about it for the past two years. At their age, they knew it was time. The crazy part was going to be telling Callie's family about their double lives.

Before she could talk to the family, she needed to understand what Brock wanted them to know about his participation. His security clearance gave him access to victims, he knew where this region's safe houses were located, and he could identify the housemothers. If the family knew about his work, he would no longer have active status. She would have to find out if *he* was ready to "retire."

****

Brock waited for her in the parking lot at the University of Florida's hospital. When he saw her car approach, he motioned for her to park, and he climbed in the front seat.

"I just got off the phone with the nurse in ICU in Orange Park and Mom's condition is basically the same. She woke up earlier this morning and they allowed Dad to sit with her. Apparently, he said something that upset her, and she was so agitated he was asked to leave so they could calm her down." His voice gave away his concern. "Miss Grace, how much can you tell me? I need to know what's going on."

"Your mother and I have a long history that is larger than me being your housekeeper. By telling you our story, I am guaranteeing our retirement." She laughed. "You can see that we have reached that age, can't you?" When he smiled at her, she continued with their story.

When she finished, she watched him for his reaction.

"I can't believe I grew up in a house with FBI agents and never suspected. Wow, Miss Grace, that's the last thing I would have expected from you and Mom. But, on the other hand, neither of you had a clue that I was on your team. If we hadn't had an accidental meeting, you still wouldn't know. That was the first time I went to a safe house that wasn't in my area." He threw his head back and looked at the ceiling of the car. "I guess it was meant to be."

"Seems like it. I just need to know how much to tell your family. You know if I say anything about you, you'll no longer be able to do this work."

"Miss Grace, you and Mom are going to retire, but I'm not ready. Please let this be our secret."

"There's no problem with me, and if your mother is lucid, there will be no problem from her. If she says something while she's under the influence of all the medications, we'll blame it on the drugs."

"Do you know why Mom was targeted?"

"There's a huge case coming to court next month and she's a prime witness. Brock, they've been making threats for months and we've been careful. Now they're getting serious and we're both in danger. Our agency missed something, and they got to your mother. When she made the decision to drive to Gainesville, she somehow lost her security detail. You can bet some heads are going to roll on that one. Our security has been doubled, and Matt and Connor are using their resources to cover us, too. Your brother and Matt still don't know the full story. However, with the pace that Matt is working on this, it won't be long before they put some of the pieces together. I needed to talk to you before I talked to them."

He took his time responding. "If you're telling me that you and Mom are witnesses in the Mario Villa trial, then I have questions."

"I figured you'd have lots of those. I'll answer if I can."

"Who are you, Miss Grace?"

"My name really is Grace Samuels, and I was born and raised in Jacksonville. I'm widowed and I have two adult daughters. You know that part of my story. What you don't know is I graduated in criminology from Bethune Cookman College, I received my master's from Howard University before going to work with the FBI in Washington, DC.

"I became a field agent in the Miami office when trafficking on college campuses expanded and Florida grew into one of the major trafficking highways. I was assigned to the University of Florida since I was familiar with the area. My cover was an advanced studies program which I really worked to obtain. Later, I received a PhD in Criminal Justice from the University of North Florida.

"Because I was working, it took me years to earn that degree, but I'm one of those people who love learning." She smiled at him. "Many days, I'd be studying right along with you while you were doing your homework. I moved from Gainesville to Shamrock Beach when your mom and I became partners." This was the most she had told anyone about her life in years.

"I knew you weren't an everyday housekeeper, but I never figured you for all those degrees. I'm impressed, but it's going to take some time for me to get used to calling you, Dr. Samuels. You and Mom are something else." He reached over and gave her a hug. "With your credentials, why did you stay in Shamrock?"

"Your mom and I made a good team and I like living here. I work with other agencies as a consultant and, in the last ten years or so, I've spoken at conferences around the country. I like the work I do." She hesitated. "Brock, when I was younger and more ambitious, it wasn't easy for a black woman to move up in the agency. I was passed over several times before I gave up and accepted that I was supposed to be the best field agent I could be. That's changing, but it's still a man's job."

"I'm honored to know who you really are. Just one more question. Who is Paula?"

"I can't answer that right now, except to tell you she is one of the good guys. You do understand that nothing is as it seems. I have a meeting with my boss when I leave here and, based on what he allows, I'll call your family to a meeting. It's important for you to be there and act as surprised by what I'm going to say as the others do. I hope you'll get all your questions answered."

"I'm in the hospital until six o'clock, and Marti already knows I'm going to Orange Park after that. I can be there by seven o'clock at the latest."

"Honey, I'm glad you've made the decision to remain in the program. Unfortunately, most of the rescued victims need good doctors. The work you do is vital."

Smiling at the young man she helped raise gave her hope for the future. "I'm proud of you, but then, you *are* your mother's son."

****

The man sitting across from her had gray streaks in his hair and wrinkles around his eyes. Grace didn't want to admit they had worked together for decades. In her mind they should still be in the middle of their careers, not nearing the end.

"Martha, I've never been this concerned about Callie's safety, or my own. When I saw her in that hospital bed, it frightened me. After this case is closed, both of us will be retiring. The enemy knows who we are. We'll never again be safe in the field."

"The office agrees with you, Grace. You and Callie

have had a long run. In fact, the three of us have probably overstayed our welcome." He didn't smile.

"Depending on your directive, I want to tell her family the truth. No more secrets, no more lies. They need to know what we're up against and why we're under protection until this trial is over. I've heard from Washington that as soon as Callie can be moved, she will be relocated."

"Yes, my last assignment will be to expedite that move. Like you, I'm retiring the minute Mario Villa and his thugs are behind bars. I've got my eyes on a mountain house in the Carolina's loaded with books and good wine." Martha took a sip of his iced tea and gave Grace the go-ahead to provide Callie's family, and her own, some pertinent information. "You may not name names or discuss any particulars of the Villa case."

"I understand. Also, I just met with Brock McBride, and he's made the decision to remain on the inside. The family won't hear his name from me."

"I hadn't heard that good news. I hope someday I'll get to meet him." Martha stood to leave, and his expression softened. "Grace, I'm sorry about Callie. This shouldn't have happened. An investigation is already underway on what went wrong, and I promise you the person responsible will be dealt with. You and Callie have done great work over the years. Your partner will be okay. She's tough."

"Thank you for that recognition." Grace got a lump in her throat and was silent for a moment. "If this is our last meeting, do you think you could tell me your real name? I've called you Martha long enough."

The meeting was over, and they said their good-byes. Their relationship didn't invite small talk.

****

Matt was furious and he didn't care if the woman sitting before him liked it or not.

Paula leaned forward and waited. "What is your point? We're on the same side. Yes, it was a setup. Yes, I hurt the judge's reputation. Yes, I cost you money and time." Her voice grew louder as she talked. "You'll have to agree, it was necessary. It was well planned and part of my cover. Everything I did was a calculated risk. Ultimately, I kept Callie and Grace safe until last night. Other details will emerge, Matt, that will convince you that what I did is justified."

"Are you serious, lady? You've hurt some people I care about, and you want me to say it was all right? In my opinion, it was downright Machiavellian. And when did you break into the McBride's home and steal that brooch? The end of this fiasco better justify the means." Matt's anger mounted as he thought about all the things Paula had done over the past weeks. "I've vented, so I'll shut up for now. I don't know how long it will take for me to cool down."

"I'll try to put myself in your place if you'll at least try to see things from my perspective. I had to be visible, yet invisible. When I got to that retirement dinner, I knew the original plan was going to hurt some good people and I cringed. Everyone in town loves the McBrides and they needed to hate me if I was going to be able to do my job. It was the best way to keep them tight together—they circled the wagons, didn't they?" She faced him with her own version of anger showing. "I had a job to do, and I, too, would have been in great danger if I hadn't done it. Don't you understand?"

Connor opened his office door in the middle of this

boxing match. "What are the two of you screaming about? If you want everyone in this building to know what's going on, you're doing a great job of it." He marched to his desk and sat down. "If I'd known you were going to war, I wouldn't have asked you to meet in my office."

"Sorry, buddy. I let my emotions get the best of me." Matt turned to Paula. "Truce?"

"Okay, but I hope you've had your say." She sat down and turned her attention to Connor. "Your friend is concerned I've done too much damage to your family. Let me start by telling you I'm sorry, but it was necessary."

"That's a beginning, but it doesn't answer any of my questions. So, start talking. Tonight, at seven o'clock, Grace Samuels is holding a family meeting and we need to be on the same page."

For the next hour, Paula furnished Connor and Matt the background and details of the work she'd been assigned. The three of them decided which information to share with the family and who would do the talking.

As they got ready to leave, Paula stopped Connor. "For the record, I never broke into your house. The brooch was found in the home of Mario Villa."

"You're not kidding, are you? I'm flabbergasted." Connor dropped back into the chair and ran his hands through his hair. "One part of me admires Mom and Miss Grace, and the other part can't believe they've pulled this off. They've been at this all my life."

"It's not over, Connor. The challenging part is still ahead of us. We've got to make sure your mom and Grace can give their testimony." She paused. "I'm not being callous and uncaring, but they are crucial if these people are going to be convicted and put out of business."

For a long moment the three were silent. Matt sighed. "Well, we know that now, and we'll do whatever you need," he promised.

"Paula, my family is not going to go easy on you. Are you sure you're ready to face them?" Connor took her arm as they walked out of the building.

****

"I've known this family for forty-some years. I've dried your tears, cleaned up your messes, and given you as many hugs as I gave my own children. You know how much I care. What you don't know is who I am." Grace stood before the group and hoped her legs would hold her up until she finished talking.

"Now, stop looking at each other like this is a B grade horror movie. Judge, you've had a few shocks in the last couple of weeks, but what I've got to tell you is going to be even harder than all the other stuff." She tried to soften her expression before continuing. "First, I've got someone else you all need to meet."

She looked across the room. "Connor, go let her in, please."

Connor walked to the door and opened it wide enough for Paula to enter. There was a collective gasp before Dara stood up. "What is she doing here? Hasn't she caused us enough trouble?"

"Dara, sit down and listen. What we've got to tell you is more important than your anger and indignation," Grace commanded. "This is Paula Felton and she's a big part of this story. But I'll get to that in a minute."

When everyone was quiet, she continued. "I met your mother when she was in grad school and pregnant with a baby she knew she couldn't bring to Shamrock Beach if her marriage to you, Charlie, had any chance. I understand she's told you all that part. What you don't know is the part I played in all of that. I was a fledgling FBI field agent working on the university campus. In exchange for helping your mother with the finances of her pregnancy and the adoption of the baby, she was recruited and eventually joined the FBI as an intake counselor. There are other details to this story, but they're Callie's to tell, not mine." She watched their mouths drop and eyes widen. She watched the expression change on Charlie's face and wished she didn't have to go on with her story.

"Callie and I have been partners for more than forty years in a program enacted to eliminate human trafficking. She meets with rescued victims, trains other staff, and delivers messages under the cover of her museum work. And she's very good at what she does. We are trained professionals, and we have a good support team. Over the years, all has gone well. Neither of us has ever felt we were up against something we couldn't handle, until last year." She looked at Paula and motioned for her to take over. "The next part of the story belongs to Paula, and I need to sit down."

Connor stood up. "Before Paula begins, you all need to know Matt and I learned all this today. We were in the dark, the same as you." He smiled at Grace. "Our Miss Grace forgot to tell you she has a doctorate in criminology and is respected as a consultant in the field of human trafficking. This brave woman knows how to do more than bake great scones." He blew her a kiss. "Now listen to Paula and try not to interrupt her."

Paula nodded at Connor, then looked around the

room. "I'm Paula Felton, FBI special agent. Before you all nail me to my cross, please know how sorry I am for hurting you. Judge, when this is over, I'll move mountains to repair the damage I did to you and your family." She held his gaze a moment, then cleared her throat.

"Two years ago, while on duty, Callie witnessed a malicious murder. She was in the process of preparing a fifteen-year-old girl from Honduras for entry into the rehabilitation program when the safe house was raided. Callie had gone to the restroom when the raid took place. The perpetrator didn't take time to search the house, but Callie saw it all from the crack in the bathroom door. Right before her eyes, she watched that girl's life snuffed out. It's believed the young girl was part of a prostitution ring in Jacksonville and was a personal favorite of the man who has been on our 'most wanted' list for ten years. To this day, we still haven't uncovered who leaked the rescue operation or how the safe house was compromised." Paula paused.

"The girl stole some money when she made her escape and could positively identify the kingpin. During her intake meeting, Callie convinced the girl to tell her that monster's name. After the murder, Callie passed the name to us, and Mario Villa was arrested on a money laundering charge, and the trafficking and murder charges were held back. We thought Callie and Grace were safe by doing it that way, but as part of my undercover work, I found out they were in danger, and I was sent to protect them. To do that, and to finish the case, I had to find a way inside your family. The retirement party gave me my chance and I took it."

"God in heaven. You have got to be making all of

this up." Charlie jumped to his feet. "How could Callie have lived with that knowledge and never let on? How did she hide all the grief I know she must have felt?" He narrowed his eyes. "I don't believe a word you're saying. Why would you lie to us again?"

"I'm telling you the truth, sir. I understand you don't want to believe me, but it's true. The case goes to trial next month and, as you can see, this group of criminals is intent on making sure Grace and Callie don't give depositions or testimonies. I've been living at Grace's for the past few weeks as part of her protection and she and I have tried our best to protect Callie. Her protection detail couldn't prevent the accident that happened when she made an unexpected trip to Gainesville yesterday. That opened the door for Mario's people to get to her. His influence is far reaching and had his plan worked, Callie would be dead."

"Judge, she's telling you the truth. You've got to help her." Grace held on to Charlie and looked him in the eyes. "I know you don't want to accept any of this. You'll remember when Callie was sick for days. Brock thought it was probably a case of the flu, but it wasn't. What Callie had seen and was unable to prevent made her physically ill. We'd been debriefed and we knew we couldn't talk about it outside of the agency and the courtroom. Now, you've been told the truth and until this trial is over, you and the kids have got to be on our team."

Brock nodded. "Dad, I'm as dumbfounded and upset as you are. Mom's life is at stake. We're in this together now. She'd want us to do all we can to help. Do you understand she has devoted her life to getting rid of this horrible crime?" Brock put his arm around Grace and looked at Paula. "Count me in. I'll do anything you need."

"Thanks, Brock," said Paula.

"It has taken me a minute to find my voice," said Adalyn. "But I'm in and I know Dara feels the same way." She stood next to her dad and put her hand on his arm. "Daddy, you've been our leader forever. Mom needs all of us to do whatever it takes."

Paula realized Charlie needed time, so she continued. "What has been said in this room cannot leave it. The entire family is under an upgraded protection order. As soon as Callie can be moved, she's going to the hospital in Shamrock Beach. We can't have the family traveling back and forth to Orange Park.

"Brock, your family will be moved to the house in Shamrock Beach, and you'll have protection in the hospital in Gainesville. Sorry, but you won't be able to travel to see them. Unless you want to take leave and move with them. The threats have taken on a more aggressive and sinister nature and the enemy will be looking to do more harm to all of you. They will do anything to make sure Callie and Grace do not testify."

"Judge, to ease your mind, Callie and I have already let the agency know we're retiring as soon as this case is closed. I hope that makes you feel better." Grace could see that the judge was too rattled to care about her declaration. "Callie would want you all to help her put these monsters behind bars."

"I can tell you one thing, Grace. You and my wife deserve Academy Awards. Why couldn't you all trust me enough to tell me this years ago?"

"In your position as an attorney, and then a judge, we were dealing with some of the same people you were. The agency had to make sure there were no compromises or conflicts of interest. Judge, you've handled several cases involving human trafficking, and Callie's integrity had to be maintained. She couldn't tell you what she was doing."

"I feel out of the loop and, again, angry that you felt I couldn't be trusted. This whole situation has set me on my heels and a longer conversation is going to be required. For now, Grace, I'm in." He sighed and looked around at his children. "Your mother will have a lot of explaining to do when this is over. Until we have more answers than questions, we'll do our part to make sure she recovers and can appear in court. I'm tired of all the lies and pretense, but I can't wear my heart on my sleeve and do what's needed to protect her and Grace. You can count on me."

"Thank you for including me," Grace said softly. "Your wife has known all along she could count on you, and now I know that I can, too." Grace nodded at Charlie before she continued. "The McBrides have always been as close to me as my own family and, more than ever, I need your prayers and support."

Paula nodded. "Judge, if you're staying at the hospital tonight, an agent will be assigned to stay with you. If you look close enough, the rest of you will probably be able to spot the escort that has followed you back and forth to Shamrock Beach." Paula smiled at Adalyn and Dara. "I tried to select the best-looking agents for you."

****

"I need your assistance." Paula began the meeting with Connor and Matt promptly and professionally. "I won't waste your time with facts, figures, and platitudes. Grace has filled you in on the pertinent information.

Mario Villa was apprehended several months ago and is awaiting trial. The charges at the time included money laundering, human trafficking, drug sales, and attempting to bribe a federal officer. He was denied bail because he's a flight risk. He has the means and the money to flee. His trial begins in three weeks, and based on Callie's deposition we think we have sufficient evidence to get those charges upgraded to include first-degree murder."

"So, why do you need us?" Connor couldn't imagine how a small-town lawyer would be of any use to the FBI.

"The two of you have information you don't even know you have. If you'll agree to help me, I know we can bring the organization's kingpin to justice, too. In turn, we may be able to identify the man who ran Callie off the road."

"I thought Villa was the big boss. Are you saying there's someone else pulling the strings? Do you already know who this guy is?" Matt chimed in.

"Yes, but he's slippery and, on the surface, squeaky clean. I was able to get close to him, but I'm convinced he's suspicious of who I am. To make sure the investigation wasn't compromised, I dropped out of sight." She hesitated. "Connor, this man is the reason I hurt your family so badly. For that I'm sorry."

"How can we help?" Connor and Matt asked at the same time.

"You deserve to know the whole story before you decide. The plan is simple."

****

Her phone had been ringing and vibrating off and on all day. She wasn't ready to go back to New York, and she'd told her director, her agent, her co-stars, and her friends that it might be weeks before that was possible. Exasperated, Adalyn pulled off the road and answered the call. "Hello. I'm putting you on speaker because I'm on the road."

"What is this craziness I'm hearing? You need to get yourself back to New York as soon as possible. We've already started filming, and you have a contract. Don't give me any more excuses." Her director ranted.

"Lenny, my mom is in critical condition, and I can't leave. Why can't you understand? Just write me out of a dozen episodes. You can always say I've gone to rehab or some such nonsense."

"Sweetheart, the sponsors are clamoring. I've done all I can to buy you some time, but I'm running out of options. I'll do my best to give you two more weeks, but that's it." His voice calmed. "Oh, and I hope your mom is okay."

She started the car and pulled back out on the highway. The car that had been following her drove around her and she gave the driver a thumbs up to let him know she was all right. *When is this nightmare going to end?*

The moonlight peeking through the tall pines kept the highway from appearing ominous. The occasional houses were set back from the road far enough that light from their windows didn't interfere with the beauty of the scenery. Adalyn needed the tranquility of the moment to keep her fear and worries from overwhelming her. She hadn't seen any progress in her mother today, the studio needed her in New York, and the revelations of the past twenty-four hours had unsettled the world she thought she knew.

Someday, because truth was stranger than fiction,

she would sell this story to the writers of her soap opera. The FBI, human trafficking, a small-town museum curator, and a housekeeper. Who would believe it?

She drove into the hospital parking lot and found an empty space near the door. Her protector drove past her and parked at the end of the row. She had yet to meet the young man who had become her shadow, but he felt like an old friend. She smiled as the automatic double doors swung open for her and wondered if the young man even knew who she was. It was a sure bet he didn't watch the afternoon soap operas.

Dara and her dad were waiting for her to take over the watch. It was their turn to drive home and get some rest. She and Connor were on duty for the night.

"You all look like you're ready to break out of this joint." She tried to lighten the mood as she walked into the waiting room. Dara's fatigue showed, and her dad looked older than she ever remembered. "I left you a plate of meatloaf and mashed potatoes in the fridge. Warm it in the oven. There's more than enough for the two of you."

"That's great, sis. Food here at the hospital leaves a lot to the imagination. You know, I try to imagine what most of the meals are supposed to be." Dara made a grotesque face and then grinned.

"Your mother's been very quiet today. I've read to her from the Bible and talked about the weather. Nothing that might upset her." Charlie moved to give his oldest child a hug. "You can tell her all about the latest fashions, or some such nonsense. Whatever you ladies like to talk about."

Adalyn chuckled. "I'll settle in for the night and see you in the morning. Connor should be here soon. Your escort is waiting on you."

When Dara and Charlie were out the door, she walked to the nurses' station to ask if she could see her mother. If she could find even a small sign that Callie was improving, it would make the night go faster.

She moved close to the hospital bed and took her mother's hand. The coolness alarmed her, and she turned to the nurse. "Her hand feels cooler. Should I be worried?"

"Her fever broke this afternoon. It's a good sign that you can detect the difference in temperature. The doctors are pleased and they're starting to talk about moving her out of our ICU to progressive care in Shamrock Beach." The nurse continued to check the monitors. "Can I ask you something?"

"Sure. I'll answer if I can."

"You're the actress Adalyn McBride, right? My mom and I love your show."

"Thanks, and yes. For now, that's who I am. If I don't get back to New York soon, I'll probably be killed off or something. My director is getting antsy."

The nurse took a piece of paper from her pocket. "I hate to ask, but it would thrill my mom if I could take her your autograph."

"I'll be glad to do that for her, but you can't give it to her until my mom is released from the hospital." Adalyn hesitated. "You know it would create a commotion if people knew I was here."

"I can do that for you." She handed Adalyn the paper and a pen. "Mom has a birthday next month. I'll give it to her then."

After she signed the paper, she glanced toward the door to see Connor standing outside watching her. "I know I've been here longer than usual but is there a chance my brother can come in for a few minutes? He hasn't seen Mom since last night."

Adalyn changed places with Connor and walked back to the waiting area. She had read a few pages in the novel she picked up in the gift shop when he came in and sat down next to her.

"I think she looks better tonight. Don't you?" Connor remarked.

"The nurse told me Mom's fever broke. I'm taking that as a good sign."

Connor nodded. "I hate to do this to you, but early in the morning Matt and I are taking a trip out of town. We'll be gone at least two days, maybe three." He held up his hand. "Before you say anything, that's all I can tell you." He shifted in the chair so he could see her face. "Grace has agreed to take over for me. She'll be here tomorrow night with you."

"That's fine, but why all the secrecy?"

"For your safety. Trust me one more time. If we do our job right, this whole ordeal may be over sooner rather than later. You'll let Dad know. I don't want to call the house this late."

"What are you doing about your practice? Don't you have clients that need you?"

"I do, and there are a few headaches looming. You know how that goes." His voice held a hint of laughter. "I've tried to take care of as much as I can, but I'm leaving a load of work for Annie. She's the best paralegal around, so I know she can handle it. Boy, is she going to read me the riot act when I get back to the office." He leaned back in his chair and closed his eyes. "A few minutes of shuteye will help me. Are you okay with me taking a little snooze?"

Adalyn picked up her book and tried not to overthink why her brother was leaving town.

****

Paula sat at the kitchen table finishing a huge breakfast. "You're spoiling me, Grace."

"Honey, if you stay with me much longer, you're going to turn into a real southern lady." Grace was happy to have someone to cook for. She had lived alone since her children had moved away.

"I've reviewed everything we know and studied each detail of this operation. All the evidence points to Mario Villa, but from everything you've told me, he isn't the number one guy. Even though we have Callie as an eyewitness to the murder of Elena Juarez—she watched him shoot that poor girl, no mistake about that—we may not be able to pin anything on the big boss."

"Okay, let's talk it out. What's causing you to disconnect from Villa?" Paula asked.

"What if we have it wrong and Villa is the head? What if the guy you've been covering is a henchman? For all we know Villa killed the girl because she could identify him as the real boss. Callie has said over and over the girl didn't appear to be afraid of Villa. She stole a large sum of money from the man who had enslaved her and held her captive for years. If that man was Villa, she would have been afraid. If she thought she was in danger, you'd think she'd have begged him to take her back. But she didn't."

Paula shrugged. "Legitimate points that Callie might have misunderstood. Remember, she was hiding in a bathroom and probably thought she was going to be the next victim. That degree of fear colors the way you think and makes the details fuzzy. There's no denying he pulled the trigger, and Callie can testify to that."

"You're right, and every time I go over the scene with Callie, her story never varies. What if he's not the real boss? If we don't have all the facts, it could put all of us in harm's way."

"I know you have a strong attachment to Callie and her family, so you've got a right to be concerned about their safety. Don't let that attachment get in the way of the evidence. Yes, Callie witnessed the murder, but we have other witnesses who have pointed the finger at Villa. I think we've come to the correct conclusion that Villa is a big deal in this operation, but we want the top. Let's see what transpires over the next few days."

"Finish up your breakfast and get on the road. You've got a long way to go today."

****

The man sitting next to her looked calm, but his voice was unyielding. "We've tried several different ways to infiltrate the McBride's household and the obstacles have stymied us. Your 'I'm his daughter' scheme was genius, but it backfired. You almost capsized my plan with the way you handled that one, and now you want me to give you another chance? You're as laughable as your scheme."

"I saw my chance and I took it. How was I to know they could do that DNA thing so quickly? You know you can trust me. I did everything I could think of to embarrass the judge, didn't I? Now that Callie is in the hospital, she'll never be able to testify against Mario." She smirked. "And the Feds think they've got the guy who runs this operation, don't they?"

"Callie will never get out of that hospital. But what

about Grace? What are you going to do about her? She's the one who has all the incriminating evidence."

"I've got a plan for Grace. You need to trust me."

"You're still alive, aren't you? How much more trust do you want?"

"I need to know I'll still be alive when this is over." Her tone softened and she rubbed her hand across his thigh. "Sweetheart, you know I'd do anything for you. Before you decided to do away with the McBrides we talked about all the fun we could have. I've missed you." She let her hand wander as she whispered in his ear. "Take me back to your house. I need you. I need all of you."

"We'll get a hotel; nobody goes to my house."

"If you really trusted me, you'd take me home with you so I can meet your mother. After all, this plan was your revenge for her. Your mother is the one Judge McBride betrayed years ago. Come on, Edward, you've been the man I've wanted for a long time, and I know you'd like the way I would treat you, wouldn't you?" Her touch became more forceful. "I'm ready and so are you."

"You think you're so clever. Do you think the promise of sex with you is going to get to me? I can have all the sex I want, as often as I want it. I've got hundreds of nubile young things who'll do anything I want them to. So, get that idea out of your head."

She leaned away from him. "I wish I could believe you. I think all you've really got is me." She nuzzled closer. "Show me all these sex slaves who are so eager to please you. Maybe they can please me, too. Wouldn't that be delicious? Wouldn't you like to watch? Every fantasy you've ever had could come true and we could do it together."

"You're talking crazy." She knew Edward's breathing changed as she talked.

"I know all the tricks. I could teach all those young things how to thrill you and your friends. Take me home with you, now. We're so worked up, our coming together will be glorious."

He started the car, and they sped off into the darkness. "Where are we going?"

"To a place where you can prove what you just promised."

****

"They're on the move. Don't lose them. The back-up is in place. Be careful." Connor turned to Matt. "I guess she didn't need us to confront Edward. Looks like she's switched to Plan B."

****

The car lights and traffic noises were left behind as he turned his car into the alley between two buildings that looked abandoned. He slowed and when they were close to the far end of the alley, he flashed the car's bright lights five times.

A gate she hadn't seen in the darkness slowly opened. He eased the car through it and waited for it to close behind them. When the car stopped, he turned to her. "Show time, sweetheart. Let's go." He walked around to her side of the car.

"Wait a minute. I thought we were going to your house. This place gives me the creeps."

"All you women are alike. You think you can run the show, but you don't get to make the decisions. Now, get out. You've got work to do."

Roughly, he grabbed her arm and pulled her out of the car. With one hand securely holding her, he unlocked a door with the other and ushered her inside.

"What is this place? Why did you bring me here?"

They walked down a corridor toward a large room that was dimly lit. As her eyes adjusted, she gasped. She scanned the more than twenty-five faces of people who were chained to the walls: teenaged girls and boys, young women, and two small girls who were probably no more than eight years old. They were sitting on the floor with their wrists chained and their feet shackled. Most stared glassy eyed, a few kept their eyes closed. The small children slept.

"Now you can believe me," he shouted. "Teach them well. Show them all your tricks. They just arrived, so they don't know what I like." He flung her forward. "I'll try out each one of them when you're finished, and they better be good. They better be very good."

When she regained her balance, she turned to him. "Where did these people come from? Why do you have them locked up in this horrible place?"

"You already know the answer to that, don't you? You thought you were so smart." His voice had reached a frenetic pitch. "When you're finished breaking them in, I'll be able to get a good price for them and for you. Or, better yet, I'll keep you to break in every new group." He kicked at her feet, and she fell. "Get out of your clothes and go to work. You promised I could watch." He became more menacing. "Every time you're finished, I'll be ready for you to show me what you taught them. I have an insatiable appetite."

His laugh sent chills through her entire body, but she knew better than to show fear. She had to buy some time.

"These people are too drugged for me to teach them anything. They can't even hold their heads up. What do you think I can do with zombies?" she yelled at him.

"That's for you to figure out, sweetheart. You made the promise."

Slowly, she stood up and began to unbutton her blouse. "Where did this bunch come from? Will they be able to understand what I'm saying?"

"They're from Honduras, but they don't need words for what you're teaching. Stop stalling."

She had reached the last button on her blouse when the FBI burst through the door, followed by Connor and Matt. All the agents had drawn guns and were shouting for Edward to surrender. Instead, Edward pulled his gun and started firing without regard to what he hit. When he was brought to his knees by a shot to his stomach, there was chaos in the room.

Paula had taken a shot to her shoulder and one of the chained victims had a chest wound that needed immediate attention. The shouting and crying didn't stop until the agent in charge demanded silence so his orders could be heard.

Matt called for an ambulance and Connor raced to help Paula. "How bad is it? Hang on, we've got an ambulance on the way."

"It's just a surface wound. I'll be fine," she whispered before she passed out.

One of the agents stood over Edward and said with disgust, "This guy is in bad shape, but he'll be able to stand trial and live happily ever after in prison."

Two ambulances arrived as the FBI agents continued to assess the carnage. The teenager that Edward shot was dead, and the other victims seemed to be in shock. Three men who were supposedly on guard outside had been arrested, Paula and Edward had been transported to the hospital with wounds that weren't life-threatening, and the EMTs were attending those who needed help.

"Who has a key to these chains?" Connor was anxious to release the victims, but no one seemed to have a key. "We need a locksmith, a doctor, and a safe house, pronto."

****

Connor sat beside Paula's bedside and watched as she awakened from the surgery to repair her shoulder. He had many questions and hoped she had a few answers. "You don't look like a hero right now, but we're recommending you for all kinds of metals." He smiled when she opened her eyes and glared at him. "Hey, I had to say something to get you to open your eyes. I take it all back. You look like Wonder Woman."

"Go away and let me sleep." She was groggy and her words were slurred. "Go away."

"No fair. You get to sleep, and I don't. Matt and I have been answering questions and filing reports all night, while you've been getting your beauty sleep." He kept talking even though her eyes were closed, and she had turned her head away from him. "I thought you'd want to know Edward survived his surgery and he'll be headed to jail, the victims are sheltered at a safe house, and the FBI is trying to find the identity of the young girl who was killed. They will make sure she is returned to her family in Honduras for burial." He hoped she could hear him. "Not bad for a night's work, Paula."

"More like a couple of years," she murmured.

"I'm leaving, but I'll be back later." He took her hand as he stood up. "Well done, Paula Felton. Well done. By the way, thanks for making sure this creep could never lay his hands on Dara again."

Matt was talking to one of the agents assigned to guard Paula when Connor walked out in the hall. "Good morning. Is there anything I need to know before I head back to the hotel?"

"Nothing that can't wait until we've caught a couple hours of sleep. It's been a long night," Matt said on a yawn.

****

Her shoulder hurt, her head hurt, and her mouth was dry. She pushed the call button for the nurse and prayed she would get some relief. There was no one in the room with her, so she must have dreamed Connor McBride.

"Good morning. My name is Barb and I'll be taking care of you today. How can I help?"

"Can you bring me a glass of water? My mouth is so dry, and I need an aspirin."

The nurse poured the glass of water and lifted her head so she could take a sip. "It's almost time for your next pain meds," she teased. "I think you need something more than an aspirin. I'll be back in a few minutes with your shot. Do you feel up to talking to people? They've been waiting for you to wake up."

"It depends on who it is."

"I'll check and let you know."

Grace walked into the room and waved at the nurse. "I think she'll want to see me."

Paula nodded her head at the nurse. "She's my good friend. It's all right for her to stay."

"How are you?" Grace gave her a big smile.

"I'm uncomfortable and I'm glad to see you. My memory is fuzzy right now, so tell me everything you know."

"Edward is alive, and he'll be able to stand trial. Callie McBride is doing better and they're hoping she can be moved to the hospital in Shamrock Beach tomorrow. Those poor people in that abandoned building have been moved to a safe house and the intake counselor is working with them. The teenager who was killed has been identified and arrangements are being made to have her body escorted home to her family. So far, of the three men arrested last night, one is singing his head off. He's naming names in hopes of a deal. If all goes well, we should be able to shut down Edward's operation permanently." Grace stopped talking while the nurse checked on Paula and gave her the medicines.

"That's about it for now. They say you should be here for another day or two. Then you'll be on medical leave for several weeks. Tell me, Paula, how did you know it was Edward?"

"It's a long story." Her eyes were beginning to droop, and she was slurring her words. "We've got to finish up this case. I can't go on leave."

"Your part is done. Your reports can be finished while you're recovering. From what the doctor told me, you've got weeks of physical therapy ahead of you."

Paula groaned. "I'll be fine without all that therapy and stuff."

"Wait until you can't have any more pain medicine to make that statement. That bullet really tore up your shoulder. Recovery might not be as easy as you're hoping. The next question is where you want to go when you leave here? If you don't want to go home to Miami, you can come back to my house. I'll take care of you, and you can do your therapy in Shamrock Beach." When she looked, Paula had closed her eyes again.

"You don't have to make a decision today."

****

"It's been two days and Connor isn't back. Did he tell anyone where he was going?" Charlie was frustrated and angry. "I need to talk things over with him and he's not answering his phone. The doctor told me this morning they're planning for your mother to be moved. Most likely tomorrow."

"I'll call Brock. He'll help. Don't get upset with Connor. Whatever he's doing is something he felt was important." Dara tried her best to stay calm, but Charlie had been voicing his frustration all morning. "The doctors will take care of everything. Brock tried to tell you to stop worrying last night."

"What did Connor tell you when he left? It's not like him to disappear for days."

"Why are you so concerned about Connor? He's a big boy. I'm sure we'll hear from him soon."

"All right, you seem to be handling everything that's going on. Why have you and your sister been so quiet these last few days? What do you know that I don't?"

"We're in shock, we're concerned about Mom, we're worried about you. We'd like to get off this roller coaster. It's not every day one finds out her parent has been living a double life." She sighed. "I've spent a couple of sleepless nights looking back on my life and who I've always imagined Mom to be. None of what I heard the other night from Paula and Miss Grace matches my image." She stopped talking and looked directly at her dad. "Daddy, I'm afraid you might change your mind about Mom." Tears flowed down her cheeks. "Please tell me you still love her."

Charlie rushed over and gathered her in his arms.

"Honey, don't even think that. I'll always love your mother." He lifted her chin. "Dara, marriage isn't easy and what we were told the other night makes me question the trust issues between your mom and me. But I signed on for 'better or worse.' This family won't divide; you can count on that." He sat with his arm around his daughter until her tears were dry. "Come on, let's go ask the nurse to let us see your mom."

When they walked in the room, the head of Callie's bed had been lifted so she was partially sitting up, and the nurses had combed her hair. Charlie thought she looked beautiful.

"You must be feeling better. That's the best news we've had in a week."

"Have I been here that long? I can't seem to remember." Her voice was not as fragile, and her eyes looked bright for the first time since the accident.

"Do you remember what happened, Mom?" Dara asked.

"I went to Gainesville on an errand for the museum and a truck ran me off the road. I don't remember anything after that."

"We'll have plenty of time to talk about what happened. Right now, we just want you to get better." Charlie sat on the side of the bed. "You've had a rough time, but yesterday we got some good news from the doctors. They think you're strong enough to be moved over to our hospital."

"What do you mean? Where am I now?" She looked around bewildered.

"You're in the hospital in Orange Park. They've taken great care of you, but we want you closer to home."

"Tell them to let me go home. I'm feeling fine. I

don't need to be in the hospital any longer."

"Going home will happen soon enough. For now, the hospital is the right place for you."

Callie frowned. "Where is Grace? Have you all seen her? I need to talk to her."

"She was here earlier in the week, but we haven't seen her in the past two days. I'll give her a call later to let her know you're doing so much better. She'll want to know the good news; she's been worried about you." Dara took her mom's hand. "So many prayers have been answered. You won't believe all the people who've been praying for you."

"Is it that bad? I thought I just had a bump on my head."

Charlie shook his head. "It's a bit more involved than a bump on the head. You've had multiple surgeries. You've been in ICU for over a week, and the kids and I have taken shifts to be here with you around the clock. Dara and I have the day shift, Adalyn and Connor have the night shift, and Brock comes whenever he has a minute. The McBrides have had you covered." Charlie was trying to get her to smile. "Grace has come and gone, and so has Matt. You really had us worried."

"What an ordeal for all of you. I'm sorry to be so much trouble," she whispered.

"Nonsense, Callie. Your family loves you." He leaned forward and gave her a tender kiss. "You're worth every minute."

Chapter Twenty-One

Grace pulled her car away from the portico at Tallahassee Memorial Hospital where she had waited for the staff to wheel Paula out the front door. Paula decided to stay with her until physical therapy was done. It would take them about three hours to make the drive to Shamrock Beach and Grace was eager to get on the road.

"You look better than you did last night. I hope that means you're feeling better?"

"I hurt and I'm hungry. Do you think we could go through one of the fast-food places to get me a hamburger?"

"As long as you're willing to eat in the car. Even though we've got an escort, I want to get home before dark." She looked behind her to make sure the agents in the black SUV were not too far behind her.

Once they were on I-10 headed east, Grace began asking questions. "How did you manage to get Edward to take you to the abandoned building?"

"A little bit of female persuasion, but I thought he'd take me to his house, and I could do some snooping around. Never did I expect what happened. I'm glad I had a tracer on my phone, and Connor, Matt, and several agents were only a few blocks away when Edward started driving. Grace, this wasn't even Plan Z."

"I wondered if you had changed plans when I got the call. I thought Connor and Matt were supposed to pretend to go after Edward for messing up Dara's face. You gave me a bit of a scare. I'm glad I wasn't here when it all went down."

"What's next? I know you and Callie are retiring, and there will be a lot of repair work for the McBride family. Including my part in humiliating the judge. I couldn't believe the looks on the faces of the family when we told them what was going on. How is Callie, by the way?"

"She's doing miraculously well. They're going to transfer her to Shamrock Beach today or tomorrow. She's got a long way to go and, who knows, the two of you may be in physical therapy together." For some reason, Grace thought that was funny.

"I followed Edward for almost a year. I knew what he was capable of, but I didn't have any proof. When I discovered he was dating Dara, I knew he was going after the McBrides. Years ago, Edward's mother, Julie, thought the judge had taken an interest in her, and she told Edward the judge would be his new daddy. Of course, the judge had no idea of this woman's fantasies. She led Edward to believe the judge had tricked her, and she made him promise to someday make the judge pay. When Edward discovered Callie was a witness against Mario, he put his plan in motion. He could get revenge on the judge and kill Callie. I had to do something drastic. He thought I was working with him, and he baited me to come up with some way to infiltrate the family. We had false documents drawn up and letters to make the case that I was the judge's daughter, and I was supposed to make the family believe me. Edward was furious with me for what he called my aggrandizing stunt at the retirement dinner. I hadn't planned it that way, it just happened. But it created the diversion I needed, and he went back to Tallahassee in a huff. When he attacked Dara, I knew I had to ramp up our protection of the family. I had some of our best field agents following their every move." Paula got quiet. "Grace, even with all I know about this man, I was appalled at what I witnessed at that abandoned house. It made me sick to my stomach to see those people chained, nearly naked and drugged. The worst part was the two youngest girls. Their little bodies, so vulnerable, and so totally out of it. Maybe I'm getting too soft for this job." Paula finished her burger and turned to stare at the pine trees whizzing by. "This is the most boring interstate around. Aren't we there yet?"

"We're about halfway." Grace tried not to show how much concern she felt for Paula. "Edward wasn't given bail. The judge thought he was a flight risk and he'll be remanded into federal custody. That ought to make you feel a bit safer. The goons that were picked up the night of the raid are spilling their guts in hopes of a deal. They fingered four others who have been arrested, too. But human trafficking operations go way beyond Edward and Mario. One by one we'll get them, Paula. Someday it's got to stop." The sadness in Grace's heart echoed in the car.

"You've given your whole life to this cause, Grace. This little victory is in large part your reward for working so hard and diligently. Callie's testimony will ensure Mario is behind bars for the rest of his life, and we've got enough evidence against Edward to close his sordid business. We can't stop it all, but we did stop this part. We can't get discouraged."

"There's so much more to be done, but I'm tired. Retirement is looking better and better. It's time for me and Callie to give the younger generation a chance. One question. Matt's team found the shamrock brooch in your hotel room. How did you get it?"

"The agents found it when they searched Mario Villa's house. When he was taken off to jail, he told them to 'Tell the lady, I've got her brooch and soon I'll have her daughter to go with it'. Apparently, he's had his eyes on Callie for years. When I realized it was Callie's, I signed it out. I intend to give it back to her."

"Oh lordy, all these years, I thought we were safe. If he hadn't killed that girl, there's no telling what direction this story would have taken." Grace was almost sick with the realization that Callie had not been safe for a long time.

****

Connor and Matt had answered question after question for the FBI, the Leon County Sheriff's Office, and the Tallahassee Police. Edward Jenkins was a respected member of the FSU faculty with no prior arrests. His only black mark had been the domestic issue with Dara that resulted in a restraining order but no charges. No one wanted to believe he was the mastermind of a trafficking operation, but Paula had evidence that couldn't be refuted.

As the men who had been arrested at the scene began to tell their stories, there could be no mistake that Edward was a dangerous man.

His guard detail was increased at the hospital, and the judge refused to give him bail. His gunshot wound was serious, not life threatening. Arrangements were being made to move him from the hospital to a secure medical location under the supervision of the FBI.

Mario Villa's trial was still three weeks away and

much of the evidence they had gathered against Edward was now coming from Villa. Connor was convinced they had an ironclad case against both men. His concern was his mother's role in all of it.

"Matt, I think we've been dismissed, and I'm ready to get out of here. I need to get to Orange Park to see about my mom. Will you drop me off at the hospital? Somebody will give me a ride home."

"I'd like to see what's going on with your mom before I stop by my folks to pick up some things. You're welcome to ride back to Shamrock with me," Matt offered.

"I'd hate for you to hang around until I'm ready to go. Surely someone in my family loves me enough to give me a ride home. If not, you're it, my friend," teased Connor. "Wait till I fill them in on this caper before you disappear."

"I won't stay long at the hospital. I need to go on to Jacksonville tonight. I think I've spent more time this past month at my folks' than I've spent at my place. They're probably ready for me to go."

"There are so many love stories mixed up in all the lies my family has been living. There's no telling what we're going to walk into when we get to the hospital. I can't imagine how my dad's reacted to all this."

****

After Callie's release from the hospital, she and Charlie had been sequestered in a rehabilitation center until it was time for her to testify. On that day, she was wheeled into a room in an undisclosed location where she, like Grace, would give her testimony against Mario Villa via videoconferencing. She was wearing a mask to protect her identity from the public. Mentally and physically, she felt able to do what was necessary to put such a despicable man behind bars forever. All she had to do was remember what she had witnessed that day in the safe house.

Grace, also wearing a mask, had participated in the same protocol the day before and her testimony laid the groundwork for what Callie had to say. Grace had years of facts, but Callie was there, she saw the murder, and she could identify the man who pulled the trigger.

She glanced around to make sure Charlie was seated where she would see him when she began her testimony. Things weren't settled between them, and the kids avoided talking about the new facts they'd learned about her life. Instead, everyone had gone overboard to let her know she was loved. For now, that's what she needed, and it would carry her through the ordeal of the trial.

The agent who had been her guardian since the accident, helped her walk from the wheelchair to the table where she would face the camera. He made sure she was comfortable, then via camera, he declared to the judge that the proceeding could continue.

The judge informed the jury that the witness's identity was being protected, but both the prosecution and defense team were aware of the process used to vet the witness. With her hand on the Bible that was held by the FBI agent, she was placed under oath. "Do you swear to tell the truth, the whole truth, and nothing but the truth, so help you God?"

"I do."

And so, it began. She was scrutinized, questioned, and asked the same questions in different words. The prosccutor and the defense attorney took their turns. Every now and then, she had to take a deep breath and remind herself that what she was doing was vital. With every answer and explanation, she looked directly into the camera. She knew the jury would be listening to the inflection in her voice and would wonder what her expressions were behind the mask. They would look and listen for gaps and discrepancies in her testimony.

She was asked questions about human trafficking and her role as an intake counselor. Over and over, she was asked why she was at the safe house and whether she knew the murdered girl. For an hour that seemed like forever, the grueling ordeal went on. And as the time passed, she grew weary. At one point when she hesitated a moment too long, the judge asked if she was able to continue.

"Yes, your honor. I'm a bit slow, but I'm able to go on."

When she was asked to tell the jury, in her own words, what she had seen, her heart began to race.

"I was the intake counselor for a young girl from Honduras who had been kidnapped and brought to the United States at the age of eleven. She told me her captor had not sold her but kept her locked in a room for his own pleasure. In her words, she explained to me how she was enslaved, how she was given drugs, and how she became addicted. She had no idea what city or state she was in, but she told me she had stolen money from her captor so she could get away.

"Our rescuers found her in a hotel used for prostitution located in Jacksonville and she was taken to the safe house. Her addiction was severe, and I was trying to make arrangements for her to enter a drug rehab center. On the afternoon she was killed, I was alone in the safe house preparing her for that move. The house

315

mother had gone to the convenience store down the street to purchase some feminine hygiene products the girl needed. It's rare that any of us are ever in the house alone, but we agreed to make this exception because of the situation. I was waiting for the housemother to return but needed to use the restroom. It was just down the hall, and I left the door cracked open." Callie clutched her hands in her lap. For a second, she closed her eyes. "I hadn't been gone five minutes when the front door was busted down and a man forced his way into the house. I hid in the restroom and hit the emergency call button on my phone. I knew I had to figure a way to get us out of the house. The man kept hitting her and asking her where his money was. I managed to open the bathroom window and was planning to get out and go around to the front of the house to create a diversion when the man shouted, 'Enough is enough. Give me the money or you're dead.'"

She was oblivious to the tear that escaped down her cheek under the mask. "I went over to the door just as the man pulled out his gun and opened fire on that poor girl. I don't know how many shots were fired, but it was several. He was ransacking the room when the house phone began to ring. It must have startled him because he stopped what he was doing and fled. When he left, I ran to see if I could help the girl, but she was dead. I sat by her side holding her hand and within minutes two policemen arrived. The man who had killed the girl was gone."

"Can you identify that man?"

"Yes, I can. He is sitting at the defense table in the courtroom. His name is Mario Villa."

The questions continued, the cross examination was

intense, and Callie felt drained. The defense attorney was trying to force her off track, and on two occasions she had to request a moment to gather her thoughts.

No matter how tired she was, she knew the jury would react negatively if she lost her train of thought or seemed unsure of what she was saying. With every question she answered she knew her only responsibility was to tell the truth. She owed it to that little girl and all the little girls just like her.

****

When Callie's testimony ended and the video camera was turned off, the agent approached and offered her a glass of water. "I know that was exhausting for you, but you handled it very well. The car is waiting if you're ready to leave."

The agent helped her get seated in the wheelchair and then he whisked her out of the building. Charlie followed closely behind her. "I will be glad when I can remove this mask. How about you, Callie?"

Before she could answer, the agent interrupted. "I'm sorry, sir, but both of you will have to keep those masks on until the car delivers you to the rehabilitation center. They don't want to take a chance on your identity being discovered."

They were hurried into a waiting car and driven out of the city.

"You were great. The nightmare is over for you and Grace." Charlie had his arm around her to stop her trembling. "You gave the jury what they needed to convict. With Villa and Edward Jenkins in prison, you don't have to be afraid anymore."

She closed her eyes and leaned into his chest. "When will they let us go home? I just want to go home.

317

I want to see my kids. Hear the waves. I need to talk to Grace."

"When the jury has rendered their verdict, we won't have a reason to be in hiding. It may take a few more days, but it'll be soon. We'll be able to leave the rehabilitation center and our family will be able to leave their location. Everyone will be able to go home. Now, why don't you close your eyes and rest while we're on the road?"

"Why haven't we talked, Charlie? Don't you have questions you need answered? Aren't you angry with me?"

"When this is behind us, we'll have time to talk. I'm not angry, I'm hurt. I understand and I don't understand. It's complicated and I have questions that only you can answer. But I'm not ready to throw away forty-four years. We'll be fine."

****

Grace had left the video-conference location the same way Callie did. She and Paula were still under the watchful eye of a security team. Thankfully, her protection would end soon; Paula's would continue until Edward's trial was over. Then, for their continued safety, Paula would be transferred to another division, and Grace would move to Oregon where her daughter lived.

"My daughter is looking for a small house for me in her neighborhood. I'm looking forward to it and dreading it. My roots are in Florida and here I am moving to a place where there isn't a palm tree or a lot of sunshine. It's going to be different. You know, Paula, there's a big university in Eugene where my daughter lives. Maybe I can teach in the criminal justice department."

"That's the best idea you've had. You're a great teacher. It'll keep you out of trouble." Paula smiled. "I'm going to miss you. I've gotten used to you being around."

"Honey, you're not going to have time to miss me. You've got the other trial coming up in six months, you're still in physical therapy, and there's a certain young man that has been calling you almost every day. I'm not trying to be too nosy, but what's going on with you and Connor?"

"Absolutely nothing. It's all been work related." She grinned. "He is cute, isn't he?"

"That man will always be a little boy to me. He's mischievous, too big for his britches, and the best thing since grits. If, and I'm just saying if, you decide to take a liking to him, you'll never be sorry. But don't you do anything to break my baby's heart."

"Whoa, you're getting ahead of yourself." She stopped to think about it. "I've been warned. Changing the subject. Do you think the jury heard what Callie said today? Was her story strong enough to sway them?"

"You saw the video. She did a good job, and everyone could see that her emotions were real," Grace said.

"All the facts you added to the case yesterday were so horrendous and atrocious there is no way the jury can decide anything other than guilty. Mario Villa is going to prison for a very long time."

"I can't believe Callie and I thought he was the head of the dragon."

"Edward Jenkins is more intelligent than most of the people in this line of work. He is so cagey, it's a wonder we finally nailed him."

"What made you look in his direction? I don't

remember ever seeing him in Jacksonville, or even seeing his name on any of the memos or briefings."

"When I started tracking the money, I discovered he was listed on the board of a business named EWJ, Inc. It's a legitimate company that owns several large office buildings in the southeastern United States and Central America. I kept digging and found out the company also owned a string of economy hotels in port cities like Miami, Jacksonville, and Savannah. Hidden in all the legitimacy were several hotels that were on our list because of alleged prostitution. His company owns that hotel in Jacksonville. I got very suspicious when I couldn't find any of the other members of the board. He was covering everything under the guise of his professorship at FSU. A year ago, I started trying to cozy up to him. I took one of his classes and followed him around like a groupie. He wasn't interested, but I kept at him. I took a job in a diner I knew he frequented and kept pushing until he asked me out. We were having dinner one evening when he told me he was headed to Shamrock Beach and wanted to know if I'd ever heard of it. When I asked why in the world he wanted to go to a small town that didn't have a good beach, he told me he had been dating Dara McBride and her family lived there."

"I'm glad to know you weren't that cozy with the creep," Grace growled.

"We got cozier after that dinner conversation, and he eventually told me some made-up story about the judge and his mother. That's when he asked me to help him embarrass the judge. It was my chance to prove my loyalty to him, and I had to take it. Edward had false papers drawn up, drilled me on what I needed to know,

320

and persuaded Dara to invite him to Shamrock Beach for the judge's retirement dinner. His plan was for me to meet the judge at the dinner and challenge him privately. Edward was as surprised as you were that I went public with the challenge."

"That's what all that nonsense about you being the judge's daughter was about?"

"I knew he was seeking revenge against the judge, but when I figured out that he was really after Callie, I had to find a way to get inside the family."

"Let me tell you, girl. You messed up that family something awful. After it got so deep, I called Martha and found out you were on the team. That's when I knew I had to start being more careful."

"You and Callie have had a surveillance detail ever since Mario Villa was arrested. Way before the retirement dinner. It's amazing how good Callie is at losing her protectors."

"Paula, how are you going to make it up to the judge? This is a small town with big ears, big mouths, and big grudges. You are public enemy number one around here."

"Before I do anything, I've got to be sure you and Callie and Brock are protected. They've relocated all the safe houses in this area and that's had an impact on Brock. Right now, he's not on the medical call list and it'll probably be at least a year before he has to decide whether he's going to continue."

"Goodness, I already know the answer to that question. Brock isn't going to quit. You can bet on that."

"When the trial's over and you and Callie are officially retired, Martha will let me have a private talk with the judge. Maybe he'll go easy on me when I put the shamrock brooch in his hand."

Chapter Twenty-Two

"The jury convicted Mario Villa and he's been sentenced to life in prison without pardon." Charlie sat down on the couch beside Callie. "It is over."

"A weight's been lifted off my shoulders, and my prayers have been answered."

"Put that book aside, Callie. It's time for us to go home, and there are things I hope we can settle before that happens. I've poured us some wine and we can talk. How's that?"

"I appreciate your thoughtfulness." A gentleness crossed her face. "Do you think a glass of wine will make this any easier?"

"It can't hurt." He handed her a glass and settled in one of the chairs facing the couch.

"Charlie, it started a long time ago and you'll have to understand if I don't remember every detail. You had graduated from law school, and I was finishing grad school when I found out I was pregnant. That part of the story you already know. I was scared and financially in a bind when I met Grace."

"I thought you told me someone named Martha helped you."

"Martha is a code name for a field director. Field agents from the Miami office use it when they are talking about the one who supervises them." She waited to make sure she had his attention. "Grace Samuels, our so-called housekeeper, is the person who helped me." And in her own words, Callie confirmed for Charlie all that Dr. Grace Samuels had already explained to him. "The victims of trafficking have stories that are similar," she said, her fatigue beginning to show. "They were taken by force, usually drugged, and sold. Most of the males are sold as forced labor in the fields. Most of the older women are sold into servitude as domestics in wealthy households. Younger females and males are sold into prostitution. It is a sordid, ugly business that we were trying to eradicate."

"How have you worked in this world for so long and stayed sane, Callie?" Charlie's voice cracked as he spoke.

"I had a job to do that would hopefully bring these unfortunate people out of hell. Grace was my sounding board when I became overwhelmed. Then, Grace discovered that our daughter, the one I gave up for adoption, was missing. She was eleven years old and had been abducted at her school bus stop. I'm still looking for her, Charlie. It's been years, but I'm still looking for her."

She took a deep breath. "You and our family are the glue that has held me together, but I prayed every day that she would be found. I couldn't walk away knowing she might be out there somewhere. That thought has been my driving force all these years."

"I really wish you'd shared this with me. Why all the lies? Why couldn't you let me help you look for our daughter? It's unbelievable to me that you and Grace could pull this off without anyone suspecting. How could you keep this from me for so many years?"

"This wasn't an every day job, Charlie. I only

worked when I was needed. Sometimes there would be months in between assignments. Once, Grace and I went two years without a call. We covered for each other." She sank back into the couch and took a deep breath. "I didn't like keeping all of this from you, but it was necessary for the integrity of the program. After you became a judge, Martha was concerned about conflict of interest. And, as it turned out, you handled one or two of the cases we were involved in."

"It will take me years to unravel all this in my head. Half of me is proud of you for doing this and the other half wants to shake you for doing it."

"I knew you would ask me to stop if you ever found out. I couldn't risk it. And, if I thought our daughter might need me, I couldn't turn away."

"We agree. I would have insisted you stop." He put his wine glass down and stood up. "Do you still feel like you must pursue this search for our daughter?"

"I've discussed this with Martha and with Grace. They've convinced me that finding our daughter is no longer viable. Maybe years ago, there was a chance, but, at her age, the likelihood of her being alive is non-existent."

She closed her eyes and let the tears fall. Charlie's arm went around her, and he held her until she stopped crying. "I'll continue to pray for her every day, and I'll probably never stop asking myself what if things had been different. In my heart, I've always called our first daughter Hope."

"There will be one big difference now. When you feel that way, you can talk to me, and we can grieve for Hope together." The silence between them grew louder before Charlie finally spoke again. "I see you, Callie. For the first time in forty-four years, you have finally let me see you."

"Thank you," she whispered.

"You are retiring, aren't you? Grace said you were." His smile reached his eyes, and he threw his arms around her and hugged her tightly. "I love you, Callie. But I'll love you even more if you retire!"

"It's already official. Grace is in the process of getting ready to move to Oregon to be near her daughter, Shannon, and I'm packing my bags for Ireland. You owe me a trip."

He laughed out loud. "My dear, you never cease to amaze me. Our love story will go on whether we're in Shamrock Beach or Ireland. You can count on that."

A word about the author...

Proud to be a native Floridian, Jeanne Moon Farmer, loves to set her stories in the diverse cities and towns of her beautiful home state. Like her characters, her life has been lived against a background of sandy beaches, palm trees, and unbelievable humidity. And she sees a story behind every hibiscus.

As a wife, mother, daughter, teacher, writer, and friend, she is curious about the threads that bind us to other human beings and searches for significance in the life dramas that teach us who we are.

Her writing reflects the journey of people who have been tried and tested by their own choices. Some have been defeated by those choices while others learn they can rise above the consequences through forgiveness and love.